More Than Once Upon a Time

KRISTY DIXON

MEEGORE PUBLISHING LLC

More Than Once Upon a Time

Book Cover by Getpremades

Edited by Whitney Morsillo

Edition 1 edition 2023

ISBN 978-1-960841-09-4 ebook

ISBN 978-1-960841-10-0 paperback

ISBN 978-1-960841-11-7 hardback

For Kent and April Thompson

Chapter 1

O livia dragged behind her sister as they entered what felt like the twentieth shop. How could this many bridal stores stay in business? Her feet were tired, and her head throbbed. Emily was being picky, and Olivia was excited to be done.

"This is the last store," Emily promised.

"It's going to be like all the others," Olivia said with a sigh. She didn't even bother examining the bright lacy shop. "They all carry the same brands, so we're just wasting our time."

"My wedding has to be perfect," Emily said, with a dreamy look on her face. She picked up a bride and groom cake topper. "I don't want to miss anything."

"You could have looked online."

"That's no fun," Emily pouted.

Olivia noticed two rows of chairs pushed into one corner. "I'm going to wait over there."

Emily nodded, not paying any attention to her. Two men occupied a couple of the chairs. They were both zoned out, staring at their phones. Olivia chose a seat on the end and pulled her phone out of her purse, mindlessly scrolling through social media.

"Not your type of store?" an older woman asked. Olivia glanced up as a smiling, elderly woman sat next to her. Didn't the woman know the rules? If there were a lot of chairs, you never sat next to someone. It was just common courtesy.

"Not really," Olivia answered, glancing back at her phone.

"You don't like weddings?"

"I don't like shopping for them."

"Who are you with?" the woman asked, running a hand over her silver hair.

"My sister," Olivia said, not looking up. Why was this woman still talking to her?

"I love these stores," the woman gushed. "And I love happily ever afters."

Olivia put her phone away. It was obvious the woman wasn't going to stop talking. "I don't believe in happily ever after."

The woman frowned. "How sad. Why not?"

"I've never seen it."

"Oh, I find that hard to accept," she said, patting Olivia's hand. It took all her focus not to pull away. "You can see happily ever afters everywhere."

"Maybe in fairy tales."

"So, you don't believe in fairy tales?"

Olivia shook her head. "Of course not. I don't waste my time with them."

A wide, wrinkled smile appeared on the woman's face. "But they can be fun. My name is Nancy, by the way."

"Olivia."

"Well, Olivia, I hope you give fairy tales another chance."

Olivia sighed. "They make people hope for things that aren't going to happen. I hate that. Each story has a girl that falls in love with someone they don't really even know, and it all works out perfectly. It's silly."

Nancy cocked her head. "Perhaps, but they are still fun. It looks like your sister is getting ready for her own happily ever after."

Olivia glanced over to where Emily was trying on tiaras and rolled her eyes. "Emily has always been into true love and all that garbage."

"You don't even believe in true love?" Nancy asked, the gleam leaving her eyes.

"I believe in love. I just think it's more rare than people say. I've gone on tons of dates, and I've never come close to it."

"That may be because you haven't found the right one yet."

Olivia laughed. "The right one? How can there be a right one? There are billions of people out there. If you have to find the right one, I say the chances are slim."

The man next to Nancy scooted to a further chair and turned the other way. He wasn't enjoying the conversation any more than she was. Olivia had had plenty of crushes over the years, and they had never amounted to anything. All the guys that were interested in her were weird. She shuddered at the memories. She had yet to meet a guy she liked that liked her back.

Nancy studied her. "So, you're content to go through life alone? How sad."

"It's not sad. I've already accepted that true love won't happen."

"You don't seem old enough to give up on happiness."

Olivia pushed her wavy blonde hair over her shoulder and looked at the concerned woman. "I'm eighteen, and I'm not giving up on happiness. I just don't expect it to be a fairy tale or a relationship. It's not like I'm saying I'll never have a relationship, but I'm not looking for it and getting disappointed."

She knew that wasn't completely true. She wasn't looking for a relationship, but she was already disappointed that it hadn't ever happened to her. That was why she was being careful. Dwelling on it only made her sad. If she decided it wasn't ever going to happen, she would save herself from heartbreak.

Nancy tapped a finger on her lips. "I rarely aid people unless they are a lot more bitter than you seem to be, but something about you makes me want to help."

"I don't need any help," Olivia assured her. She wondered what made the woman assume she could do anything.

"I'll be excited to see you change your mind. It will be a process, but you're far from the worst case I've seen."

Emily bounced over to show Olivia a cake topper with two dragons blowing fire into the shape of a heart. Emily was obsessed with dragons. "Look what I bought!"

Olivia stood and turned to Nancy. "I doubt we'll ever meet again."

Nancy winked and grinned. "We will. Oh, we will."

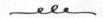

Olivia put all her muscle into pulling the window shut, but it refused to budge. "Come on!" she said, as she struggled. She wouldn't have to deal with the stubborn window for much longer. Once Emily and Trent were married, Olivia was going to have to move back home with her parents or find another roommate. Finding a new apartment for a good price was rough. Rent wasn't cheap, and her job in retail wouldn't pay a full month's bills.

There were cheaper apartments. Emily had insisted on having a nice beige apartment. Beige was actually on the list she made when they were searching. The walls and carpet both matched the requirement, and Emily had quickly filled the place with beige furniture. It was all of high quality, and as bland as anything. Olivia had run out and gotten the brightest blue comforter and curtains she could find, so her room wouldn't be quite so—beige.

"Just leave it open," Emily said, entering the bedroom with a pile of clean towels. "It's muggy in here."

"Are those mine?" Olivia asked, pointing to the towels.

"They mysteriously ended up in my wash again," her sister said, cocking her head to one side.

Olivia grabbed them, placed them on her dresser, and faced her sister. "Sorry. I don't understand how that keeps happening."

"For all your talk of being self-reliant, it sure happens a lot."

"I did your dishes last night," Olivia reminded her.

Emily sat on Olivia's bed. That meant she wasn't leaving. "Have you decided what you're going to do when I get married? I'm sure you don't want to move back in with the parents."

"I have a few leads on roommates, and I'm trying to get more hours at work."

"You can stay here with us for a while," Emily said, running her fingers through her light brown hair. "Trent doesn't mind."

"No," Olivia said, shaking her head. "You're getting married. You don't need me tagging along everywhere."

"I've always enjoyed you tagging along."

"Yes, but that'll get old fast. You need your own space."

"But you'll remember I'm always here for you, right?"

"I know," Olivia said. Emily had always been the best big sister. They had little in common, but they always had fun together.

"I wish you would start dating again. You don't do enough socializing."

"I've told you about every date I've ever gone on. You should understand why I don't do it."

Emily sighed. "You can't give up just because you had some unpleasant experiences. I'm twenty-five, and you've heard my bad dating stories. It took me until I met Trent to fall in love. You're giving up way too easily."

"Now you sound like the nosy woman at the bridal shop."

"Part of finding someone you love is going through weird dating experiences and finding out who you're compatible with. True love rarely happens in high school, and you only graduated a year ago."

Olivia shook her head. "I've never been asked out by a single guy I liked. It was always the boys I tried to avoid. I don't see that changing. I'm not doing pity dates anymore, so that means I'm not dating."

"I don't get why you won't give Trent's cousin Brian a chance. Every time I see him, he mentions you."

She rolled her eyes. "I said no more pity dates. If I went with him, it would be a pity date. The day I met him, he spent an hour telling me about the best ways to milk a cow and why it's different from milking a goat."

Emily smiled. "He grew up on a farm."

"You know he's weird, though, Em."

"It's possible that the reason the boys you like don't ask you out is because they don't realize you like them. Maybe you need to be more straightforward. Ask them out."

"I don't like anyone, so that's not going to happen. Why do people that fall in love suddenly think they are love experts?"

"I'm just trying to help. I don't want you to end up old, cynical, and alone. You don't want to be like Ebenezer Scrooge."

Olivia grinned. "He was old, cynical, alone, and rich. I'm pretty sure I'm never going to be rich."

"Just go on one date with Brian," Emily begged.

"Bah humbug."

"Not funny."

Olivia pulled her hair into a ponytail and grabbed her shoes. "You don't have to worry about me becoming a hermit. I have friends and a job. It's not like I'm just sitting around wasting my life."

Emily frowned. "Yes, but I still worry. It's getting late. You aren't going running, are you?"

"Running is how I deal with life's stresses. If I don't run, I'll go crazy."

"Make sure you come back before it's dark."

A cat meowed. "Is that Toby?" Olivia asked, walking back to the window. She usually left it closed because the crazy cat liked to walk on the ledge outside, and they were on the third floor.

Olivia poked her head out the window and saw the tri-colored calico walking on the ledge. "Toby, come here," she commanded. Toby stared at her with his big dark eyes and took a few steps away. "Come on, sweetheart, I'll get you some dinner."

"He probably just wants to visit the Jensen's cat," Emily said. "You worry too much. Cats are pros at walking on small ledges."

"Yes, but it stresses me out. Come on, Toby. I'll give you a treat." Toby turned toward her but didn't come any closer. "Are you going to make this complicated? Come on." Olivia leaned out the window and tried to grab him.

"Don't lean out there like that," Emily said. "It makes me nervous."

"I've almost got him," Olivia said, touching the cat's paw. Toby backed up, and Olivia leaned forward. She felt her foot slip. The last thing she heard was Emily screaming her name.

Olivia groaned as the sun streamed onto her face. It couldn't be morning already. She was exhausted. A pounding at the door caused her to pry her eyes open. She sat up with a start and glanced around the unfamiliar room. Where was she? Paint peeled from the white walls and there was a small wooden wardrobe in the corner. It was the only piece of furniture, besides the small creaky bed she was in.

"What are you doing in there?" a woman's voice demanded from the other side of the door.

Olivia jumped out of bed in a panic and glanced down at the faded blue linen nightgown she was wearing. She had a vague memory of falling out the apartment window. Was she in a hospital? It didn't look like a hospital. The blanket on the bed was brown and worn. A hospital wouldn't use old bedding with holes.

The doorknob rattled, and she inched nervously to the door. Unlocking it, she pulled it open and peeked out. A stunning woman with large eyes and perfectly curled brown hair stood before her. She wore an old-fashioned dress that would have looked ridiculous on most people, but it was elegant on her. It had a high neckline and a tight-fitting bodice. The skirt cascaded gently to the floor. The woman appeared to be in her mid forties.

"Still in your nightdress?" she huffed. "You should have been up an hour ago. Don't just stand there looking stupid. Why aren't you working?"

Olivia stared at the woman and blinked twice. "Who are you? Where am I?"

"Of all the silly nonsense," the woman said. "Are we pretending to have lost our memory to get out of a punishment?"

"What are you talking about?" Olivia asked, taking a step back. "I don't know who you are or where I am."

The woman's eyes narrowed. "I don't have time for this. I'm late. When I get back, you better be dressed and working."

She turned and slammed the door. Olivia put a shaky hand to her heart and willed it to slow down. What was going on? She needed to get out of here.

Hurrying to the wardrobe, she threw open the doors and found two tattered dresses. She grabbed the closest one and quickly put it on. It smelled funny, but she had to wear something. A pair of worn slip-on shoes sat on the bottom. She grabbed them and shoved them on her feet. Now, she needed to figure out what was happening.

Olivia opened the door and stepped out into an elegant hallway. She was taken aback by how fancy it was after the room she had just vacated. The carpet was red and paintings of landscapes with gold-colored frames lined the walls. She didn't take time to admire them. She rushed to the staircase and flew down the red steps. When she reached the bottom, she grabbed what she hoped was the doorknob to the outside.

"Ella!" a feminine voice said from behind her. Olivia turned to see a younger replica of the woman from before. "Where do you think you're going?" the girl demanded. She appeared to be the same age as Olivia.

Olivia tried to turn the knob, but it wouldn't turn. She fiddled with it for a moment.

"Are you ignoring me?" the girl asked.

"Let me out," Olivia demanded. "How does this lock work?"

"Have you gone mad? First, you don't show up to make breakfast, and now, you can't open the door?"

"Why would I make you breakfast?" Olivia asked, turning to the girl.

"Because it's your job. Mother was angry this morning. I bet she'll make sure you are punished tonight."

"I don't know you or your mother," Olivia said, trying the door again. "If you don't let me out, I'll call 911." She realized it was a bluff as soon as it came out of her mouth. She didn't have her phone.

"Call 911?" the girl asked. "I swear, Ella, you need to get more sun. Or perhaps less."

"My name isn't Ella."

The girl laughed. "Isn't Ella? Pray tell, what is it then?"

Another girl, slightly younger, joined them. She resembled the other two, except her hair was a darker brown.

"What's funny?" the younger girl asked.

"Ella isn't Ella today, it seems."

"What do you mean, Lottie?"

"She can't seem to remember her name or how to open the door."

"One of you better open this door before I have you all sent to prison!" Olivia growled.

Both girls glanced at each other and broke into hysterical laughter. Olivia was done. She couldn't figure out what was happening. She glanced at the window to the side of the door and tried to open it.

"Look, Mara," Lottie giggled. "She's going to go out the window."

Olivia studied the large immaculate entryway. There was nothing there except some large paintings of the ocean and two decorative chairs. She grabbed one and held it in the air. "You've got two seconds to open the door before I break the glass."

Lottie snorted. "You wouldn't dare."

Olivia turned and smashed the chair into the window and watched as it shattered. Lottie and Mara stood with their perfectly pink, heart-shaped mouths hanging open. It would have been funny if Olivia wasn't so terrified. She quickly scampered out the window, cutting her leg on the way out. She ignored it. Stepping out onto the hard packed dirt, she ran away from the house.

"You are in so much trouble!" one girl yelled from behind her.

Ignoring the girl, Olivia darted down a dirt street, glancing back at the elegant estate. Nothing about this situation made sense. The house had large, intimidating pillars and huge windows. It didn't look familiar in any way. Her stomach fluttered more the further she ran. There weren't any houses that she could see and only the occasional tree on the side of the road. The shoes weren't made for running, and her feet hurt.

Her run became a brisk walk, and after about ten minutes, she saw a house up ahead. With luck, the people who lived there would let her use their phone. The house was enormous, with large gray columns and wide windows. It was almost an exact replica of the house she had just escaped. Not wasting time, she hurried to the front door and knocked.

Olivia ran a nervous hand over the ratty blue dress and tried to smooth back her blonde tangles. She must look like a colossal mess. The door opened and a man in an old-fashioned black suit stood before her. He had a neatly trimmed black mustache and was bald on top.

He studied her and frowned. "Ella. Is something wrong? My mistress will not be happy if she sees you at the front door."

"My name isn't Ella," Olivia said, wrinkling her forehead. "Which door should I go to?"

The man stepped outside and closed the door, his eyebrow raised in concern. "Has something happened? Are you alright?"

"I need to use your phone," she said. "I woke up in a house I've never seen, and I need to call the police. Or at least my sister."

The man furrowed his brow. "I'm not sure I follow. What do you need?"

"Your phone."

"I don't understand what you mean."

"You don't know what a phone is?"

"No. I better go tell my mistress something is wrong and I will take you home."

"I have no idea where I am. Nothing around here is familiar at all. Am I still in Colorado?"

"I've never heard of it."

"Where are we?"

The man ignored her and looked concerned. "There's blood on your dress. You need a doctor."

"I'm fine. I had to break a window to escape wherever I was."

He raised his eyebrows. "You were abducted?"

"Possibly. I just need to get out of here and find my sister."

"Lottie and Mara rarely leave the house during the day. I'll take you to them."

"What? No! Why would I want to go there? I just escaped from that place."

The door creaked open, and an elderly woman poked her head out. "What's the problem, Charles?"

"Something has happened to poor Ella here. Her mind seems to be confused."

The woman glared at Ella. "Take her home. I don't want her making a scene on my porch."

"Yes, ma'am," Charles said, as the door closed. "Come, Ella. Let's get you home." He took hold of her arm, and she jerked away.

"My name is Olivia, and why is everyone in this place crazy? I'll get help somewhere else!" She turned and bolted down the dirt path and back to the street. Her leg pulsed, but she continued to ignore the pain as Charles followed behind her. "Go away, or I'll send the cops for you as well!"

"I will not leave you in this state of mind," the man said. Olivia walked quickly and tried to breathe normally. The man looked concerned, but he made no more sense than the women in the other house.

"Where's the nearest town?" she asked, keeping a steady pace.

"Ten minutes down this road. Same as always. You should know that."

"Why? I've never been here before."

"You've lived here since you were born. I've known you since before your father died."

"My father isn't dead."

"We need to get you to a doctor."

"I'm the only one that doesn't need a doctor around here," Olivia said, wishing for her running shoes. "I've never seen you before."

"I wondered if you would snap one day," Charles said, huffing. He didn't seem to be in the best of shape. "You were always such a happy child until your father married that evil woman. She works you too hard. Her and those two spoiled daughters."

Olivia shook her head. "You're talking like I'm Cinderella or something."

"I would never call you that, but I know your stepsisters do. You need to learn to ignore them. It's the only way to survive."

Olivia glanced sideways at the middle-aged man. His face was red from the fast pace. "I don't have a stepfamily."

"Did you hurt yourself? Bump your head, perhaps?"

Olivia stopped, and so did Charles. "I did hurt myself. At least, I'm pretty sure I did. I fell out of a high window. I bet I'm having a dream or something." The cut on her leg made her rethink that. There was genuine pain there.

"Well, that makes sense. You have a head injury. When we get to town, I'll take you to the doctor. Your family probably won't be too happy about that, though."

"I'm not really here," Olivia said. "I must be unconscious. My leg probably got hurt when I fell so I can feel the pain, even though I'm not awake."

"Ella, you're awake. Let's go get you help."

"I'm going to stay here and wait until I wake up," Olivia decided. She glanced around and spotted a large rock off to the side of the road. She would sit there until she woke up. Going to town wouldn't help if she wasn't actually here. She must be hurt and having a crazy dream because of that Nancy woman she talked to earlier. That was why she was imagining fairy tales.

"You can't stay here," Charles said, following her.

She sat on the rock and folded her arms. "I'm not leaving. I'll wake up, eventually."

Charles looked around like he was searching for help.

"You can leave. I'm fine."

He threw his hands in the air. "I can't leave you here! You don't even know who you are."

"I know exactly who I am," she said. "My name's Olivia Saunders, and I'm from Boulder, Colorado. I spent yesterday shopping with my sister Emily and then I fell out the window trying to get my cat. Now, I'm supposed to believe I'm in some fairy tale? I'll never believe it."

"Your stepmother is going to be furious when she finds you."

"I'm not going back."

Charles sighed. "I'll go for help." He turned and walked away.

"You go for help," Olivia said under her breath. "I'll just hope I wake up before it comes." She watched the man get smaller as he scurried down the road to town. Olivia sighed. Who was she kidding? Sitting here, even if she wasn't here, was going to be boring. She might as well go to town to pass the time in the dream. She stood and hurried after the man. Hopefully, someone in town would be a little more helpful.

Chapter 2

P rince Jerron laid back on his uncomfortable purple sofa and crossed his ankles. He put his arms behind his head and studied the ceiling as a short thin man stood in front of him, talking himself blue. Jerron wasn't listening to a word the man said, but he had no doubt it was something about getting married. That was all the little man seemed to talk about.

"Your father is getting impatient. He won't let you go on unmarried much longer. If you want him to force you into marriage—"

"Blah, blah, blah, I get it Richard," Jerron said. "There's nothing you can say that will change anything. My father wants me to get married. He wants you to bother me until I find a girl, blah, blah, blah."

Richard sighed. "You should obey your father. He is the king."

Jerron propped himself up on his elbow and turned to Richard. "Yes, well, here's the problem. I can look for a girl, but we won't ever have a connection. It doesn't matter how hard I try. I can't find anyone I can stand to be with. I can't even tell you how many times I've tried."

"I've never seen you try very hard," Richard said.

"Yes, well, I don't tell you everything. I'm never going to get it right, and I'm exhausted from trying."

Richard shook his head. "You're a prince. You don't have to try. Any girl in the kingdom would marry you."

Jerron rolled his eyes. "Yes, they would marry me because I'm a prince. Do you really want some silly girl running around the castle, all ridiculous and giggling, with no thought in her head except that she is a princess?"

"So, you want a girl that doesn't want to be a princess?"

"Something like that."

Richard paced for a moment and then his eyes lit up. "I know what you need! You need to go slumming."

Jerron laughed. "Slumming, huh?"

"Have you heard of it?"

"You want me to dress up like a commoner and go mingle with the people?"

"Yes. It's the perfect solution. You can meet women, and they won't know who you are. Then, you won't have to worry about them liking you only because you're the prince."

Jerron sighed and sat up. "I've done something similar before. It didn't go well."

"Can we try? Just once?" he begged. Jerron studied the man for a second. He looked so hopeful. It wasn't fair to Richard that he had to deal with Jerron and the king. It wasn't his fault they were both so stubborn and each wanted different things.

"I suppose," he said. "It is boring around here."

Richard clasped his hands together in delight. "I'll arrange it," he said with a huge smile.

"You do that," Jerron said. He wouldn't tell the man, that prince or not, Jerron's love life was pathetic.

"This is so much fun!" Richard said, adjusting his tunic as they walked down the dirt packed street. "I've never dressed like a commoner before."

Jerron grinned at the bounce in the man's step. Richard needed to get out more. He couldn't be over twenty-five, and he spent all his days with Jerron. That couldn't be healthy—or fun.

Jerron was more at home in his brown tunic than he was dressed as a prince. It was so much more comfortable. He hadn't been to town much, and he felt more relaxed walking down the street than he had driving through in the royal carriage. The shops they passed were all small, but clean and well kept.

"Where do we go first?" Richard asked, his eyes dancing. "The tavern? Perhaps the store? I brought some money. We could go watch the blacksmith, or perhaps the hatter. I've heard good things about the food at the inn."

Jerron grinned. "Calm down, Richard. You're going to overdo it. Let's go to the inn. I'm in the mood for some non-palace food."

Richard's eyes lit up, and Jerron felt a wave of guilt. The king had assigned Richard to him for almost all parts of the day.

Jerron was boring, so it must be even worse for Richard. He would try harder to let the man have more fun.

The inn was a white two story building with a bright red door. They scanned the place and found the dining area. It was small with six tables, only one of which was occupied. He better enjoy every second of this because when the king found out what they were doing, he would put an end to it.

"There aren't any girls in here," Richard observed after they ordered their food.

"That's too bad," Jerron said, not even pretending to care. Eventually, the story would force him to find a girl, but why rush it? If he could put it off for a few months, it would be ideal. Once he settled on someone, that would be the end.

A serving man brought out their roast and potatoes, and they both eagerly dug in. The servings at the palace were always too small for Jerron's liking. This place didn't hold back. It might be worth sneaking out now and then. The king believed that if he needed to diet, everyone else did as well.

"What type of girl are we looking for?" Richard asked. "You must have some preferences."

"My preferences don't matter. I should search for some strange princess or a girl that's in trouble. That's how it works."

"How what works?"

"My life."

"You are confusing lately. I rarely leave your side, and you keep talking like you've had all these experiences you couldn't have had without me knowing."

"I can't explain it to you. I can't explain it to myself," he said, forking a large bite of potatoes into his mouth. Trying to tell anyone about his life was a waste of time. He'd tried it a few times, and all that came from that was people branding him crazy.

Richard raised his eyebrow. "Are you sneaking out at night?"

"No. Don't worry about it." They finished the rest of their lunch in silence. Jerron wanted to order more, but his stomach was already uncomfortable. They paid and left the inn.

Richard pointed down the street. "What's going on up there?"

Jerron squinted against the bright sun and watched as a well-dressed woman tried to pull a younger servant girl down the street by her arm. The younger girl wasn't taking it. Jerron sprinted toward the two, and Richard followed. They stopped when they reached the pair, and the door to the doctor's office opened. Doctor Smedley exited and frowned at the scuffle.

"Lady Anna, the girl needs time to heal," the doctor said, removing his spectacles.

"What she needs it's a good whipping!" the elegant woman said, letting the girl free of her grasp. "She broke the window to our house. On purpose!"

The girl rubbed her arm and glared at the woman. "I am not going anywhere with you!" she exclaimed. She pushed a strand of blonde hair behind her ear. Her dress appeared faded and worn, and she had a streak of dirt running across her face. Even in that condition, she was one of the prettiest girls Jerron had ever laid eyes on.

"What's going on?" he asked.

The older woman wrinkled her nose as she studied him. "I don't believe this is any of your concern. You are dismissed."

Dismissed? Jerron smiled. It had been a while since anyone had dared to dismiss him.

"Lady Anna, the girl is hurt," the doctor said. "She fell from a window. She doesn't remember who she is. I bandaged her leg, but she shouldn't be walking on it. The cut was deep."

"The window was only two feet off the ground, and she was acting strange before that," Lady Anna said, crossing her arms and glaring at the doctor. "Ella is my servant, and she will come with me."

The doctor nodded in defeat.

"I'm not going anywhere with you," the girl said. "My name isn't Ella, and the police should arrest you for keeping me locked in your house."

"You see? She needs rest," the doctor said.

"I will let her rest today," the woman finally agreed. "Come now, Ella."

"I'm not going with you."

"You don't have a choice. You have nowhere else to go."

The girl clenched her fists. "I do. I just need to find out where I am so I can leave."

"Ella, you really should go home," the doctor said, rubbing the lenses of his glasses on his shirt. "You need to rest."

Lady Anna grabbed for the girl's wrist, but the girl moved away. "Touch me again and I'll punch you in the face!" she threatened.

"I don't have to deal with this!" Lady Anna growled. "I'll send Stephan for you!" She turned and stomped toward a burgundy carriage and disappeared inside.

"Take care of yourself, Ella," Doctor Smedley said. "You just made things harder for yourself." The doctor nodded to all of them and returned to the building.

The girl glared at Jerron with her bright brown eyes. "What?" she snapped.

"Nothing," he said. "We just want to help."

"I just need to wake up. I don't need any help."

This had to be the girl he was looking for. She had more attitude than most, but she must be the one. If she wasn't, why would she be in his path? Jerron wasn't ready to leave the palace, though. He'd been in a lot worse positions. He wondered what would happen to her when they forced her back to Lady Anna's house.

"You said you aren't Ella?" he said. "So, who are you?"

"It doesn't matter," she muttered. "That woman thinks she's my evil stepmother, but she's delusional."

"Evil stepmother? Ella . . ." It was coming together. "I suppose you have two evil stepsisters to go with that?"

She tilted her head as she studied him. "It would seem that way."

Jerron nodded. This made things easier. Now that he knew what story he was in, he could predict what would happen. There was something odd about this girl. Wasn't Cinderella obedient? Perhaps, she was like him. He hadn't run into anyone like him since he came here. He reached out a hand and touched the girl's cheek.

Richard sucked in a horrified breath, and the girl took a step back. "I swear this place is crazy," she said. "How do I get out of here?" she muttered, gazing down the street.

"No way that I know of," Jerron said. "You're stuck here."

"Then, I need to find a job until I figure this out."

"A job?" Richard asked. "You won't find a job here. There are no respectable jobs for women."

The girl rubbed her forehead and closed her eyes. Something was definitely different. This girl didn't fit the mold of other people he had met. And she was confused. He was usually the only one that didn't understand what was going on, but after all this time, he was getting good at pretending to fit in. Maybe she really had a head injury, or maybe she'd been sent here the same way he was.

"It's not ideal," Jerron said. "Your best hope is to go back to that Lady Anna's house and wait for things to improve."

Her eyes shot daggers at him. "Best hope of what?"

"Getting out of here. I know it doesn't make sense. Play the story out."

"The story?"

"I probably shouldn't say anything. It's probably supposed to be a self-discovery kind of deal."

"I'm leaving," the girl said with a look of pity on her face. She thought he was crazy. That was alright. She wasn't alone.

"Where are you going?" Jerron asked, as she walked in the opposite direction Lady Anna took.

"Somewhere that isn't here," she said.

Jerron glanced at Richard, and the man shrugged.

"She'll be back," he said.

"Why do you care?" Richard asked, and then his eyes lit up. "Did she catch your attention?"

"Of course she captured my attention. She captured yours as well."

"You know what I mean," the man said, rubbing his eyes.

Jerron glimpsed someone out of the corner of his eye. An older woman was watching them. When they made eye contact, she lifted her pink skirts and darted around the doctor's office. "It can't be," he muttered.

"What?" Richard asked.

"No time to explain," Jerron said, sprinting after the woman. He had wondered more than once if that woman was behind his mess of a life. He'd hoped to find her somewhere but had no luck. He wasn't going to lose her now. Jerron rounded the back of the building, and the woman stood there, smiling.

"Good to see you again," she said, studying him.

"Nancy, wasn't it?" he asked.

Her smile widened. "You remember. How thoughtful."

"I've been hoping to run into you for years," he said, not getting too close. "What have you done to my life?"

"Done? What do you mean? We've only met once, and it wasn't here."

"Yes, and ever since we met, my life has been a disaster."

She brushed at her dress. "No more of a disaster than it was before."

"What are you?" he demanded. "A witch?"

Her lip twitched in what Jerron could only guess was amusement. "A witch? Why would you say that?"

"You gave me that whole spiel about fairy tales and true love and the next thing I know, I'm in a never-ending loop of nonsense."

"It's only never-ending as long as you think it's nonsense."

"So, as soon as I decide this is all normal, it will end?" Jerron crossed his arms and glared at the woman.

"Oh, it's not normal, but it isn't nonsense. I thought you would come around faster. You've been here for much longer than I supposed you would. That's why I've changed some things this time."

He scowled. "The girl? You're messing with her too?"

"Helping. It's helping, Jerron. The same way I'm helping you."

"Funny," he said through clenched teeth. "I haven't felt like I've had any help since I came to this crazy place."

"I've helped you. I send you memories now."

"It was better before you did that." When he first came into this confusing world, it confused him every time a new story happened. He fumbled through it all and would eventually move on once he got the story right. Now, when he started a new story, he had a vague memory of the character he was supposed to be.

He must be failing at whatever Nancy wanted him to do because he had been flipping through different lives often enough to give himself a headache. He had strange faded memories of so many things it confused him.

This time when he woke up, he decided to drag this story on as long as he could. It was always better when he was a prince. Sometimes, he was a stable hand or a merchant. As a prince, life was comfortable. He hadn't been sure what story he was in until today. Now, at least, he knew how to finish the story properly and on his own timetable.

"I'm as surprised as you are that it's taking you this long," Nancy said. "That's why I'm changing things this time. Perhaps you need something a little more real."

"So now you have another victim?" he said, swallowing the bitterness in his throat. "How does that help anything?"

Nancy's mouth turned down. "You will thank me someday." She turned and walked away from him. "And don't tell the girl," she said over her shoulder. "It will only make it harder."

"Are the people in these stories real?" Jerron asked. He'd been wondering since Nancy dragged him into the mess. "Is Richard real?" Richard was the first person who he had become friends with.

"That's not something to worry about. I really need to get going. I have a lot to keep track of. Do your best, and I'm sure you'll figure things out."

Jerron leaned against the building and watched as the woman vanished into the trees. He pondered on how long she had trapped him in this world. It seemed like years. He wondered if anyone back home was missing him. His sister had probably given up on finding him by now. She was the only one that would care.

Richard came around the corner and gave him a curious look. "Where are we going next?" he asked.

"I don't care," Jerron said, shrugging. "I've lost my enthusiasm."

"Did you ever have any?"

"Nothing I do matters, so we can do whatever you want."

Richard's eyes lit up. "The bakery has some nice-looking pastries."

"Didn't we just finish eating an enormous meal?" Jerron asked with a crooked smile.

"There is always room for a pastry," Richard said, raising his dark eyebrows.

"I guess you're right."

"I'm right about a lot of things."

"Oh?"

Richard nodded. "Right about pastries, and right about you needing to find a bride. If you don't start cooperating, your father is going to send me packing."

"I doubt it. Where else is he going to find someone that's willing to follow me around and nag me all day? I'm sure it's not a simple job."

"Not at all. I'm glad you recognize that."

Jerron laughed and clapped Richard on the shoulder. "Alright, let's go."

"Go find a wife?"

"Go find a sweet roll."

"Alright. First, the sweet roll, and then, a wife."

"And they lived happily ever after, but did they?" Jerron asked, sitting on his large four-post bed. He kicked his boots to the floor and rubbed his temples.

"Who?" Richard asked, picking the boots up and placing them neatly against the wall.

"Anyone. They always say happily ever after, but what happens after the story? No one knows, because that's where it ends."

"Is that why you don't want to get married? You're afraid it will all end badly?"

"Perhaps," Jerron said, peeling off his socks. "I've never met a girl I wanted to spend the rest of my life with. Most of the girls I knew growing up only liked me for pathetic reasons."

"Because you're a prince?"

"No." Jerron leaned back onto his elbows. "It all started with Rachel Jenkins in fourth grade. She seemed to like me, but it turned out she only liked me because I had a really cool eraser collection. As soon as Paul Goldberg got a cooler pencil collection, I was old news. Same thing repeated with Hannah Chesten in high school, but that time it was cars. It's always like that."

"Sometimes, I wonder if the doctor should examine your head," Richard said. "You've made little sense this past month."

"I'm tired of trying to make sense. Maybe if I just try harder, Nancy will take whatever curse she's cast off me."

Richard's forehead creased. "Who is Nancy?"

Jerron shook his head. "It doesn't matter. You should go to bed. You seem tired."

"I will," Richard said, making a beeline to the door. He probably wanted to get out as fast as possible, so Jerron couldn't change his mind.

Jerron blew out his lamp and crawled under his down comforter. He didn't bother putting on pajamas. He rolled to his side and tried not to feel bad for himself. This was a cushy life. If he avoided throwing a ball and getting married, he could live here forever. That wouldn't be fair, though. The 'Cinderella' girl from today would be stuck here as well, and she wasn't in the comfortable position he found himself in. If they didn't end the story, she would go on serving the wicked stepmother for eternity.

Obviously, Jerron didn't get the game. If he did, he assumed it would have ended. All he'd learned in his time here was that he had to play out the story, and as soon as he kissed the girl, it would fade into a new one.

The first time he had woken up in a fairy tale, he had fumbled around for months. Every time he ruined the story, the day would start over. Now, he did his best to figure out what story he'd been dumped in and get it over with as fast as possible. Well, unless it was a more comfortable story. Some were easier than others. Most, he wasn't familiar with.

It was careless to let Nancy leave today. He had been hoping to run into her for a long time. Before this all happened, his sister Maggie had dragged him to a movie. It was a ridiculous romance that was completely unbelievable. He made sarcastic comments to Maggie throughout the show. He regretted it now because that was when he met Nancy. She'd sat behind him and heard him complaining.

When the movie ended, Nancy cornered him and asked him why he'd been so cynical. She seemed genuinely concerned about his lack of believing in silly endings. She grilled him for a few minutes until he got tired of being polite and he left. He remembered driving home, and the next thing he knew, he was waking up in a place he didn't recognize.

There were a few times he thought he spotted the old woman, but she always disappeared before he could get to her. That was, until today, and he had wasted the time he had. Next time would be different. Next time, he would convince her to send him home. He couldn't do this forever.

Chapter 3

Olivia kept her eyes shut and ignored the pounding on her door. Emily was going to have to let her sleep a little longer. Her nightmare from the night before must have messed with her sleep because she was exhausted. The pounding didn't stop.

"Go away, Emily!" Olivia yelled, opening her eyes. She drew in a sharp breath as she saw the claustrophobic bedroom from her nightmare. She sat up and covered her face with her hands. "No, no, no."

"Ella! Open this door!" Lady Anna barked. "I don't have time for any nonsense. I'm in a hurry."

Olivia leaped from the bed and pulled open the door. Lady Anna's eyes were wide as she studied her. The woman was wearing the same dress as yesterday.

"How did you get me back?" Olivia demanded. "I'll just leave again!" Olivia had spent the entire day trying to put as much distance as she could between herself and this place. When it started getting dark, she had found a covered place in the trees and had quickly fallen asleep.

"Back? Leave? What are you yammering about?" the woman asked. "You are late this morning. Get dressed, and get to work. You don't get breakfast. It will put you behind." Lady Anna slammed the door, and Olivia stood there, staring at nothing. What was going on?

Rushing to the wardrobe, she pulled it open and put on a gray dress that wasn't any less tattered than the one from before. It had the same smell. She wrinkled her nose and hurried out of the room and down the stairs. When she got to the front door, she was surprised to see the window had already been repaired.

"Ella!" Lottie's voice said from behind her. "What are you doing?"

Olivia ignored her and lifted the hem of her dress. Her leg wasn't cut. How was that possible? She looked at the doorknob. Why couldn't she figure out how to unlock it? She didn't want to break the window again.

"I think there's something on the porch. A parcel perhaps?" Olivia bluffed.

"Let me see," Lottie said, pushing her out of the way. She grabbed the doorknob and pulled up, opening the door. Olivia felt ridiculous. The door wasn't even locked. "There's nothing there," Lottie said.

"My mistake," Olivia said, walking out into the sunshine.

"Where are you going?"

"Wherever I want to."

"Mother is going to be angry."

"That's too bad," Olivia said, scurrying toward the road. What was she going to do? All the walking yesterday, and she had gotten nowhere. Something really odd was happening, and she didn't know how to process it. She turned in the opposite direction from the day before. She already knew what she would find that way. A whole lot of crazy townspeople. This direction appeared the same as the other direction.

"Ella, wait!" a man's voice called out. She turned her head but kept walking. The strange man from town was jogging in her direction. She frowned and pressed onward. What could he want? He had made less sense than everyone else. He caught up and matched her pace.

"What do you want?" she asked.

"I just wanted to make sure you were alright. How's your leg?" he asked. She came to an abrupt stop and turned to stare at him. He was tall with dark brown hair and a tan. If she hadn't sworn off dating, he was someone she would be interested in.

"How do you know about my leg?"

"I was outside the doctor yesterday. Remember?"

"So yesterday did happen," she muttered. "It doesn't matter." She started walking again.

"Well, it happened for some of us," he said. "I'm Jerron, by the way."

Olivia side-eyed him. "What do you mean for some of us?"

"This is a weird place. I'm not sure how to explain it to you without seeming like a crazy person."

She laughed bitterly. "Everything I've seen has been crazy since I woke up yesterday."

"I believe it. Let me warn you, though. You can run away a hundred times, a thousand times, and it won't change anything. You'll wake up every day in the same place until you do things right."

"That doesn't make sense."

"I'm not supposed to tell you anything, but for the first time since I've been here, someone else is affecting my life repeats. I usually only relive a day if I screw up. I had to repeat yesterday, and I'm guessing that was your fault."

"What are you talking about?"

"Is your leg healed?"

Olivia bit her lip. "Yes."

He raised one eye brow. "How do you explain that?"

"I . . . can't."

"Take it from someone who understands what you're going through. The only way out of this place is to learn to accept happiness. At least, that's my guess. Go back to the house with Lady Anna. Do the cooking and cleaning, and follow the story."

"The story?"

"It's the only way to move on."

She narrowed her eyes. "What do you mean, move on? Am I dead?"

He chuckled. "No. Well, I don't think so. It's more like—stuck in some weird limbo. I get put in a fairy tale, and if I follow it close enough, I wake up in a new one. If I don't, I will wake up to the day I messed up."

Olivia kept going forward. She thought about her leg. How could she explain that away? And how had she returned to Lady Anna's house? She'd put several miles between her and

34

this place yesterday. She was in good shape, and she had walked most of the day.

"You're still here," she finally said. "If you've figured out how this all works and you can't escape, then why should I listen to your advice?"

"Look, Ella," he said, taking her shoulder and stopping her. "Olivia."

"Olivia. I don't understand most things here. I only know what I've learned. If you want to keep repeating this day, then that's fine. I'm in a comfortable position right now, so it won't bother me to keep repeating. I've had it a lot worse. You, though, aren't in the greatest position."

She studied him. He seemed sincere. He was also really handsome. She shook her head. She would not dwell on things like that. Good-looking guys were always a bad idea—At least, that's what Emily always said. Olivia figured she said it because Trent wasn't handsome. He wasn't ugly, just average.

"So, if I follow the story, I move on to what?" she challenged.

"Another story."

"And it keeps happening forever?" Panic rippled over her body, and she tried to remain calm.

"No idea. Someone is trying to teach us a lesson, and it won't stop until we learn it. I try to follow the stories now, but I'm still here, so I'm obviously not getting whatever they want me to."

Olivia frowned and thought about the bridal shop and the elderly woman. "Is this because I said I don't believe in happily ever after? It had to be that Nancy woman."

"My guess is yes, and it is Nancy."

"Can I find her somewhere?"

Jerron sighed. "I've tried several times. I actually talked to her yesterday, but I didn't get anywhere. She thinks she's doing us a great service."

"What you're saying is impossible," she said, continuing on her journey. She couldn't explain any of this, but that didn't make his explanation sound.

"Where are you from?" Jerron asked, keeping up with her.

"Colorado."

"Same."

"What happened to you?" she asked.

His brow wrinkled. "What happened to me?"

"How did you get here? I fell out a window and the next thing I knew I was here. That's why I figure I'm unconscious or something, and this is all in my head."

"The last thing I remember is driving. Nothing big happened that I can remember."

"How long have you been here?"

He tilted his head. "Here as in Cinderella land, or here as in Nancy's crazy world?"

"Both."

"I've been here for about a month. I'm not sure when the whole adventure started. It seems like years." The corners of his mouth turned down. "I tried to keep track at first, but that just got depressing."

Olivia frowned. What if she spent the rest of her life here? She wasn't leaving a lot behind, but this wasn't ideal. She already wished Emily was here with her. "If I have to do the story right, that means it ends when I marry the prince? I'm really not looking to get married."

"From my experience, you only have to kiss him. Once that happens, a new story starts."

She bit her lip. "Interesting. How many people has Nancy dragged here?"

"No clue. Until I saw you yesterday, I thought I was the only one."

"So, are the other people here actors? Are they all just playing a role?"

He rubbed his scruffy chin. "In my opinion, they believe they are the people they are supposed to be."

"Are they real?"

"Sometimes, I'm sure it's all happening in my head, but then I hurt myself and figure it has to be real. I've had some serious injuries since I've been here. I can't imagine hurting that bad and it being in my head. As for the others? They seem real, but hollow."

"What's your real name?"

"It's Jerron. It would surprise you how many characters don't have names. If it's a nameless character, they always use my real name."

"What if I can't do this?" Olivia fretted. "If I'm supposed to be Cinderella, that means I have to go to the ball and stuff. I'm terrible at dancing, and everyone's going to be watching. And do I have to make myself cry so a fairy godmother will come? I'm not sure if I can do that."

"Things don't need to be really specific. If you follow along, instinct usually takes over. I even get memories of some characters now. It's annoying sometimes when I'm trying to pull out my own memories. I don't want to lose myself because of the fake ones."

Olivia's stomach tumbled. "This is all so crazy, but I'm starting to believe it. I can't come up with anything that makes sense. I mean, I still won't be surprised if I'm unconscious somewhere, but I believe you when you say I can't run away from it."

She couldn't believe she was having this conversation, and it was equally hard to believe she was so easily convinced. There just wasn't a way to explain away her healed leg and ending up at Lady Anna's house again.

"Do you want me to walk you back?" he asked.

She sighed and rubbed her eyes. "I suppose." She switched directions. Part of

her wanted to spend the day getting away, but yesterday's walk was still fresh in her mind.

"Is there anything besides trees around here? I walked forever yesterday, and I only passed a few houses."

"I haven't really explored. The village seems pretty small. Most of the houses are clustered together, except on this road. You're right about the trees. They do seem to have a lot of forest."

"I should have ignored Nancy."

Jerron nodded. "Nancy is all about happy ever after. My guess is we have to do this until we find or believe in happiness. I've really tried, but it hasn't changed anything."

Olivia sighed. This wasn't going to be easy. She enjoyed cleaning about as much as she enjoyed shopping for weddings. "Maybe we're supposed to help other people find happiness? If Nancy likes helping others, maybe she thinks it would help us understand what it's like to do that for people."

"I never considered that," Jerron said, his eyes lighting up. "That could be it. I've been too self-absorbed to think about helping people around me. I'm going to try that. Thanks, Olivia."

"I might be wrong."

"It's something to try, though. That's more than I had this morning."

ele

Jerron set a brisk pace after he left Olivia at her new home. He was eager to try following her advice, and he knew the person he wanted to start with. Richard definitely deserved something better in life. What did Richard want, though? That was a tough one.

He found Richard pacing in Jerron's room.

"Prince Jerron! Where have you been?" the man asked, looking relieved. "I've been so worried the king would appear and I wouldn't be able to tell him where you were!"

"Sorry. I went for a walk."

"You aren't allowed to do that without supervision."

"Yes, I realize that. Sorry. I'm glad I didn't get you in trouble. How can I make it up to you?"

Richard scratched his head. "Nothing comes to mind."

"I've got an idea. A ball."

"A ball?"

"Yes. We throw a ball. The dance kind, not the bouncy ones. You can tell the king that I promise to decide on a bride within a week after the ball." Jerron grinned as he watched a smile spread across Richard's face. "There is a condition."

"What's that?" Richard asked.

"You have to dance at the ball."

"Me?" Richard squeaked.

"Yes. That's my condition."

Richard looked green. "One dance."

"Deal. And I get to choose the lucky lady."

Richard groaned. "You're trying to punish me, aren't you?"

Jerron laughed. "Not at all."

"Fine deal. I'm going to talk to the king now. He's going to be ecstatic!"

"I'm sure he will." Jerron smiled as he watched Richard scamper out of the room. Even if he wasn't looking forward to it, he would make sure Richard benefitted from the ball.

His smile slid from his face when he thought of Olivia. He hadn't told her he was the prince. Would she be disappointed? It was strange knowing she was a real person. All the other girls in the stories had seemed fake. Their responses were all automatic and followed the fairy tales as far as he could tell. Olivia was real, and he liked her more than he should. Probably because they were in the same situation. It had been a while since he'd had a conversation that felt genuine.

It might all turn out wrong. The other girls had no choice but to fall for him. It was their story. Olivia possessed a will of her own, and from what he'd seen, it was a strong will. She might not follow through. Why was he getting nervous? Perhaps because he knew he could get rejected this time. Not that his ego was getting big from all the stories, but he always knew or could guess how it would end. He didn't love fairy tales, but there was a method to them.

Jerron paced across the room. He hoped Olivia understood what they were up against. She wouldn't really be expecting anything from him. He rubbed a hand across his face and told himself he believed it. She would cooperate. She had to.

Olivia stared in horror at the outhouse. The small wooden structure was located at least a hundred feet behind the main house. She could smell it as soon as she saw it. This was worse than cleaning.

After returning to Lady Anna's, she'd asked Lottie where the cleaning supplies were. Lottie mocked her, but eventually showed her a closet full of mops, brooms, buckets, and rags.

The house was large, and she wasn't sure where to start. She wasn't a stranger to cleaning, but things here differed from what she was used to. Olivia walked around the house, trying to decide what to do. She'd never been in a house this fancy. Most of it seemed clean and probably wasn't used very often.

It would probably be easy to slack off. Everyone had been ignoring her so far, and she would not create work for herself if it didn't need to be done. There was enough intricate woodwork around the house to keep a person busy dusting forever.

Things had been going well until she needed to use the bathroom. She searched the house, and when she couldn't find one, she realized the horrifying truth. No indoor plumbing. There was a pump in the kitchen, but that was the only indoor source of water she could find. It only made sense to go search out back, but now that she was here, she was having second thoughts.

The small wooden structure appeared well kept and clean, but she didn't want to open the door. She'd only been camping a few times in her life, but she always hated the camp bathrooms, and those had running water.

Slowly opening the door, she peered in. A powerful smell assaulted her nose, and she gagged. Flies buzzed past her face. Slamming the door, she took a step back. How did people get used to something like this? She peered into the woods behind the house and sighed. There was a choice. The outhouse or the trees.

She should have asked Jerron where he lived. It was possible he'd figured a way around some of these things. Would he come looking for her again? He was her only link to her world—the real world.

"Fairy godmother!" Olivia called. It was worth a try. She would rather be granted indoor plumbing than a fancy dress and a prince. Perhaps the prince had indoor plumbing. There must be some advantages to being royal.

When no sparkling fairy appeared, Olivia toughened up. She studied the assaulting shack and wondered how long she could hold her breath.

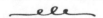

Olivia placed a platter of burned potatoes on the dining room table next to the scorched chicken.

"Ew," Lottie complained, inspecting the food. "What is wrong with you today?"

Olivia shrugged. She hadn't been this tired in a long time. She wasn't a skilled cook even when she knew what she was doing, so dinner had turned into a gigantic mess. Figuring out how to light the oven had been a chore.

"You have been ridiculously out of character today," Lady Anna said, glaring at the food. "Late to wake up, no lunch, now this."

Mara snickered. "You should have seen her cleaning today. Every time I passed her, she looked like she didn't know what she was doing. It was ridiculous."

"I'd like to see you do better," Olivia said, sinking into an empty chair.

"What are you doing?" Lady Anna demanded. "You know you are not to sit with us."

Olivia narrowed her eyes. "You can't expect me to work all day and never eat. I feel like I might pass out."

"You'll survive without food for one day, and perhaps tomorrow you will remember to wake up and make breakfast."

Olivia took a deep breath and tried not to imagine herself flinging the hot potatoes at the woman.

"Come, girls," Lady Anna said, rising from her seat. "We will go to town for dinner."

Mara squealed, and Lottie smirked.

"As for you," she said, glancing at Olivia, "You give this mess to the pigs and clean up. I don't want any excuses when we get back." The three of them strutted out of the room.

Olivia had never been so happy to see the backs of anyone. She waited three minutes, but that was all she could take. The pigs could wait. She grabbed a piece of burned chicken and stuffed it in her mouth. It tasted heavenly. After she filled her empty stomach, she took the leftovers and went searching for the pigs.

As she rounded the corner of the house, she almost bumped into a tall, muscular man in a dirty tunic with muddy boots.

"Sorry," she said, as she stepped around him.

"That for the pigs?" he asked in a deep voice.

"Yes," she said. She wondered if this was Stephan, the man Lady Anna had threatened her with the other day.

"I'll take it," he said, relieving her of the plate.

"Thanks."

"Why are you acting so peculiar?" he asked, studying the burned chicken. "Are you trying to get in trouble? I hate it when they make me punish you."

Olivia studied the man. He didn't look mean, and he seemed concerned.

"I can't explain," she admitted.

"Well, stay out of trouble. Alright?"

"I'll try."

"Lady Anna was upset when she left this morning. She was mumbling about you, and she told me to keep an eye on you. You're lucky she wasn't here when you left after that. Who was the man that brought you home?"

"Someone I met in town yesterday."

"You didn't go to town yesterday," he said, shifting the plate. "You never go to town. Lady Anna will be angry if she realizes you have a gentleman friend."

Olivia chuckled. "It's not like that. He's trying to keep me out of trouble as well."

Stephen nodded. "Just be careful. She doesn't like you to talk to anyone. I don't want to see what might happen if she finds out."

Olivia wasn't sure what to say, so she just shrugged and returned to the house. This morning she had been dreading the ball, but after a few more days of this, she was going to be more than ready.

Chapter 4

Jerron stood in front of the fancy house and wondered what he could do to get Olivia to come out. He had stayed away for two weeks. That should be long enough for her to figure some things out. She must be doing alright because he hadn't had to repeat any more days. That meant she was learning faster than he had. Of course, she had the advantage of him telling her some things. He'd been on his own.

A scream came from behind the house. Jerron darted around the corner of the building and ran to the back. Olivia was standing by the outhouse, hugging herself and shaking.

"What's wrong?" he asked, moving in closer. She looked up with wide eyes. She probably hadn't expected to see him again.

"What are you doing here?" she asked with a tremble in her voice.

"I came to check on you. What's going on?"

"It turns out part of my job is to rid the outhouse of spiders."

"And you hate spiders?" he asked, holding back a smile.

"The spiders here are not normal!" Olivia said. "I've never seen anything like them! Every night I have dreams about them. It's horrible."

"That was a pretty loud scream a minute ago. Do you want me to go take care of them?"

"It's not a spider today. It's a big, evil snake! I do not do snakes. I don't care what punishment Lady Anna wants to give me, I am not touching that thing! When is the stupid ball? I'm ready to marry the prince or anything else to get away from this place!"

Jerron chuckled. "I'll go take care of the snake for you."

"Be careful. It's huge."

"How huge is huge?"

"I didn't measure, but I would guess three feet."

That was pretty impressive for a snake around here. The only ones he'd seen were pretty small. Jerron had snakes as a kid, so they didn't bother him. He opened the door to the outhouse and peered inside. He inspected the space and saw nothing.

"Can you hold the door open so I can see better?" he asked Olivia.

She pulled the door wide and stood as far away as she could without letting go. Where was it hiding? Something brown moved near his foot and he stepped back. A baby snake slithered against the ground. He grinned and picked it up. It wrapped itself around his hand. He came out of the enclosure and held it up.

"Get rid of it!" Olivia commanded. "I can't believe you're holding it!"

"It's a baby. It's not going to hurt anyone."

"I don't care. Get it far away from here!"

"Alright," he said, walking toward the trees. He wasn't sure if he should tell her there were probably more around. When he'd gone a fair distance, he released the snake and then returned to her.

"Thank you," she said.

He smiled. "Any time. Do you want to go for a walk?"

"I'll probably get in trouble."

"Have you been staying out of trouble?"

"Not really," she admitted. "Thankfully, the man who is supposed to carry out my punishments is really a softy named Stephan. Lady Anna tells him to beat me. She sends me out to the stable, and Stephan makes whipping sounds while I scream. Then, I pretend to be sore."

Jerron clenched his fists. Nancy better not be leaving Olivia in danger. "Has he ever hurt you?"

"No. He's not the type."

"I'm glad he doesn't really hurt you. Does Lady Anna?"

Olivia shook her head. "Usually, they just make me miss meals."

Jerron forced himself to stop grinding his teeth. "Are you hungry? I can bring you food."

"No. I'm not as passive as the Ella they are used to. I just eat while I'm burning their food. They never notice."

He grinned as some of his tension slipped away. "You burn their food?"

"Not on purpose. I've never been a great cook, and I don't know how to cook on their stove. That's the biggest reason I get in trouble. They think I'm ruining the food on purpose.

I'm starting to hate the Ella that was before me. She must have been perfect at cooking and cleaning. I can't live up to it."

"Who is this?" a young woman asked, approaching them.

"Just a passerby," Olivia said. "He came and rid the outhouse of a snake."

"Oh, how kind," she said, batting her eyelashes at Jerron. The girl was pretty, but she had nothing on Olivia. "My name is Lottie. Why don't you come inside for some tea?"

"No, thank you," Jerron said. "I really need to be on my way."

"You can't do us such a great service and not let us repay you," Lottie said, linking her arm with his and tugging him forward. Olivia's mouth turned up slightly as he allowed himself to be led to the house. "Ella, bring us some tea and shortbread."

"Of course," Olivia said from behind them. Jerron wondered if Olivia knew how to make tea.

"Don't scald it," Lottie warned. The girl smelled of strong floral perfume. Jerron hoped it didn't give him a headache. He didn't do well with flowery smells, and she must use it liberally.

"I really should be leaving," Jerron tried again.

"Don't be silly. There's always time for tea. What's your name?"

"John." Jerron glanced over his shoulder. Olivia looked amused, but he didn't understand why. He couldn't give his real name because he didn't want Lottie to know he was the prince. She led him into the house and to a sparkling clean parlor. Olivia must be keeping up with her work.

"Please, sit," Lottie said with a smile that reminded him of a terrifying clown. He sat on a small sofa and looked around uncomfortably. The room was pleasant enough. Lottie sat on the sofa beside him, and he held in a sigh. She was much too close for comfort. He should have dressed shabbily and skipped his bath. That probably would have kept her away.

"Why haven't I seen you before?" she asked. Jerron tried to lean farther away. He could feel her breath when she talked.

"I don't live close," he said, hoping Olivia would hurry. He could gulp down a cup of tea and be on his way.

"I hope you'll come around more often. I'm sure my mother would love to meet you."

"Who is this?" a younger girl with dark brown hair asked, entering the room.

"Go away, Mara," Lottie said. "This is none of your concern."

"I never get to talk to anyone!" Mara protested. "All the guests are always for you. It isn't fair!"

"Excuse me a moment," Lottie said to Jerron. She stomped over to her sister and whispered loudly, "As soon as I'm married, you get to have all the company! It would be in your best interest to go away!"

"Fine, but it's not fair, and I'm telling Mother when she returns."

Lottie glared at her sister. "She'll side with me. I'm doing this for you, you know."

Jerron wondered if she really thought he couldn't hear her. He had never heard anyone talk so loudly when they were trying to be quiet.

"How are you doing it for me?" Mara whined.

"If I make a good match, I can send eligible men your way."

"Oh, alright," she muttered, turning and stomping from the room.

Lottie turned around, and her fake smile returned. "Sorry about that," she said. "My sister isn't always as refined as she should be. I imagine it's because she's the youngest."

Jerron nodded as she returned to sit next to him.

Olivia entered the room with a tray and placed it on the table in front of them. "Will there be anything else?" she asked.

"No, now go," Lottie commanded. Olivia did an exaggeratedly bad bow and turned to leave.

Jerron smiled. "Wait. Where I'm from, it's customary for the servant who makes the tea to sit with the guests."

"That's a silly tradition," Lottie said. "The help shouldn't sit with their betters."

"I insist," he said.

"Fine," Lottie said, staring daggers at Olivia. "She can pour the tea."

Olivia nodded and poured tea into the two cups. Her eyes sparkled as Jerron took his first sip. It was awful. He couldn't imagine anyone making tea taste that bad— unless it was on purpose.

"Oh, Ella!" Lottie spat, slamming her cup against the table. "That tastes terrible! I don't know why you can't do anything anymore! I'm sorry, John. She'll be punished."

"I really need to go," he said, standing.

"Don't leave!" Lottie protested, grabbing his sleeve.

He pulled it from her grasp. "I have some beautiful roses at my house that would be lovely in this room," Jerron said. "As punishment for your servant, have her follow me, and I will send some back with her."

"You're going to send me flowers?" Lottie asked, beaming. "How delightful! You heard that, Ella. Follow him, but don't talk to him. Stay at least ten paces behind."

"Of course," Olivia said, rolling her eyes. Jerron smiled as he left the house, with Olivia behind him. Today was turning out to be entertaining.

"Thanks for getting me out of there," Olivia said, as she strolled down the dusty road with Jerron.

"Sure," he said. "Is it horrible?"

"It's not as bad as I thought it would be," she said, reflecting over the past two weeks. "I don't know what I'm doing, but the house doesn't get very messy. It's mostly dusting. The cooking is terrible, and getting rid of the outhouse spiders. Lady Anna is rarely home, and Lottie and Mara don't want to be around me any more than I do them."

"Are you getting any memories?"

"No. I'm not trying to remember anything. I don't want to get confused between my real life and this place."

Jerron nodded. "I understand that. It is easier to adjust when you have the memories, though. It might help you with the cooking."

"It would be worth it if it made me brave around spiders."

"So, are you really that bad at making tea, or did you do that on purpose?"

Olivia grinned. "I don't drink tea, so I don't know what it's supposed to taste like."

"That didn't answer my question."

"I know."

"I feel bad you're spending all your time cooking and cleaning, and I'm having a cushy time in this reality. I always hate when I get stuck in an uncomfortable place."

"What was the worst story you've been in?" she asked.

Jerron thought for a moment. "*Robin Hood* was awful."

Olivia thought of the cartoon fox and smiled. "You were in *Robin Hood*?"

"I *was* Robin Hood. I had to sleep outside and hang out with a bunch of odd guys. Thankfully, I got memories with that one so I could actually use my bow. I hated every minute of it. I'm not really into robbing the rich, or anyone else. I hate to admit it, but I'm a wimp when it comes to sleeping outside and cooking over a fire. I love comfort."

"This is all so strange," Olivia said. "I still have a hard time believing it's happening. So, did you fall in love with Maid Marion?"

"Not even close. She was the most boring character I've met. I did my best to follow the story, and it ended. Getting away from her was a bonus. She cried a lot."

"Why?"

"I have no idea. I was so happy to be done with her."

"What was the weirdest story you've been in?"

"*Peter Pan*."

Olivia laughed. "You were Peter Pan? Could you fly?"

"I wasn't Peter Pan. I'm too old for that."

"Who then? Hook?"

"I wish," Jerron said, flashing a bright white smile at her. "I was Wendy's father."

She grinned. "You're not old enough for that."

"I agree. I was about nine years older than Wendy. It was ridiculous. It was almost as bad as *Robin Hood*, but at least the house was comfortable."

"Aren't Wendy's father and Hook usually played by the same person?"

"Maybe. I think you know more about fairy tales than I do."

"I used to watch the movies when I was little. I guess I didn't get cynical until high school. The father in *Peter Pan* never goes to Neverland."

"Nope. I spent the entire time comforting Mrs. Darling. She was upset by her lost children. Still, she didn't cry as much as Maid Marion."

"What have you been doing for the last two weeks?" she asked.

"Not a lot. I have a servant that I've been trying to help. I decided that perhaps I can make him happy and Nancy will give me points."

Olivia could see a house up ahead. There weren't many on this road. "I was going to try to help my wicked stepsisters learn to be happy, but I haven't been feeling it. They are both so self-absorbed and petty. I'd rather keep burning their food."

"You should try. I don't want you to end up here forever."

Something fluttered inside her stomach, but she quickly squashed it. Just because Jerron was nice to her didn't mean he liked her. She would not let herself feel anything for him but friendship. Wishing for the impossible only made a person miserable.

"Does this house have any roses?" Jerron asked, studying the house they were approaching.

"I see some yellow ones on the side."

"I'm going to run up and ask if I can cut some. I'm not going to make you walk all the way to my house. It's way too far."

"I'll wait here," Olivia said, watching him jog toward the house. She smiled as he stumbled over a fallen branch. He really was a nice guy. She shook her head and told herself to behave. With everything that was happening, she didn't need to add a broken heart to it.

ella

Lottie ripped the yellow flowers from Olivia's hand and inhaled their fragrance.

"How lovely!" she cooed. "Look at the flowers that gorgeous man sent to me, Mara."

Mara sank angrily onto the sofa and crossed her arms. "Why don't men ever send me flowers?"

"Why would they send you flowers? I'm the oldest, and so I'll inherit. Remember what I told you. If I make a good match, it will help you make one as well. Now, Ella," she said, turning to Olivia. "Tell me about John's house. Was it large?"

"Oh, umm, it was nice," Olivia said. She wasn't really sure what to say since she hadn't seen Jerron's home.

"Was it bigger than ours?"

"Yes."

Lottie glared at her. "It took you long enough."

"He lives far away," Olivia said. She didn't actually know where Jerron lived, but they had spent an hour walking around talking.

Lottie squealed with happiness. "I bet he's back before the week is over. He couldn't stop staring at me."

Olivia rolled her eyes, and Mara harrumphed. Lottie hugged her flowers and bounced out of the room.

"I hope they have bugs in them," Mara muttered. "Big biting bugs that bite her face and make it swell."

Olivia grinned. "It's not always easy having a sister."

Mara gave her a strange look. "I wish I was as pretty as she is. Then, men would notice me."

"You are as pretty as she is," Olivia assured her. The girls actually looked similar.

"Then, why do the men only like her?"

"I'm not sure they do. She scares them, and they don't know how to get away."

"Really? What about the man today? He sent flowers."

"He only did that, so he had an excuse to leave."

"You think so?" Mara asked, the corners of her mouth turning down.

"Lottie's never going to be happy because she only cares about appearances. Let me give you some advice. Don't be like Lottie." Olivia wondered if the girl would turn on her and tell Lottie everything she was saying.

"Then how do I catch a man?" Mara asked.

"First off, change your mindset. You're young. Don't try to catch a man. Try to get to know lots of men and see if you are suited to any of them. If you are, be yourself. If he doesn't like the real you, he isn't worth it."

"Wow. That's deep," Mara said with wide eyes. "Sometimes, I wish we were allowed to like you. You're a lot nicer than Lottie."

Olivia smiled. "Maybe you can like me secretly."

"Perhaps," Mara said, tilting her head. "But I'll still have to be mean to you when anyone's watching."

"I understand that."

"There actually is a man I'm interested in," the girl confided.

"Oh?"

"There are two major problems. The first is, he doesn't like me. The second is, my mother would never approve." Mara dramatically slumped against the sofa and sighed. "My hopes and dreams will never be realized."

Olivia held in a laugh. Who would have thought she would be trying to give someone relationship advice? She'd sure never had a successful one. Perhaps, it was easier to tell someone what to do than to do it yourself.

"Who is this man?" she asked.

Mara sat up straight and glanced around, as if she was expecting someone to be hiding behind the furniture. She leaned forward and whispered. "It's Stephan."

"Oh," Olivia said. A girl could do worse than Stephan. He had shown he was a kind man more than once in the last two weeks. He was young, but a little rough around the edges. "Does he know how you feel?"

"Of course not!" Mara exclaimed. "If he did, I would die!"

"Well, that's a bit dramatic. How often do you talk to him?"

"Never! I just spy on him from the stable window. I climb up the woodpile and peek in."

Olivia tilted her head. "Do you only like him because he's handsome?"

"No. He's really nice. He helped me last year when I got my leg stuck in the woodpile. He was even nice enough to not ask me what my leg was doing there in the first place. Then there was the time I almost got attacked by a momma pig. Let me give you some advice. Never pick up a baby piglet when the momma pig is around. Stephan saw her chasing me and saved me."

Olivia tried not to laugh at the image playing through her head. "So, you like him because he's saved you twice?"

"More than twice," the girl said, bowing her head in shame. "He actually had to get me out of the woodpile twice. It was really embarrassing the second time."

"I would imagine."

"Remember when you had that fever last year? There was a beehive on the outhouse, and I couldn't make you deal with it because you were sick. I decided that bees probably wouldn't sting me because they die if they sting. I figured it would be silly of them to sting me and die, so I threw a rock at the hive to break it down."

Olivia could see where this was going.

"The bees flew at me, and guess what? They did sting me! I ran into the trees, and I guess Stephan saw me. He ran after me and threw me into the creek. He said they weren't actually bees. I forgot what he called them, but I guess they can sting over and over. There were some other times, but talking about it's making me depressed," she said, resting her elbows on her knees. "I'm sure you don't understand heartache. You don't even get to meet anyone."

"Oh, I understand," Olivia said, shaking her head. "When I was in school, I liked the same boy for over a year. I thought about him all the time. One day, he passed me in the hall and called me Olive. I was crushed."

"I forgot you went to school. Did you like any other boys after that?"

"Sure, but they never seemed to like me. It was always the weird boys that wanted to be around me."

"I doubt that's true," Mara said. "You're even prettier than Lottie and you're a lot nicer. I bet plenty of nice boys liked you. Weird people are just louder and don't seem to get as nervous."

"I suppose it's possible. Perhaps, you should try talking to Stephan instead of spying on him," Olivia suggested.

"I can't do that. I have nothing to say. My life is boring because I never get to do fun things like Lottie."

"You don't sound boring," Olivia said.

"He doesn't know I exist."

Olivia smiled. "I'm pretty sure he does." It would be hard to not remember someone he had gotten out of trouble so many times.

"I wouldn't know what to say."

"I take the dinner scraps out to the pigs every night, and Stephan usually comes and takes them from me. Maybe you could take them out tonight?"

"Scraps? To the pigs? Mother would never allow it."

"You don't have to tell her."

Mara's eyes opened wide. "I'm not sure if I can pull off a deception. Mother can see through everything."

"That's because you always look guilty."

"What do you mean?" Mara asked, crossing her arms.

"When you sneak extra dessert from the kitchen, it's always obvious because you open your eyes wide and walk slowly with your hands behind your back. It would be less obvious if you just grabbed the food and walked confidently away. That's what Lottie does."

"Lottie sneaks extra?"

"Every day."

Mara's brows came together. "But you notice."

"But I don't care. Your mother only catches you, not Lottie. You're usually the first one finished with dinner. Take your time and don't leave the table until your mother and Lottie do, then you can take the scraps out."

"Will you come with me?"

"Won't that make it more awkward?"

"No. If I can't talk, you can."

"Alright," Olivia agreed. This might be entertaining.

Olivia held the door for Mara as the girl balanced a plate full of scraps in her hands. They walked over to the pigs, and sure enough, Stephan approached them. Olivia studied the man. He wasn't her type, but she could see why Mara would like him. Stephan was strong from all the hard work he did, and he had a pleasant face.

"Is that for the pigs?" he asked Mara. She nodded and clutched the plate close to herself.

"I can take it for you," he said, holding out his hand. Mara kept her grip on the plate and watched the man with wide eyes.

"Give him the plate," Olivia whispered.

"Right," she said, shoving the plate at Stephan. She pushed it too hard, and the food splattered all over Stephan's shirt.

"Thank you!" she said, grabbing her skirts and dashing to the house.

Stephan's mouth turned up in a slight grin as he pulled food from his shirt and put it back on the plate. He was messy enough he was going to have to change. Olivia wasn't sure whether she should laugh or feel pity for Mara. A small giggle escaped her mouth, and Stephan glanced up at her. His eyes were sparkling, and he smiled. It was the first time Olivia had seen him look amused.

"That girl is going to be the death of me," he said. "Sometimes, I wonder if she's really as clumsy as she seems or if she's testing me."

"Oh?" Olivia asked. "Does she dump food on you often?"

"No, this is the first time. At least with food. I feel like I've spent the last five years getting her out of trouble. When I left home at fourteen to be my own man, I thought I would be doing something a lot different. Is she clumsy in the house?"

"Sometimes," Olivia admitted, "but you make her nervous."

"Nervous? Hm. It's too bad she has the mother she does."

"Why is that?"

He shrugged. Olivia wondered if the man might have some feelings for Mara.

"I better go back. I don't want Lady Anna to miss me."

Stephan winked. "Perhaps, you can send Mara out to dump more food on me tomorrow."

Olivia smiled. "I'll try." It was fulfilling helping Mara and Stephan. If they ended up together, she would be elated, and she was taking credit. Her smile slipped away as she walked back to the house. Why could she believe in love for Mara, but not for herself?

Mara was nowhere to be seen, and Olivia found herself in the empty kitchen. She sank into a chair and grabbed a cookie. What if Emily had been right? Olivia had never made any moves to let the boys she liked know she liked them. She had always hoped they would approach her without her trying.

What if she followed the advice she had given Mara? She grinned as she pictured herself shoving a plate of food on Jerron. If she had known him in high school, she would have liked him. She would probably fall for him now if he came around more. She felt the familiar pain in her heart at the thought of being rejected.

Jerron was nice, but if he ended up liking her, it might be because she was the only other person who was real. It would be depressing if she let her heart get involved and then they returned to the real world and he realized she wasn't for him.

Why was she even letting herself dwell on this? These were the thoughts she tried to avoid. It never led to anything but sadness. But still—What if Emily was right? What if her advice to Mara was right? Should she let herself hope? She could encourage Jerron a little and see what happened. If nothing came of it, it would be the final nail in the coffin.

Biting into the soft oatmeal cookie, she rolled her eyes. She didn't even know Jerron. She'd only been around him a few times. Why was she being so dramatic? Perhaps, the reason she was the way she was was because she made things more complicated than they needed to be.

Olivia told Mara to take the time to get to know people. If she was honest, she had never done that. She'd gotten silly crushes on boys she hardly knew and then taken it to heart when they didn't fall madly in love with her. She'd gone from believing in love too much to believing in it too little. Shoving the rest of the cookie in her mouth, she sighed. Could she find a middle ground?

Chapter 5

"It's set," Richard said, his deep brown eyes sparkling. "The ball will be next Friday. Your father is beside himself with joy."

"I'm sure he is," Jerron said, as he placed a chessboard on the table in his room. Being a prince in this place was boring. He always assumed princes were busy helping run the kingdom, but as far as princes in fairy tale land went, they were pretty useless. He wasn't expected to do anything. Well, anything but get married.

"He is holding you to your word," Richard said, pushing his black hair off his forehead. "He wants to be planning a wedding within a week of the ball."

"That's fine," Jerron said, placing the chess pieces down. "Sit down, and let me beat you at chess."

"I've been letting you beat me at chess for weeks," Richard said. "It's not easy, either. You used to be a lot better."

"Wait," Jerron said, looking up from the board. "You've been letting me win?"

Richard shrugged. "Of course. You always tell me to."

"Come on, Rich. I was joking. Just treat me like you would anyone else. Don't let me win."

"Alright," he said, smiling as he sank into a chair. "This will be a lot more fun. You play like a ten-year-old. A ten-year-old that's never played chess."

"Ouch." Jerron shook his head as he took his own seat. He had never been good at chess, and so it had surprised him when he kept beating the man. He should have known his skills hadn't improved just because he was playing a character that owned a chess set.

Richard began setting up his pieces and humming under his breath. "So, what made you finally decide it was time to get married? Not that I'm complaining. The king has never been so happy with me."

"I decided it's time."

"Just like that?"

"Yep. I've had a change of heart."

"What brought that on?" he asked, pushing a white pawn two spaces forward.

"I met a girl," Jerron said, watching the other man's reaction.

Richard's eyes widened, and his mouth dropped. "What do you mean, you met a girl? I'm with you all the time! You can't make me believe you met someone. Are you sneaking out at night?"

Jerron grinned. "No." He moved his black pawn forward. "Remember the girl in front of the doctor's office?"

"Doctor's office? When have we been in front of the doctor's office?"

"Right—I had to redo that day. Well, remember when you couldn't find me yesterday? I was with her."

"But when did you meet her?"

"I was with you, but you don't remember."

Richard took one of Jerron's pieces and shook his head. "Some days, you make little sense. You will not convince me you met a girl when you were with me and I don't remember. I don't drink, and I have an excellent memory."

"Sometimes, I like to mess with you."

"Don't I know it? So, who is she?"

"A servant girl."

Richard raised his eyebrow. "Lovely. Your father will be thrilled."

Jerron grinned as he took one of Richard's pieces. "He said I could marry anyone, and his opinion isn't my concern."

"I don't care who she is, I'm just happy I won't have to have any more lectures from the king. He seems to expect you to obey me. How is this girl different from any of the other girls?" he asked, taking Jerron's knight.

"It's weird," Jerron admitted. "I'm not well acquainted with her, but talking to her just seems natural. She isn't fake. She says what she thinks. I've never had a connection like this before."

He frowned. Everything he was saying was true, but it didn't matter. Once they kissed, she would disappear, and he would never see her again—unless they both found their way back to Colorado someday.

It was also possible that she had captured his attention because she was the first person he knew was real. He would have to be careful and make sure he understood his own mind. He really didn't know her well at all. Still, he had to move things along. He couldn't force her to stay here being a servant. That wouldn't be fair.

"You are terrible at this game," Richard said, scooping up another piece.

"I thought I was getting better. You were so easy to beat. I can't believe you were letting me win. I command you to never lose to me at anything on purpose. Deal?"

Richard grinned. "Yes. I'm enjoying this much more than usual."

"So, back to the ball," Jerron said, feeling mischievous. "I'm still trying to figure out which girl I should get you to dance with."

Richard groaned. "I hoped you forgot about that."

"Never. What type of women do you like?"

"I'm not that particular. The problem is there isn't a type of woman that likes me."

"Have you tried?"

"Well, no. Not really. When I was in school, all the girls teased me because I was short. It made me shy about courting and such."

"So, do you want me to find a short girl?"

"She doesn't have to be short, but not taller than me."

Jerron held back a smile. That meant short. Richard couldn't be taller than five foot three. At six foot, Jerron felt like a giant when he walked with him.

"Checkmate," Richard said, beaming.

"Already?"

"It's like I said. This isn't your game."

Olivia smiled as she entered the kitchen and saw Mara peeking out the corner of the window. She glanced out and saw Stephan chopping wood. "What are you doing?" she asked.

Mara jumped and spun around. "Nothing," she said, rubbing her arm.

"I made some more cookies," Olivia said. "Why don't you take him a couple?"

"Oh, no. I couldn't do that."

Olivia didn't know how to cook, but she could make a decent cookie. Once she had figured out the oven, she pulled the recipe from her head and tried it a few times. Of course, there weren't any chocolate chips here, but they still turned out well enough for Lady Anna to demand she make them again. She could have used raisins, but there was little in the world that annoyed her more than biting into a cookie and finding a raisin masquerading as chocolate.

"Most people like cookies. I bet Stephan doesn't get many desserts."

Mara bit her lip. "What would I say?"

"Would you like a cookie?"

"Just like that?"

"Why not?"

She fiddled with her hands. "I'm too nervous. What if he says no?"

"Then, take a bite and smile. Tell him it's his loss."

Mara raised an eyebrow and sighed.

Olivia handed her a small plate with three cookies. "He won't say no. He's too polite."

"Alright," Mara said, taking a stabilizing breath. "If I pass out, I will blame you."

"Just don't lock your knees or forget to breathe and you'll be fine."

"Thanks, Ella. You've been good to me this week. I'm sorry for all the times I've been nasty. You're so much more pleasant to be around than Lottie." Mara rushed out the back door, cookies clutched in her hands.

Olivia watched out the window as Mara made her way to Stephan. When he saw her approaching, he put down the ax and wiped the sweat from his brow. Mara shoved the plate of cookies into his hands and turned and dashed back to the house. She crashed through the door, slammed it shut, and leaned against it, panting.

"I did it!" she exclaimed, grinning from ear to ear. "He took them and everything."

Olivia smiled and shook her head. Stephan was standing out there holding the plate and staring at the door. "You sure did."

"I'm so invigorated!"

"Next time, you should stay and talk to him."

"Possibly," she said. "I can't believe I did that!"

Olivia felt like a hypocrite. She'd never done anything like give a guy cookies.

"What's going on in here?" Lottie asked, waltzing into the kitchen. She grabbed a handful of cookies and studied her sister. "What happened to you? Your appearance is awful."

Mara frowned and ran a hand over her windblown hair. "Do I look that bad?"

"Disgraceful," Lottie said, stuffing an entire cookie in her mouth.

Olivia bit her tongue and began cleaning up her cookie mess. Getting into a fight with Lottie was pointless. There wasn't a way to win, and it would end in a punishment. Olivia had always thought Cinderella was a pushover, but she was understanding some of it. If her stepmother kicked her out, she would have nowhere to go, and times were different, so she wouldn't be able to get a job. It made a person rethink their opinions.

Was it ridiculous to fall in love with a person you didn't know? Of course it was, but maybe it was the only way poor Cinderella could get away. Olivia scrubbed the table top and ignored Lottie's loud chewing.

"Girls!" Lady Anna exclaimed, bursting into the room. "Look at this!" She held a paper in the air. "There is going to be a royal ball, and we are invited!"

Lottie blew cookie crumbs from her mouth as she squealed and snatched the invitation from her mother's hand. "Oh my! I may faint!"

Olivia and Mara shared a glance. Olivia kept scrubbing and ignored the tight knot that was forming in her stomach. Was she ready for this? Meeting a prince and having all eyes on her was going to be horrible. Not only that, but she was going to have to kiss him, eventually. There hadn't been a lot of kissing in her past.

"It says the prince will choose a bride one week after the ball!" Lottie said.

"When is it?" Mara asked.

"In a week!" Lady Anna said, tapping her chin. "There is so much to do. We must have the best for Lottie. She's sure to catch his eye."

Mara rolled her eyes and sat at the table. "Hopefully, they don't have any food for her to spit out every time she gets excited."

"Uncalled for Mara," Lady Anna hissed. "You will have a nice dress as well, but it would be silly to hope a man would choose you over Lottie."

Olivia pressed her lips together and resisted the urge to kick Lady Anna in her dainty little backside. It was time to take the attention off Mara. "Do I get to go?" she asked.

Lady Anna turned to her in surprise, and Lottie laughed like a braying donkey. Mara studied her hands.

"You? At a ball?" Lottie snickered. "How ridiculous! Can you imagine it, Mara? Cinderella in her tattered dress and soot covered face. I'm sure the prince would have you exiled!"

Olivia returned to her scrubbing. Soot covered? The real Cinderella might have a smudged face, but Olivia had kept herself clean. Once she realized she was stuck here, she had scrubbed her dresses until they no longer smelled, and she made sure she always had one hanging on the line every morning.

"You may be my stepdaughter," Lady Anna said, "but no one will expect us to bring you."

"Won't they?" Olivia couldn't help asking, as she tossed her wet rag to the table. "You and Lottie care so much about how others view you, but you don't realize how you appear to people."

"Oh? And how is that?" Lady Anna asked, fire flashing in her eyes.

"Do you really believe people think highly of you for making your own stepdaughter an unpaid servant? And Lottie runs around chasing every eligible man for as far as the eye can see." Olivia couldn't believe she said eligible. It almost made her smile.

Lady Anna's eyebrows came together, and her face turned purple. Olivia didn't give her a chance to explode. "You live in luxury because you married my father, not because you are better than anyone. You dress Lottie up like a princess because you need to distract people from her horrid personality!"

Lottie darted at Olivia and lifted her arm to strike. Before her slap could connect, Olivia caught her arm and pushed her back. Lottie screamed dramatically and did a fake fall to the floor. So much for following the story. This day was probably going to repeat, so there was no reason to hold back now.

"Ella! How dare you lay a hand on Lottie!" Lady Anna yelled, taking an angry step towards her.

"She broke my arm!" Lottie cried from the floor.

"Don't come near me!" Olivia said, grabbing the closest pan and holding it up threateningly.

Lady Anna stopped and pointed her finger at Olivia. "You better weigh your options, Ella," she growled. "If I cast you from the house, you will have to beg for your food and live outdoors. Is that really what you want?"

"Better than spending any more time with you!" she said, backing out the door. She threw the pan onto the dirt and walked to the front of the house. That felt good. She'd been holding back a lot of comments since she came here. It might be worth doing the day over. She could handle them being mean to her, but they were crushing Mara's spirit.

Olivia couldn't decide what to do. There was still a lot of daylight left. She needed to keep occupied until today started over. She looked down the road and saw two men walking in her direction. If she wasn't mistaken, one was Jerron. Her heart seemed lighter as she hurried toward them.

"Hey, Olivia!" Jerron called, as she came closer. "I was just coming to find you."

"Good timing," she said, glancing at his companion. The man was short with black hair and dark brown eyes. He looked familiar. He might have been the man Jerron had been with the day she met him. "Do you want to do something fun?" she asked Jerron.

"Something fun?" he asked, stopping as they reached each other.

"I'm sorry, I completely ruined today. Tomorrow is probably going to be a repeat."

"No way to salvage it?" Jerron asked with a twinkle in his eye. "I had runny eggs for breakfast. I'm not looking forward to repeating that."

"Doubtful. I just pushed my stepsister over and threatened my stepmother with a pan. I'm not sure I can come back today."

Jerron laughed. "It sounds like a productive day. Richard, why don't you go have fun in town," he told the man with him. Richard raised his brow and took the wad of money Jerron handed him. He said nothing. He just turned and walked the other way.

"So what did you want to do?" he asked.

"I'm not sure. Is there anything to do around here?"

"Not that I know of."

Olivia thought for a moment. "There's a stream that runs behind the house. If we go diagonal, we should be able to run into it somewhere over there," she said, pointing away from the house. "We can follow it for a while and wade or something."

"Sounds good," he said, taking her hand and walking in the direction she pointed. Olivia's heart was pounding, and she willed her hand not to sweat. A guy had never taken her hand before. She tried to appear casual as they made their way to the stream.

"We should probably get farther from the house," she said. "I'm not sure if Lady Anna will send someone after me or not."

"Is it okay that I'm holding your hand?" he asked. "It's just really nice to be with a real person for a change. I haven't felt a connection to anyone in a long time."

"It's fine," Olivia said, as they walked along the stream. She tried not to let disappointment creep in. He was only holding her hand because she was the only person he knew was real. The only person going through the same thing he was. Why was she like this? She needed to stop over-analyzing every situation.

"This seems like a pleasant spot," he said, dropping her hand and bending over to take off his boot. "I wonder how cold it is."

Olivia leaned over the stream and stuck her fingers in. "It's not too bad." She kicked off her own shoes and stepped into the tepid water and sighed. It felt nice. Her feet were not enjoying the shoes she was stuck in. They pinched and were probably a size too small.

"I love all of these big trees, but it makes everything feel the same. If I were to spin in a circle with my eyes shut—I would probably be completely lost."

Jerron grinned. "We could make that into a game."

Olivia glanced around. "Do you think there are any snakes in the water?" The thought caused a shiver to ripple over her spine.

"I don't see any. I wonder if there are any places to swim around here," he said, stepping in beside her. "This water isn't very deep, so I doubt it."

"I don't swim," Olivia said. "Deep water scares me."

"I love swimming. You don't swim at all?"

"No. If I ever get forced to go, I sit on the stairs with all the three-year-olds. I've tried to get over it, but I can't."

"Swimming can be relaxing, but I can understand it scaring a person." Jerron paused and studied her. So, what made you snap at the steps today?"

"I don't know," Olivia shrugged. "Mara isn't bad, and the other two are always rude to her. She was rude to me at first, but with time, we could become friends. They act like Lottie is so much better than everyone else. It makes me crazy. The invitation came for the ball, and I just snapped. I didn't mean to push Lottie, but she was trying to slap me, and I wasn't in the mood."

"I get it."

"Sorry I'm making you redo the day."

"It's fine. It doesn't really change much. One day isn't much different from another."

"What if we never get out of here?" Olivia asked. "I'm only on my first story, and it seems like it's been a long time."

"Try not to obsess about it. I've been meditating more on my life and why I'm here. I wonder if that's what I should have been doing from the start. Trying to finish the stories might not be all there is to it. Maybe I need to change as a person, or figure out why I've always been bitter about certain things."

"Are you making any progress?" she asked, kicking the water.

"I might be. My parents were never into family stuff. We didn't do activities like other families. They were both hyper focused on their careers and making money. They fought a lot, and they competed with each other. Every time there was a school performance, they would argue about who had to go, and in the end, neither one would come."

"That would be rough."

"I didn't really care because I thought they were embarrassing. They never gave in, though. One time, my sister suggested my mom go to her band concert and my dad go to my basketball game. They wouldn't even do that. Both wanted the other person to do it all. They never compromised. I thought that was just the way parents were until I got older and realized it wasn't true."

"That's why you don't believe in happy endings?"

"It's not that I don't believe in them. I just don't imagine they happen by chance. I've been pondering about it a lot lately. My parents were so concerned with making themselves happy that they made themselves miserable. That's the conclusion I've come to anyway. They didn't care about the happiness of anyone else in the family.

"You can't be happy if you only care about yourself. I've heard plenty of people say that you need to do what makes you happy. If that comes at the expense of making others miserable, you won't be truly happy. Selfishness isn't the answer. That's what I'm coming to understand."

Olivia waded to the other side of the stream and sat on a raised spot of ground, dangling her feet in the water. Jerron joined her. "I probably care too much about myself," she said.

"Me too. That's a big part of my problem. Lately, I've been focusing on making my friend Richard happy. I realized I was the one choosing everything, and he has to follow me around doing whatever I want. Now I try to choose things he likes. He's happier, and so am I. I'm getting some things right."

"So, we're happier when we focus on others and not ourselves," Olivia said, tilting her head as she studied him. "That sounds like a lesson we should have learned in kindergarten."

"It's possible some of us need more of a shove than others."

Olivia nodded. "I've been thinking about how I deal with people. Our lives are like a movie. In our own story we are the main character. In other people's story we might be a supporting character or even a background character. Everyone influences other's lives to different extents, and so we need to decide how we want to be reflected in everyone else's story. Mara has a crush on their stable hand. I've been trying to help her, and it makes the time pass a lot smoother. Well, not smoother, but it's been more entertaining. I have been happier watching her. I'm not sure I can do anything to help Lottie, even if I wanted to."

"How does Lady Anna feel about Mara's crush?"

"She doesn't know, thankfully. I'm not sure it can ever work. Lady Anna won't ever accept it, and if Mara defies her, Stephan will lose his job and they won't have a way to be together."

"I could get him a better job," Jerron said, scratching his chin. "I just need to remember to do it before this tale ends."

"You would do that?" Olivia asked, smiling. "That would be great."

"Sure," Jerron said, playfully bumping his shoulder into hers. "What is he qualified to do?"

Olivia thought for a moment. "I'm not sure. He seems to do everything around the outside. I wonder why clearing the outhouse from spiders isn't part of his job. I bet Lady Anna just wants me to do it to be mean."

Jerron grimaced. "I wouldn't doubt it."

"He would probably do it if I asked. He's a nice guy."

"It sounds like it." He flicked some water at her. "So I told you my sob story. Why are you against happy?"

Olivia wiped the water from her cheek. "I'm not against it. I just don't want to be disappointed when it never happens. Why spend my life hoping to find a perfect prince only to be disappointed? I won't bore you with my sad dating experiences. My sister and I watched too many movies where everything came together perfectly and then my experiences have been pathetic. I felt like I had a void in my heart, so I gave up on all of it. I focused on other things that make me happy. Now, I sound like your parents."

"Not really. You are pretty young to have given up on love, though."

Olivia frowned. "That's about what Nancy said."

"Oh man, I don't want to sound like Nancy." They laughed.

"I tried online dating as a last ditch effort. That was a bad idea. I'm not good at meeting strangers, and most of them were really odd."

"Most girls I dated were only with me because of something trivial."

"Like your pretty face?" Olivia joked.

Jerron grinned and shook his head. "My family has a lot of money. That seems to attract a certain type of person. Not the type you want to spend your life with."

"I can see that being hard. Hopefully, Nancy will see that we're trying."

He smiled at her. "We can hope."

Butterflies filled Olivia's stomach. She tried not to stare at Jerron's mouth. She wondered what it would be like to kiss him. They hadn't known each other long enough for her to be thinking about that.

"What is it?" he asked.

She stood up in the stream and bent over. "I owe you," she said, as she cupped her hands and flung a handful of water in his face. She laughed as he jumped up in surprise.

"I can't believe you just did that," he said, wiping his face. "I guess I should be happy you didn't chase me with a pan."

"So, that was the girl?" Richard asked after Jerron found him in town. They sat in the inn waiting for dinner.

"That was her."

"She's pretty."

"Yeah. Do you suppose my father will approve?"

"Not if she comes to the ball in that dress she was wearing. You should get her a new one."

"Probably," he said, taking a bite of green beans. "I'm sure she'll come up with something magical for the ball."

Richard side eyed him. "I can't believe you fell in love and I didn't even notice."

"Not in love," Jerron said. "I don't really know her that well. I just like her." He didn't add that he didn't want to leave anyone stuck in this story just because he was comfortable here. He couldn't feel good about himself if he left her in an unpleasant situation just because it benefitted him.

"Are you ever going to tell me why your clothes are wet?"

"Nope," Jerron said, looking down at his soggy clothes. He wasn't going to admit to losing a water fight. He probably shouldn't have started it. Olivia was as wet as he was and she couldn't go home and change. He smiled to himself. It had been a long time since he'd had fun, and Olivia was fun.

"Do you want dessert?" a serving girl asked, coming up to the table.

Richard looked at her with wide eyes and a full mouth. He chewed quickly and swallowed. "Um, what would you suggest?"

Jerron leaned back in his chair and smiled. Richard had acted strange earlier when he ordered.

The girl pushed a black curl behind her ear and looked thoughtfully up at the ceiling. "My favorite is the apple pie. The custard is fair, but nothing worth going on about. Don't tell the kitchen I said this, but the cake is always stale, so avoid that."

"I'll take the pie," Richard said.

"Alright, and you?" she asked Jerron.

"Pie for me as well."

"Alright," she smiled. "I'll have it right out."

"She seems nice," Jerron baited, as she walked away.

"She is," Richard said. "I came in earlier for lunch. Her name is Erabella. Isn't that the nicest name you've ever heard?"

"It's pretty." Jerron also noticed she wasn't overly tall.

"She's from the town next to the one I grew up in."

Jerron raised an eyebrow. "Did you ask her if she's going to the ball?"

"Of course not."

"You should."

Richard's eyes widened. "Why?"

"You could dance with her."

"Oh no. Stop looking at me like that. I know what you're thinking, and it will never work. Why would she want to dance with me?"

"Why wouldn't she?"

"Quiet, here she comes!" Richard hissed. Jerron watched in amusement as Richard sat up tall and smiled at the woman.

"Here you are," she said, placing the pie in front of them. "Can I get you anything else?"

"No thank you," Jerron said, as Richard shook his head. She smiled and walked away. Jerron wondered how dating worked here. Richard couldn't ask for her number since there weren't phones. Asking for her address seemed too much like stalking.

They finished their pie, and when they left the inn, Jerron made an excuse to go back inside. He caught Erabella's eye and made his way toward her.

"Do you need anything?" she asked.

"My friend was wondering if you're going to the ball."

"Yes, I think everyone will."

"Will you save him a dance?"

She put her hands to her cheeks and smiled. "He wants to dance with me? I would love to."

"Wonderful. He'll watch for you," Jerron said. She grinned and walked away. He could see why she caught Richard's eye. She looked like an exotic princess with her brown skin and sparkling rich umber eyes. Her raven hair fell in gentle waves down her back and bounced when she walked. Jerron joined Richard, and they made their way back to the castle.

"What were you doing in there?" he asked.

"I was asking Erabella if she would like to dance with you at the ball."

Richare's jaw dropped. "No! You didn't."

"I did. And I'm going to have to do it again tomorrow," Jerron said, remembering the day was going to repeat. He should have waited.

"Once is enough," Richard said, kicking at a rock. "Now everything is going to be awkward if I see her again."

"You have to see her again. She said she would dance with you."

"Out of pity?"

"No. She seemed excited about it."

Richard raised his eyebrows. "Really?"

Jerron laughed. "Yes. It's going to be great."

"Yeah, great," Richard mumbled.

"You'll thank me."

"We'll see."

Chapter 6

Olivia came to an abrupt stop when she saw Mara standing outside the stable. The girl stared at the door with determination. Olivia walked backward slowly, not wanting to distract Mara if she was about to go talk to Stephan. Mara took a deep breath and yanked open the stable door and disappeared inside.

It was too much for Olivia to resist. She creeped up to the stable and went around the back. She looked at the woodpile and thought about Mara getting her foot caught. Mara was a little clumsy, and Olivia was athletic. She couldn't understand how anyone could get their foot stuck.

Olivia quietly climbed up the pile of logs and grabbed the window ledge. She peeked in the corner of the window. How did Mara spy on anything through this thing? The window was thick and dirty. She could see movement inside, but she couldn't tell if it was a person or a horse.

"Hey!" a voice said from behind. Olivia shrieked, and her foot slipped. Her fingers tore away from the window ledge, and she clawed at the structure as she resisted falling. Her feet pushed logs from the pile and she slid with the logs until she landed on her stomach.

"I am so sorry!" Jerron said, helping her to her feet. "Are you alright?"

She glared at him. "You scared me! What were you thinking?"

Jerron shrugged as he helped her step over a log. "Sorry. I saw you up there and I thought I would scare you. I didn't think I would do such a good job."

"What's going on?" Mara asked, bursting around the corner.

Olivia felt heat creeping up her neck as Stephan came running toward them from the woods. He hadn't even been in the stable.

"What happened?" he asked, as he studied the fallen woodpile.

"Sorry," Olivia said, trying to will her face to cool down. She must be three shades of red. "I knocked over the pile. I'll fix it."

"I'll help," Jerron said, picking up a log.

Olivia grabbed a log and flinched. She must have landed on her elbows. They were both throbbing.

"You're bleeding," Stephan said. "Why don't you have this gentleman take you down to the stream to wash it? Mara can help me here."

"Help?" Mara squeaked. "Yes, I can help!" she said, awkwardly picking up a log.

Olivia and Jerron made their way to the stream in silence until they were out of earshot.

"I can't believe I made you bleed," Jerron said.

Olivia glanced at her elbow. "It's not that bad."

"Still, I should have realized scaring someone on an enormous pile of logs was a bad idea."

"Yeah, well, that's what I get for trying to spy on people."

"Who were you spying on?"

"I thought Mara and Stephan, but I guess Stephan wasn't even in there."

Jerron's eyes sparkled. "So, you were hoping to catch them making out or something?"

Olivia rolled her eyes. "No. I just wanted to see what Mara would do. I thought they might be talking."

"Are you getting invested in someone's love story?"

"Possibly," Olivia said, kneeling down at the small stream. She cupped some water in her hand and tried to wash her elbow. "I really hope something will work out for them."

"You aren't secretly a romantic, are you?" he joked, handing her a handkerchief.

Olivia grinned as she got it wet. "I didn't know anyone had handkerchiefs anymore. At least, no one under sixty."

"Richard makes sure I have one in my pocket every day. Now, answer my question."

"What was it?"

"You were about to admit to being a hopeless romantic that disguises herself as a woman bitter about love."

Olivia laughed and splashed water on him. "I'll never admit it."

"Are you hurt anywhere else?"

"No," she said, standing up. She kept the handkerchief pressed against her bleeding elbow. "We should probably go back. I bet Mara's having a panic attack."

"What's going on over there?" Jerron asked as they neared the stable.

"I can't tell," Olivia said, squinting. They picked up their pace, sensing something was wrong. Stephan was sitting on the ground, and Mara was moving her arms around like she was in distress. "Is that blood on Stephan's head?"

"It looks like it."

Mara turned and spotted them. She ran to them and grabbed Olivia's arm. Her eyes were wide, and she was pale. "I accidentally hit Stephan in the head with a log!" she cried. "What if he dies!"

"I'm not going to die," Stephan said, as they approached him. He had a bump on his forehead and blood on his face.

"That doesn't look good," Jerron said, examining the man's head.

"It's not as bad as it looks," he said. "The blood got smeared around."

"I tried to clean it with his handkerchief, but it just made a mess!" Mara sniffed.

"We'll go get some bandages," Olivia said, pulling Mara toward the house. The girl kept sniffling. Once inside the kitchen, Olivia stood on a chair to get to the cupboard with medical supplies. Mara sank into a chair and covered her face with her hands.

"What if he dies?" Mara whimpered. "It will be all my fault."

"He's not going to die," Olivia said, pulling out some clean towels and a roll of thin white cloth.

"But what if he does?"

Olivia jumped off the chair. "Don't think like that. Here, take the bandage. You can wrap some of it around his head."

Mara's eyebrows jumped off her head. "Me? I've never done anything like that."

"Well, now is a good time to learn."

"I suppose," she said, wiping her eyes. "I can't believe I hit him! He is going to avoid me like the plague."

"He knows it was an accident."

"Why do I have so many accidents?"

"Nothing good comes from worrying about things we can't control," Olivia said, cringing. She really needed to live what she preached.

"Poor Stephan," Jerron said with a grin as he and Olivia walked in the direction of town. "I've never seen a person get bandaged so thoroughly." Jerron pictured Stephan after Mara had finished bandaging him. She'd wrapped enough bandage around his head to make him look like he was wearing a turban.

Olivia giggled. "He didn't seem to mind. In fact, he seemed happy about the whole thing."

"Yep," Jerron agreed. "While you two were in the house, I talked to Stephan about switching jobs. He seemed interested."

"Really? That's great!"

"He told me he's ready to move on. He said he almost left a while back, but he realized there might be something between him and Mara, so he stayed."

"He told you that?"

"Yes."

Olivia smiled. "I'm glad. And thanks for helping him out. He's a good guy.""Have you forgiven me for scaring you?"

"It depends on how good lunch is."

Jerron smiled. "That's fair. I'm not worried though. The inn's cook is pretty good."

"Anything should be good after eating my cooking."

Lady Anna and Lottie were out of the house for the day, so Jerron had convinced Olivia to go to town with him for lunch. He told himself it wasn't a date. It was just to make up for scaring her. He kind of wished it was a date, but that might be too much to hope for.

"I left Richard at the inn. I was gone longer than I expected, so I hope he's still there." Jerron had come to talk to Stephan about a job at the castle, but he'd been distracted when he saw Olivia sneaking around the stables. When he saw her climb onto the woodpile and peek in, he couldn't help scaring her. He regretted it now. He should've realized the log pile wasn't very stable.

"I hope no one tells Lady Anna I was with you," Olivia said, as they walked through the small town. They walked up to the white inn, and Jerron opened the door. His eyes fell on Richard, who was sitting at a table with a large piece of pie in front of him.

"Can we join you?" he asked.

Richard looked up and sighed. "It took you long enough!" he said, as they sat at the table.

"Sorry," Jerron said. "I got distracted."

Richard looked at Olivia. "I can see that."

Erabella appeared behind them. "Do your friends want to order?" she asked, smiling at Richard.

"We do," Jerron said.

Richard sat up straighter and beamed at the woman.

"What would you suggest?" Jerron asked Erabella.

"We've had a lot of compliments on the chicken and potatoes today."

"I'll have that," Olivia said.

Jerron nodded. "Me too."

"Do you want anything else?" she asked Richard.

"Oh, um, maybe some coffee."

Erabella smiled. "I'll bring it right out."

As soon as she disappeared, Richard's smile slipped away.

"You don't drink coffee," Jerron said to Richard.

"I know," he said, leaning forward. "I've been here eating since you left, and I'm about to bust. This is my third dessert! Coffee was the only thing I know I haven't ordered."

Jerron laughed. "Why do you keep ordering?"

"Because you said to wait here for you! I couldn't wait here and not keep ordering. It would be rude to take up a table and not use it."

"You could've waited outside."

"You said you wouldn't be long, so I kept thinking you would appear any minute."

"Well, at least you got to talk to Erabella every time you ordered."

Richard looked horrified as he glanced at Olivia. She was pretending not to pay attention. Jerron grinned. That was nice of her.

Erabella returned and served them all water, then put a steaming cup of coffee in front of Richard.

"Are you all as hungry as your friend?" she asked. "He can probably tell you the best desserts. If you already know which one you want, I can make sure it's ready when you finish your food."

"What dessert was the best?" Jerron asked Richard.

"Um, probably the strawberry tarts."

"I'll have that."

"So will I," said Olivia. Erabella nodded and left.

"Just thinking about food makes me sick," Richard said, pushing the hot coffee far away. "I think I need to go out for some air."

Jerron laughed as Richard stumbled from the room.

"Poor guy," Olivia said. "He must really like that girl."

"He does. I probably shouldn't tease him."

She cocked her head. "He was looking a little green."

"I'll make it up to him. Are you ready for the ball?" he asked.

She tapped her fingers on the table. "As ready as I'm going to be."

"It might be fun. And you'll save me a dance, right?" Jerron smiled inwardly as her face turned a pretty shade of pink.

"Of course. I'm really bad at dancing, though."

Jerron grinned at her. "That's alright." Any chance to hold her close would be fine with him. She could be the worst dancer in the world, and he wouldn't care.

"I'm really nervous about the ball," she admitted, fiddling with the napkin on the table in front of her. "It's really out of my comfort zone, and I know people will be watching me."

Jerron placed his hand over hers. "You're going to be great." She smiled nervously at him. He wondered what would happen if he kissed her right here and now. It wasn't the right time, but would they still change to a different story? He wasn't going to chance it. He didn't want to miss the ball. Olivia wasn't looking forward to dancing, but he was. He squeezed her hand and then let go.

Kissing her might backfire. He didn't know what she thought about him. She might only be spending time with him because of what they had in common.

"What are you thinking?" she asked.

He cocked his head and studied her. "You don't want to know."

"I kinda do. You look serious all of a sudden."

Jerron definitely wasn't going to tell her what he was thinking. He wanted to ask her if she knew he was the prince, but for some reason, it seemed like an odd thing to bring up.

"I was just thinking about the ball. Once it's over, who knows what will happen? I've hated this whole experience until recently. The stories have always been annoying until I met you. I'm not ready to be placed in another story, knowing you are somewhere else."

"I didn't think about that," Olivia said, looking down at her napkin. "It will be hard to make it through another story without you there to guide me."

He touched her chin, and she looked up at him. Her eyes widened as he leaned across the corner of the table. It seemed he had lost all sense. He was going to kiss her now, whether Nancy wanted it that way or not.

"Here you are," Erabella said, placing their plates on the table. Jerron pulled back and hid a scowl.

"Thank you," Olivia squeaked. She grabbed her fork and started eating. There was nothing to do but follow her example. It looked like he would be waiting to kiss her at the ball after all.

Chapter 7

"I can't believe Stephan would leave us to go work at the palace," Lady Anna complained as Olivia brushed through Lottie's silky hair. Olivia couldn't believe it, either. She knew Jerron was going to help the man get a job, but she never dreamed it would be such a good one.

"Once I catch the prince, Stephan will still work for us," Lottie said, keeping her eyes focused on her reflection in the mirror.

"That's true," Lady Anna said, fluffing her sleeve. "And I will give him a piece of my mind for leaving us in a lurch like he did."

Olivia twisted Lottie's hair into a neat bun and left some pieces loose to curl later.

"I'm happy for him," Mara said, sitting on her mother's bed. "He can make more money now."

"That's a selfish reason to leave us," Lottie said. "He must only think about himself." Olivia snorted and tried to cover it up with a fake sneeze. Lottie was unbelievable.

"Very selfish," Lady Anna agreed. Olivia clamped her mouth shut and forced herself to stay quiet. Today was the ball, and not a day she wanted to do more than once. Arguing with people didn't seem to accomplish anything anyway.

"Will you fix my hair like Lottie's when you're finished?" Mara asked Olivia.

"No, she will not!" Lottie said, glaring at her sister in the mirror. "How ridiculous would it be if we walked in with the same style? I can't have any attention being taken off of me."

Mara folded her arms and pouted. "Perhaps, you are just worried the prince will find me more attractive and you'll be left to yourself."

"Haha," Lottie said, rolling her eyes. "Don't make me laugh. No man is going to find you more desirable than me. When we are in town, all eyes follow me, not you."

"How can you be sure?" Mara asked. "I'm always standing right by you. Perhaps you flatter yourself more than you realize."

"Mara, stop being ridiculous," Lady Anna said. "Of course they are admiring your sister. You have no reason to pout. When she secures the prince, it will benefit all of us. Men will flock to you because your sister will be a princess."

"Some men like women for more than their appearance," Olivia couldn't help saying as she secured a piece of hair with a bobby pin.

"Please," Lottie muttered, shaking her head at the ceiling. "What could a man want more than a beautiful woman at his side?"

"A woman that's kind, a good listener, not conceited, and fun," Olivia rambled off.

Lady Anna and Lottie burst into laughter. "Oh, Ella," Lottie said with a huge grin. "You are so sheltered. A man doesn't want any of those things. And even if he did, why would he choose Mara over me?"

"Because you have none of those qualities," Olivia said, mentally kicking herself. She needed to stop before it became a fight and a repeat.

"Maybe not, but those are pointless character traits in a person."

Mara looked thoughtful. "I don't know about that, Lottie. If you marry the prince, don't you want him to be all those things?"

"I'll be rich and powerful. Why would I care what the prince is like?"

"Don't you want to be treated well?"

"I repeat, I'll be rich and powerful."

Lady Anna beamed. "Yes, and it will benefit us all. Hurry, Ella. We don't want to be late."

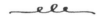

Jerron sighed as he adjusted the ridiculous cape draped over his shoulders. It was made of fur of all things. He felt like a five-year-old in this extravagant attire. The embroidery detailing his tunic seemed overly ornate and unnecessary, in his opinion. Was he a man or a peacock?

As he studied his reflection in the mirror, his thoughts drifted to Richard. Richard loved the intricacies of fashion, and he was likely responsible for the outfit. The man had gone overboard this time, but what could Jerron do about it? The ball was quickly approaching, and there wasn't time to complain or make alterations.

Jerron gingerly touched the golden crown on his head. It might symbolize his royal status, but it added to his feelings of childishness. He wondered what Olivia would say when she saw him. She would probably laugh, and he would laugh right along with her.

Straightening his posture, he steeled himself for the evening ahead. He would portray confidence, regardless of how he felt in his outlandish attire. He had a role to play, and he would play it well. Giving himself one last glance in the mirror, he stepped away. He wondered if Olivia was as nervous as he was.

Olivia paced across the kitchen floor and tried to free herself from the knot that had formed in her stomach. Her stepfamily had probably arrived at the ball over an hour ago. Her fairy godmother should have appeared. Did she need to dissolve into a puddle of tears before the woman would come? She was nervous, but she wasn't in the mood to cry. She didn't know how to fake cry anyway.

"We aren't fretting, are we?" a voice asked from behind her. Olivia spun around to see a middle-aged woman in a shimmering pink dress standing near her, holding a silver wand. Large sparkling wings fluttered around her. "I hope you didn't think I forgot about you," she said in an accent that was as fake as her wings.

Olivia examined the woman and frowned. There was something familiar about her, but she couldn't place it.

"Now, why are you so upset, my dear?" the woman asked.

"Who are you?" Olivia asked. This woman looked and sounded like a fraud.

"I'm your fairy godmother!" she said, spinning in a circle.

"Nancy?" Olivia asked.

The woman's smile slid from her face. "You recognized me? That's no fun. I even made myself younger."

"You can drop the accent. It's pretty bad."

"You're taking all the fun out of this, you realize," she said, losing the accent.

"Fun?" Olivia scoffed. "It's nice to know you think interfering in people's lives is fun."

"I wouldn't call it fun. It's fulfilling. My job is to help you lead a positive and hopeful life. That is far from what you were doing before."

"There are so many people that are doing worse than me. I wasn't unhappy. I was just skeptical of some things."

"There are many people worse off than you," Nancy said, leaning against the table. "Some are beyond what I can help. I only assist those who will benefit from what I have to offer."

"I can guarantee you, I'm not happier here. I wish you would send me home. Jerron as well. That poor guy has been through enough."

"He is hard-headed. I sense he is changing, but he's not quite ready to return."

Olivia narrowed her eyes. "What gives you the right to interfere?"

"Don't worry. You won't be here long, I can tell. You've already made better progress than most. I'll have you gushing about love in no time. I'm not here to explain anything but to create a magical evening for you!"

"How many people have you done this to?"

"What color dress do you want?" Nancy asked, ignoring her. "Blue? Yellow? Pink?"

"Not yellow," Olivia said, giving up. If Nancy spent all of her time doing this to people, she had probably had numberless victims begging her to return them to their lives.

"Blue will go nicely with your hair," she said, tapping her wand on her chin.

"Great. Sing your song, and let's get it over with."

"I don't sing. Sadly, I'm tone deaf."

"That's too bad," Olivia said.

"I don't follow one particular version of any fairy tale. I like to leave wiggle room for your own creativity."

"How kind of you," Olivia said with thinly veiled sarcasm.

"I believe so. In the beginning, I thought all the fairy tales should be close to their original stories, but those things are awful. Have you read them?"

"No."

"Be thankful. Now, mice. We need mice."

"I haven't befriended any. Sorry."

"No worries. Most don't." Nancy placed two fingers in her mouth and let out a shrill whistle. Olivia covered her ears and frowned as mice seemed to appear from thin air. Nancy scooped up four of them. "We should go outside. Horses don't belong in a house." Olivia followed her into the back.

Nancy placed the mice on the ground and swished her wand. Four white horses appeared prancing in their place. It was impressive, even though Olivia was expecting it. She ran her hand over one of their manes. She preferred horses to mice.

"There are pumpkins in the garden," she said. Lady Anna had her spend a good hour a day working in the garden. "I'll grab one." Olivia jogged over to the garden and grabbed the biggest gourd she could find. When she returned to Nancy, it was to see the woman holding a small snake.

"Look what I found," she said, holding it up. "This fellow should drive the coach, don't you agree?"

"Gross, no," Olivia said, laying the pumpkin on the ground. "I don't want to put my life in the hands of a snake."

"But see how pretty he is," Nancy said, holding him up to her face. "He's a lovely creature."

Olivia shuddered and rubbed the goosebumps on her arms. Snakes had always terrified her. It was something about the eyes. Nancy put the snake on the ground and waved her wand, causing a man to appear in its place. He stared at her and didn't blink. This could become the opposite of a fairy tale really fast.

"Hurry and clean the pumpkin out, and you can be on your way."

"Clean it out?" Olivia asked, raising her eyebrow. "You can wave your wand and turn a snake into a man, and you can't just clean out the pumpkin?"

"Hm," Nancy said, scratching her head with her wand. "I never thought about that before. I suppose I could." She waved the wand, and the pumpkin spun. The top flew off, and seeds and goop flew all over Olivia and Nancy. "I suppose I should have gone slower," Nancy said, pulling seeds from her hair.

Olivia just pursed her lips and wiped her face. She would rather have pumpkin goo on her than clean out the pumpkin at the moment. It had already been a long day.

Nancy waved her wand, and the pumpkin grew and turned into a golden carriage. The snake man led the horses around to the front. Olivia wondered if he could blink. Did snakes have eyelids? She was going to have nightmares about him.

"Now for the dress!" Nancy smiled. "It's always my favorite part."

Olivia didn't want to admit it, but she was curious about the dress as well. "Is it safe?" she asked. "I'm not sure how I feel about getting blasted with magic."

"Completely safe."

"I saw what happened to the pumpkin."

"That was my first try. I've done dresses for centuries."

"You've been messing with people for centuries?"

Nancy sighed and looked at her. "Helping. Helping for centuries."

"Are you a witch?"

"A witch? How could you ask that? You have obviously never seen a witch. I am a fairy godmother."

"I thought fairy godmothers were supposed to give people things they wanted," Olivia said.

"That is not my main purpose. I am here to help people find happiness. That's what I'm doing for you. I won't stop until you find it."

"Well, let's get moving then," Olivia said with a sigh. "I guess I can't put it off anymore."

"Alright, turn in a circle," she said, holding her wand in front of her. Olivia turned. A soft wind swirled around her, caressing her skin. When it subsided, she was wearing a full light blue dress that cascaded down to the ground. She touched her head and found a delicate tiara resting there. Her blonde locks fell over her shoulders in soft ringlets.

"Are we finished?" she asked, trying not to look pleased with the outcome. There was no reason to let Nancy pat herself on the back too much.

"Oh, you are lovely!" Nancy gushed. "And how are the slippers?"

Olivia pulled away layers of dress and petticoats to see the clear glass slippers sparkling on her feet. She took a few steps and looked up in surprise. "I thought they would hurt."

"Yes, well, I probably shouldn't admit this, but they aren't really glass. I want you to have a good time, not blisters. I have used glass in the past, and it never went well. Too many cut feet. They really don't hold together well. Even if they survive the dance, they don't make it through to the end. Some people can be rather clumsy."

"They look like glass," Olivia said, admiring them.

"It took me years to perfect them. Now, you better be on your way. I'm sure you already know, but you must leave by midnight. The magic will all be gone by then."

Olivia nodded as she climbed into the carriage. She would not be as careless as Cinderella. She would leave before midnight, with enough time to ride back. Walking would take a long time, and she didn't even know where the castle was.

Nancy shut the door and signaled to the driver. She hoped the snake had taken driver's ed.

⁓

Jerron's legs were aching, and the night was still young. Dancing with every eager woman in the room was wearing him down. Where was Olivia? It was already ten thirty. The ball had been in progress for two hours already.

He spun his partner under his arm and looked for Richard. His friend had been a bucket of nerves before the dance started, but as soon as he had his first dance with Erabella, he had changed. The couple had been inseparable since. The song ended and everyone clapped.

He tried not to gaze up to the top of the stairs, but he found himself doing it throughout the night. What was keeping Olivia? He had expected to spend most of the evening with her. It was possible she'd messed with the story, and they were going to have to redo today. He really hoped that wasn't the case.

"I believe it's my turn," said a pretty woman with brown ringlets falling from a neatly wrapped bun. He nodded and took her hand. There was something familiar about her. Recognition rained over him. It was Lottie. He wondered if she would recognize him. She didn't seem to.

She grinned. "My name is Lottie," she said, as the dance began.

"Charmed," he said, holding back a yawn.

"My mother is Lady Anna. Perhaps you've heard of her?"

"I don't believe I have," he lied.

"She is very well loved in the village," Lottie said. "Our family is quite affluent. You can ask anyone. We are trend setters, my sister and I. If we start something, you can guarantee everyone in the village will be doing it within the week."

Jerron gazed longingly at the top of the stairs as Lottie prattled on. Did she really imagine this was the sort of talk to draw a prince? It was shameless self-promotion if he'd ever heard it.

Ignoring Lottie was easy. She didn't stop for breath, and she wasn't saying anything interesting. Jerron glanced around the room, and his gaze fell on one duke that he couldn't stand. He had been in a conference with the man, and he was like Lottie in a few ways. He complimented what he thought was his own cleverness and bragged shamelessly about his summer cottage.

He grinned as an idea popped into his head. He guided her toward the duke and then stopped in front of the man. "Lottie, have you met Rodney? He is the Duke of Aldertown."

"I don't believe I have," she said, batting her eyes at Jerron. "It's good of you to introduce me to your friends."

"How lovely," the duke said, kissing Lottie's hand. Lottie pulled away quickly and rubbed her hand. The duke wasn't the most handsome man on the planet. His greasy brown hair was brushed back, making his large forehead stand out, and his hygiene could use some work.

"Lottie has been telling me about herself, and something just kept telling me I should introduce the two of you. You have a lot in common. Why don't you finish the dance with her?"

"What?" Lottie choked.

"I would be delighted!" The duke smiled, sweeping Lottie away. Jerron waved as they disappeared into the crowd. He better avoid her the rest of the night. She was going to be angry.

The song ended, and a hush fell over the room. Jerron turned to see Olivia standing at the top of the stairs. Her long blue dress billowed to the ground and her blonde ringlets framed her flawless face. She walked gracefully down the stairs, but he could tell she was aware of all the eyes following her. He grinned and made his way toward her. Things were finally looking up.

Olivia's heart couldn't take much more. It was going double time as all the people in the room watched her descend the stairs. Didn't they have anything better to do? It was a party after all. She could see someone coming toward her from the corner of her eye, but she couldn't make herself look at him. It had to be the prince.

"May I have this dance?" asked a familiar voice. Olivia's head jerked up, and she found herself looking at Jerron. He was wearing a crown. Jerron was the prince? Then, why was he running around town dressed like a commoner? She shouldn't be surprised.

"I don't know how to dance," she said, quietly.

"That's alright. I do." He took her hand and led her to a more open space, leading her through the steps. Instinct must have taken over, and she was dancing. She wondered if Nancy was responsible for that. After a minute, the curious eyes stopped following them, and she tried to relax.

"I can't believe you're the prince. Why didn't you tell me?"

"It seemed like a weird thing to bring up. I kind of figured you would come to the conclusion on your own."

"I assumed the prince was one of Nancy's puppets and he would be a stiff but decent guy."

"Prince Charming?"

She smiled. "Something like that."

"Yeah, I guess I'm not very charming," he said, spinning her under his arm.

She smiled. "That's not what I meant. Nancy is my fairy godmother."

"That figures. I bet she enjoyed it."

"She really did."

"You look great."

"Thanks," she said, not meeting his eye. She had never been good with compliments.

"You look good in your tattered dress too. I'm not just saying it because you're dressed all fancy."

Olivia's lips turned up in a small grin. He might be as nervous as she was. "I like your cape," she said. "Very regal."

"I know, it's a little much. And it's hot. I should've ditched it when the dance started. I look ridiculous."

"But you're still cute," she said, causing him to blush.

"Do you want to step outside? That's our final destination if I remember right. We've got some nice gardens we can wander around in."

"Sure," she said, letting him lead her away from the crowd. They walked out into the garden, and Olivia smiled at the wide array of flowers that blanketed the area. "Wow. Someone spends a lot of time taking care of this place."

"I'm sure they do," he said, throwing his ridiculous cape on the ground and taking her hand as they walked through the rows and rows of flowers.

"Don't let me lose track of time. I don't want to walk home with one shoe. It would take forever."

"Do you want to dance?" he asked.

"Out here? Wouldn't that be strange?"

"Yes, but what isn't around here?"

"That's true," she said. "And there aren't any people to watch me fumble around."

"You were doing great inside."

"Yeah, that was weird. I wonder if it's one of those memories you talked about, or maybe Nancy zapped me with dancing powers."

"I wouldn't doubt it," he said as he took her in his arms and they began to dance. Olivia felt silly and elated at the same time. She liked Jerron way more than she should. It was probably good that the story was almost over. It was going to be depressing when they moved on to different places.

Time flew by as they alternated between walking around and dancing. Olivia couldn't remember the last time she enjoyed talking to someone so much. Jerron was funny and thoughtful. She wondered if they would have connected if they had met under different circumstances.

A clock chimed in the background. "Oh no! It's not midnight, is it?"

"It might be," Jerron said. "Sorry, I lost track of the time."

"I need to go before I'm standing here in my old clothes." She waved as she ran through the garden and into the ballroom. She pushed her way past the dancing couples and ran up the steps. Jerron call to her from somewhere in the crowd, but she knew he was only following the story. She burst out of the castle doors and ran down the stone steps. Why did they have steps going up just to send you back down?

Olivia reached the bottom of the massive staircase and realized she was still wearing both shoes. She tried to flip one to the ground, but it wasn't coming off. She bent over and pulled the shoe from her foot. Looking back up the stairs, she saw Jerron walking slowly toward her. She threw the shoe, and he caught it. She gave a quick wave and disappeared into the darkness.

Chapter 8

Olivia hopped out of bed in a panic. She had over-slept—and not just a little. The sun was pouring into the room. Why wasn't Lady Anna pounding on the door? Olivia scurried to the wardrobe and pulled out a dress. Her legs were throbbing from the night before. She wasn't used to dancing, and the walk home had taken over two hours.

She had to take her second slipper off when she was walking because it made her lopsided and she wasn't used to being barefoot, so her feet were sore. Today was going to be hard. Hurrying down to the kitchen, she threw together a hasty breakfast. With luck, the steps were still in bed. They hadn't been home when she arrived, so they were probably tired.

"Morning, Ella," Mara said, entering the kitchen. She yawned and slumped down into a kitchen chair. Her curls were a mess of tangles.

"Good morning," she said, scrambling eggs. "How was the ball?"

Mara had a far off gleam in her eyes. "It was so dreamy."

"Did you dance with the prince?"

"Yes, Mother made me. I thought I might get out of it because he spent the night dancing with a mysterious woman, but she ran out at midnight, and Mother is very insistent."

"You didn't want to dance with him?" Olivia asked.

Mara sighed. "Not really. I don't know what to say to a man like that. I guess I don't know what to say to any man."

"What made the night dreamy?"

"Stephan was there. He was dressed so fancy, Mother and Lottie didn't recognize him. We danced a few times, and they didn't even notice. He said he's going to come call on me whether or not Mother likes it!"

"That's really neat," Olivia said, smiling. The girl deserved some happiness.

"Lottie had an awful time," Mara said with a chuckle. "The prince practically threw her at some duke, and he spent the entire night following her around. Mother made her dance with him over and over. She figures that if Lottie can't have a prince, a duke isn't bad. It sounds like he is pretty well off."

Olivia tried to suppress a smile. "It sounds like I missed an interesting night."

"I'm sure you had your own fun," Mara said, with a light tease in her voice.

Olivia turned around and studied her. Mara's eyes were twinkling. "Don't worry," Mara said, "Mother and Lottie didn't realize it was you." Olivia's heart was pounding. She always thought it was strange Cinderella's stepfamily didn't recognize her at the ball. "Where did you get the dress?"

"You wouldn't believe me if I told you," Olivia said, turning back to the eggs.

"Why did you run away? The prince looked melancholy the rest of the evening."

"I had to get home before the rest of you."

Mara's eyes widened. "Did you walk? That would take a long time."

"Two hours," Olivia admitted.

"Barefoot? I noticed the prince had your slipper when he came back."

"Yes, and my feet are killing me."

"Lottie and Mother won't be up anytime soon. They probably won't notice if you rest. I forced myself to get up so I could talk to you. We only got home a few hours ago. Just leave breakfast so they don't think you were slacking."

"I'm worn out and sore, but I doubt I can sleep anymore. My mind is spinning."

"I imagine it is. You captured the prince's eye last night. Most people wouldn't be able to sleep."

"I guess I'll go soak my feet in the creek," Olivia said, scooping the eggs onto a plate. "If nothing else, they need to be washed."

"You can't stay in bed all day," Richard said, opening the drapes.

"I could if you didn't come in here," Jerron grumbled, squinting as the sun filled the room.

"I stayed up as long as you and I've been up for an hour!" He whistled as he picked Jerron's clothes off the floor. Being a prince was making him lazy. He shouldn't be making Richard do things like that.

"Perhaps, you couldn't sleep because there is a certain Erabella on your mind?" Jerron teased.

"It's possible," Richard said, a huge grin spreading across his face. "I've met no one like her. That's not what we need to talk about, though. Your father will not forget about your promise."

"I'm planning on keeping it."

"But the girl from last night ran off. You seemed partial to her."

"I was."

"How will you find her?" Richard asked.

It surprised him that Richard didn't recognize her from the inn. Jerron forced himself to get out of bed and meandered over to his table. Olivia's slipper rested on top. He picked it up and showed it to Richard.

"You have her shoe?"

"Yes. She left it behind."

Richard's eyebrows knitted together. "So, we need to ask around and see who is missing a shoe?"

"It's more complicated than that. We're going to have to try it on every maiden in the kingdom." Jerron felt ridiculous the second he said it.

"That's a great idea! We only have a week. I'll send out a proclamation."

"A great idea?" Jerron asked. "It seems ridiculous to me. It will probably fit hundreds of women."

"We will let everyone it fits meet at the castle until we figure out who she is! I'm going to talk to the king," Richard said, bounding from the room.

Jerron shook his head. He wasn't sure how picky Nancy was going to be. If it was up to him, he would go straight to Olivia and bring her back to the castle. He didn't want to risk it. He better try the shoe on as many smelly feet as he could find.

—————

"Girls!" Lady Anna's voice echoed through the house two days later. "Girls! Come now!" Olivia tried to ignore her shrill voice. She kept dusting the parlor. Lady Anna came bursting in, followed by Lottie and Mara.

"What is it, Mother?" Lottie whined, pushing her wet hair over her shoulder. "I'm in the middle of washing my hair."

"That is trivial in comparison to what I have to tell you!" Lady Anna said with a smile. "It appears the prince never got the name of the woman he was dancing with the other night."

"So?" Lottie said, rolling her eyes. "Why should we care who she is?"

"The woman left her slipper behind in her quick flight. The prince is determined to marry her."

"And?" Lottie asked, crossing her arms. Mara winked at Olivia and sank onto the sofa.

"The prince is going to marry the girl that fits the slipper. Every woman who fits the slipper will get another chance at winning him."

"He made it quite clear what he thought of me," Lottie mumbled.

"But this is a second chance," Lady Anna said. "You can tell me everything you said to him the night of the ball, and we will figure out where you went wrong."

Olivia dusted the mantle and tried not to smile as Lottie rattled off everything she had said to the prince. The more she talked, the larger Lady Anna frowned.

"It's no wonder he pawned you off on that duke," Lady Anna said, sitting in a chair and rubbing her temples. "We won't dwell on the past. The prince won't be in our area until this evening. I'll instruct you on what to say until then."

"Perhaps, you should put your hopes on me," Mara said with a gleam in her eye. "The prince finished an entire dance with me."

"Don't be ridiculous Mara," Lottie said. "He only danced with you because he had to dance with everyone. You didn't say over two words to him."

Mara shrugged indifferently. "At least he didn't feel the need to get rid of me halfway through the dance."

"Up to my room," Lady Anna said. "I'll teach you what to say, and Ella will work on your hair. It must be perfect. We are lucky to have another opportunity."

Olivia put the duster down and followed them from the room. Spending the day listening to Lady Anna and Lottie sounded painful. She watched as Mara slipped out the front door undetected. She hoped she was going to meet Stephan.

"I don't see the point," Lottie said, as they slipped into Lady Anna's room. "The prince isn't stupid. He's going to know who he danced with as soon as he sees her. This is a waste of time."

Lady Anna glared at Lottie. "Do you really want to spend your life with that greasy duke?"

"You said you found him delightful."

"I found him disgusting, but the man has connections and money."

"Well, he has enough money that I can deal with him. If I marry him, I can demand he be less—slimy. I'm very persuasive."

"Don't be ridiculous, Lottie. You will try on that slipper, and you will try to win the prince."

The day was as long as Olivia feared. She had to fix Lottie's hair three times before Lady Anna deemed it acceptable. The entire time, she had to listen to Lady Anna quiz Lottie on the best ways to talk to a prince. Making Lottie into a thoughtful companion was not a job for the faint of heart. By the end of the lesson, Lady Anna looked exhausted and Lottie was pouting.

Olivia made dinner that evening with butterflies in her stomach. What would happen once Jerron came? Everything was going to change after today. Olivia didn't know if she should be nervous or relieved. She was ready to be done with this life, but not ready to be done with Jerron. She liked him much more than she wanted to admit, even to herself. Falling for him was happening faster than was natural. Maybe she wasn't any different from the girls in fairy tales.

She pushed a blonde lock from her eyes and glanced out the window. She could see Stephan and Mara strolling near the trees behind the house. It was a good thing Lady Anna was preoccupied. They weren't doing a decent job at hiding.

"Where is Mara?" Lady Anna asked, bursting into the kitchen. "She should at least try to appear decent for the prince. Go find her and help her get ready. Go!"

"Of course," Olivia said, hoping she wouldn't look out the window. Thankfully, the woman left the room as abruptly as she arrived. Olivia opened the back door and caught Mara's attention. She motioned for her to come to the house and then returned to the kitchen. She glanced out the window in time to see Stephan kiss Mara's hand. Olivia smiled as Mara came bouncing back to the house.

"He is so wonderful!" she gushed, as she entered the kitchen.

"I'm sure he is," Olivia said, "but your mother wants you to get ready for the prince. Come on, I'll fix your hair." They scurried up to Mara's room and Olivia had her sit in front of the mirror.

"You should be getting ready, not me," Mara said, catching Olivia's eye in the mirror.

Olivia ran the brush through Mara's curls. "I don't have time. Don't worry about me." She tried not to look at herself in the mirror. Her appearance left something to be desired, but what was she going to do? Jerron had to choose her. It was the story.

"I hear horses!" Mara squealed. "Do you suppose it's the prince?"

Olivia's stomach did a roll. "Probably."

"Do you think he'll recognize you?"

Olivia's head bobbed. "Possibly."

"I'm so excited!" Mara squeaked. "Lottie and Mother are going to be so mad!"

Lady Anna peeked into the room. "Mad about what?"

"Nothing," Mara said. Lady Anna narrowed her eyes.

"Mother, the prince is here!" Lottie called from downstairs.

"Mara, come quickly!" Lady Anna commanded. "Ella, you will stay here. I don't want to see you until they are gone." Olivia nodded and then frowned as Lady Anna closed the door and locked it. She sighed as she tried to decide how soon to break free.

Jerron had seen enough feet to last a lifetime. It was hard to believe, but the slipper didn't fit on anyone's foot. It must be magic. He hoped Nancy would be satisfied with the amount of women he had tried it on. It wasn't the entire kingdom, but it was a lot. He was looking forward to finding Olivia and returning to the castle. Lady Anna opened the door and led Jerron and Richard into the parlor.

"We are so pleased to have you in our home," the woman was saying. Jerron tuned out whatever else she said as he inspected the room, hoping to see Olivia. Lottie and Mara bowed gracefully, and Richard had them sit.

"Richard will try the slipper on you," Jerron heard himself say. He glanced into the hallway, but there was no sign of Olivia.

Lottie took off her own slipper and held her foot out. Richard tried to place it on her foot, but it was obviously too small.

"Push harder, Lottie," Lady Anna encouraged.

"It doesn't fit, Mother," she said, glaring at her.

"You aren't trying hard enough."

"Would you like me to cut off my toes?" she asked sarcastically. "That's the only way it would fit." Jerron turned away to hide his smile. Lady Anna did not seem pleased.

Lady Anna glared at Lottie. "Alright. Mara, your turn."

"I don't need to try it on," Mara protested. "I already know it isn't mine."

"Mara! Try on the shoe!" Lady Anna looked like she was ready to spit nails.

Mara sighed as she took off her shoe and put it to the side. Richard placed the slipper on her foot, and it was too big.

"It fits!" Lady Anna exclaimed.

"It's too big," Richard and Mara said at the same time.

"Nonsense! It's on her foot."

"There's no way she could walk without it falling off," Jerron said.

"Stand and walk, Mara."

Mara stood up and took one step. The slipper fell to the floor. Mara sneered at her mother and shrugged.

"Are there any more ladies in the house?" Richard asked. A thump sounded above them. Jerron grinned. That had to be Olivia.

"No," Lady Anna said, glancing nervously at the ceiling. There was more pounding and the sound of cracking wood.

"What about Ella?" Mara asked. "She should get a chance."

"Who is Ella?" Richard asked.

"Just a servant," Lady Anna said. "She wasn't even at the ball."

"Wasn't she?" Mara asked, smiling sweetly. Jerron grinned at the girl. He was glad he'd worked things out for her and Stephan.

Lady Anna's eyes widened in realization. "You might as well be on your way," she said. "We won't keep you." Another cracking noise came from above and then the sound of someone running down the stairs. Jerron grinned as Olivia launched herself into the room.

"Ella!" Lady Anna said. "Back to your chores."

"I don't believe I will," Olivia said, smoothing her hair. "I fear I might have broken the door upstairs." If she was trying to look sorry, she was doing a terrible job. "Doors just aren't made the way they used to be."

Jerron chuckled as he took the shoe from Richard and motioned for Olivia to sit. She dropped down into a chair and held out her foot. Jerron kneeled on one knee and removed her tattered shoe. Her eyes sparkled as he slid the glass slipper onto her foot.

"It fits!" Richard exclaimed. Lottie stormed from the room, and Lady Anna pursed her lips. Mara clapped, and Olivia smiled at him. Something warm filled Jerron's insides. It was a feeling he'd never had before. Olivia was someone special. Someone he could find a happily ever after with.

"Ella, daughter," Lady Anna said, opening her arms. Olivia raised an eyebrow.

"Daughter?" Jerron asked, side eyeing the woman. "I thought you said she was your servant?"

"She does some jobs around the house," Lady Anna said, "But she is my stepdaughter. I promised her dying father I would care for her, and I've done so for years."

"I would invite you to live at the palace, but there is a certain duke that is planning on asking for your eldest daughter's hand in marriage. It would be best if you lived with them." Lady Anna clenched her teeth and nodded, leaving the room.

Jerron pulled Olivia to her feet. "What now?" he asked.

"You're asking me?" she said, smiling. He gathered her into his arms and was delighted when she wrapped her arms around his neck.

"This is when we live happily ever after." He leaned in and kissed her. It was a kiss like Jerron had never imagined. All the other women he'd kissed since this whole thing began had seemed empty and cold. Olivia was definitely real and warm. He hadn't been this content in a long time.

His head started spinning, and he held on tighter. He knew this feeling. Panic filled him, and he refused to let go. Nancy wouldn't separate them now, would she? They might not be crazy in love, but he suspected they could be with a little time. Wasn't that what the fairy godmother wanted? The spinning became more intense, and Jerron felt himself slipping away.

Chapter 9

Jerron jumped out of bed and glanced around the one-room cabin. His fists clenched and unclenched. How could Nancy do this to him? Stomping over to the wardrobe, he yanked it open and pulled out the first thing he saw, not caring what it was. As soon as he was decent, he stormed outside and studied the forest scene around him. Trees. That was all he could see.

"Nancy!" he yelled. "I know you can hear me!" When he usually changed stories, he would wait and ponder until he had some memories that would let him know who his character was and what he should be doing. He didn't care this time. He moved away from the cabin and into the trees.

Everything was peaceful. All he could hear were birds chirping and the flow of water nearby. "Nancy! This isn't fair! Come out, and stop being a coward!" He spun around at the sound of footsteps.

Nancy came around a corner with a smile on her weathered face. "Hello, Jerron. No need to shout. How are you this beautiful morning?"

Jerron shifted his jaw from side to side as he tried to rein in his temper. "I thought I could leave if I started believing in your nonsense. Why am I still here?"

"You aren't as ready as you seem to believe. You just called in nonsense."

"Why did you change the story? There was more to it."

"I didn't cause the change. The story always ends when there is a kiss. You should understand that by now."

He narrowed his eyes, and he shifted from one leg to the other. "Olivia is the first person I've ever connected with like that, and now, I might never see her again."

Nancy's eyes gleamed. "You like her that much?"

"Yes, and now, she could be anywhere! I hate this game. You shouldn't mess with people's lives."

"You aren't ready, and neither is Olivia, but I've enjoyed the progress you've made. I was wondering if you would ever come around."

"I don't understand why you even chose Olivia. She isn't anywhere near as bitter as I was. Just because she didn't believe she could have a happy ending was no reason to make her fall out a window and send her to this place. I hate it here!"

"Calm down, Jerron. You'll leave when you're ready and not a second before. The same goes for Olivia. I didn't push her out the window. I just sent a gentle wind. She was the one who leaned out too far."

He could tell she wouldn't budge, so he turned and stomped back to the cabin. It was crude and old, but he didn't care at the moment. He entered the cabin and slammed the door. Jerron paced across the wooden planks that were pretending to be a floor and tried to make a plan. A plan, he scoffed. There was no point in making a plan. If he tried to leave, he would just wake up in the same place.

There was a small table in one corner with a loaf of bread on top. He plopped down into a chair and grabbed the bread. He tore off a piece and stuffed it into his mouth. It was dry and hard to swallow. He threw the loaf onto the table and covered his face with his hands. He was never getting out of here. It was time to accept it.

Olivia wrapped her arms around her knees as she stared up at the stars. She swallowed a lump in her throat and forced her eyes to stay dry. Crying rarely fixed anything, so what was the point? Whether or not there was a point, a tear ran down her cheek when she blinked. She wiped it away and refused to let more fall.

It was a shock this morning to wake up in an unfamiliar cottage with a doting mother and a cat that didn't seem inclined to leave her side. She wondered if it always felt like this. Poor Jerron had been through it so many times. The thought of Jerron made new tears threaten to fall. It would be silly to say she was in love with him, but she liked him a lot.

"Red, it's time for dinner," her new mother called from the cottage. Olivia sighed and got to her feet. It seemed strange having this woman boss her around all day. Olivia considered herself a grown woman, not a child. The woman was kind but didn't believe in being idle for any amount of time.

Brushing off her pink dress, she made her way toward the tall, brown haired woman. If it wasn't for Jerron, this would be a much better situation than she had been in before. She still wasn't having any memories like Jerron talked about, but it had taken her less than five minutes this morning to figure out who she was supposed to be. The red cloak and hood her mother handed her when she went to find the outhouse were a dead giveaway.

"What's wrong, Red?" her mother asked, as she walked past her to get in the cottage.

"Nothing," Olivia said, thinking for at least the tenth time today that it was really stupid to call someone with blonde hair Red. If she had another name, she didn't know what it might be.

"You can't tell me it's nothing," the woman said. "I can see you've been crying."

"I'm just tired," she said, sinking down onto a wooden kitchen chair. The house smelled heavenly. It was nice to have someone who could cook, feed her for a change. Her own burned food had been anything but desirable.

"Tired? You slept in today, and you've been acting like a scared mouse all day." She placed a plate with ham, peas, and potatoes in front of Olivia and sat across from her. The orange cat curled itself around her legs and refused to budge. Her mother hadn't said the cat's name, so Olivia didn't know what to call her.

"I had bad dreams last night," Olivia said. That was only half true. It was more like a beautiful dream that had been ripped away from her. She thought of the joy that filled her when Jerron kissed her and how fast it had faded, leaving her with a feeling of despair.

"No reason to let dreams ruin our day. That's why I always tell you to keep yourself busy. It's the only way to be happy."

Olivia took a bite of ham and sighed. How would this story end? She knew the basic story of *Little Red Riding Hood*, and from what she remembered, there wasn't a kiss. If she was recalling it correctly, she might end up in the belly of a wolf. It was hard to find anything comforting in that.

"Are there any men around here?" she asked. Her mother glanced up from her plate and gave her a sympathetic pat on the hand.

"You know there aren't. None besides that young woodcutter that likes to walk through the woods like he owns the place. Is that the problem? You are still quite young. In a year or two, we can worry about men, alright?"

"I'm not worried about them. I just wondered," Olivia said thoughtfully, as she chewed her food. If the woodcutter was young, he might be part of her story. She cringed at the thought. Her heart didn't want to meet another man. She wanted to find Jerron. She wasn't even sure if they were in the same world, so looking might be fruitless.

She sighed. This was the type of mess she was avoiding before she came here. She had been doing fine before Nancy came and ruined everything. She didn't even know if Jerron liked her. He had to kiss her to end the story. Still, there was the time at the inn when he'd looked like he might kiss her.

"I understand what it's like to be young," her mother said. "I know it's hard for you. We are so secluded here, but there isn't a lot we can do about it. If I could sell the cottage, we could go someplace better, but we've never had luck with that."

"I'm fine. Don't worry about me."

"But it's my job. I'll always worry."

The woodpile kept growing, and Jerron kept chopping. When he'd finally realized pouting wasn't going to solve anything, he had let the memories flood in. He was a woodcutter. All he did was cut wood and sell it. He had no family, no friends, and nothing else to do. He shouldn't have kissed Olivia, then he would still be living the cushy life of a prince. He could have taken her with him without kissing her.

Jerron split a log and threw it into the pile. There was nothing in Jerron's memories to tell him what fairy tale he was living. He couldn't recall anything with a grumpy antisocial woodcutter. He spent the day before exploring, and all he found were trees and more trees. How was he supposed to play out a story by himself? He hadn't felt this bitter since he first came here.

A wolf howled in the woods, and he decided that was his signal to stop for lunch. He stuck his ax into a log and wiped sweat from his brow. It was going to get lonely fast. He was tempted to walk in one direction until he found a woman, any woman so he could kiss her and end this.

The week dragged on like a horrible nightmare. Olivia did her best to stay away from the house. If she looked idle for more than a second her mother had her darning socks, quilting, or something equally as tedious. The woman was kind, but not one for talking. Staying around her was boring, so Olivia escaped for a long walk every morning.

It was a nice day, and Olivia lost track of time. Her red hood hung down her back, and she enjoyed the soft breeze. The sun was directly overhead, and she was going to be late for lunch. Before she could turn back to go home, she heard a sound in the woods. Curious, she walked toward it. She wasn't normally one to pry, but after a week in what felt like isolation, she was ready to meet anyone.

From the sound of it she was about to intrude on the wood-cutter. Her mother had mentioned more than once that he was unpleasant, but Olivia didn't care. This story had already gotten stale. She slowed as the sound got louder. She peered through the trees and could make out a man splitting logs. His back was to her. He was tall with dark hair, and he was strong. She could see that from a distance. He split the logs like it was nothing.

Olivia paused and hid behind a tree. She wasn't sure how to approach the man. Putting one hand on the tree she peeked around and watched him. There was something familiar about him. He turned his head to the side, and Olivia sucked in a breath. Could it be?

Stepping out from behind the tree, she stumbled into the clearing. "Jerron?" she called. He startled at the sound of her voice and then dropped the ax to the ground.

"Olivia?" he said, an enormous smile overtaking his surprise. Olivia smiled back and ran to him. He picked her up, spinning her in a circle. "I thought I'd never see you again."

"Same. I can't believe you're the hermit woodcutter my mother keeps warning me about." She ignored the butterflies that had taken up residence in her stomach and wrapped him in a hug.

"Hermit woodcutter?" he laughed. "I guess that's accurate. I haven't talked to a single person since I came here. Unless you count the first day when I yelled at Nancy. That woman's impossible. I also talk to the cow and horse I seem to own. They aren't good at holding their part of the conversation, though."

Olivia grinned and stepped back, studying him. He hadn't shaved since he'd been here. "The only person I've talked to is my mother, and she treats me like I'm eight. Still, it's better than cooking and cleaning all day."

Jerron pulled Olivia's hood over her head. *Little Red Riding Hood?* he asked, shaking his head. "Why didn't I think of that? I've been wondering what this tale could be."

"I'm too old for this character."

"Probably. I've heard a wolf a few times out here. I wonder how that will work out. You better hope I don't have to cut you out of his belly."

Olivia's eyes widened, and she shivered. "I'm not going to the grandma's house without a weapon. I wonder if that's against the rules."

"It's hard to say. Nancy seems pretty lenient on some aspects of the stories."

"Do you suppose she'll ever let us go?"

"I hope so. Now that I see you again, I have hope. I've never seen a person in more than one story. The fact that we're both here makes me think Nancy might believe we're heading in the right direction. If you're in all my stories, it won't be as bad."

Olivia wondered if that meant he liked her as much as she liked him. She wished he would kiss her again, but then they might disappear. She wondered if this was how all the girls she thought were silly felt. Perhaps, love wasn't out of reach. She wasn't sure she loved Jerron, but she liked him more than a little.

"Maybe we can make this one last?" Olivia suggested. "If we never kiss, we might just stay here, and we can do things together."

"This story is awful," Jerron said. "I like to be around people. I might not have believed in happy endings, but I've always been social. This is too isolated. I'm not sure I want to spend the rest of my life not kissing you, either."

Olivia tried to ignore the heat creeping up her cheeks. "How strict do you suppose it is?"

"What?"

"The kissing thing. Like if we kiss before any of the story happens, will we automatically end up in another story?"

"I'm not sure," he said, scratching the stubble on his chin. "I've never tested it. Do you want to?"

"Not yet. What if we aren't in the same place next time?"

Jerron tilted his head as he studied her. "I have a feeling Nancy's going to keep us together. How's your sick grandmother?"

"Sick," Olivia said with a laugh. "I haven't seen her yet. My mother goes and takes care of her every day, but so far, she hasn't let me go. She doesn't want me catching anything."

"I wonder how long this can play out. There isn't much to it. It's so boring. Do you want to come in for lunch?"

"Sure," she said, taking the hand he offered. "I'm already going to get a lecture for being late. I might as well make it worth it."

Jerron watched Olivia as she tried to cross the creek without getting wet. She jumped from one stone to the next, nearly falling in every time. They had been meeting every day for the past week, and today, he wanted to show her the swimming hole he found. They needed to cross to the other side of the creek to get there faster, and she was doing her best to stay dry. Jerron plunged into the knee deep water and walked slightly behind her.

"When you fall, you're going to get wet and hurt yourself," he warned.

"*If* I fall. Not when," she said, jumping to the next rock. Today was the first time since coming here that he'd seen her without her cape and hood. She was wearing a red dress, and her blond hair fell in gentle curls. This week was a lot easier than the one before. It was nice to have her company. It was going to be even harder if they got separated again. Every day, he fell for her a little more.

"I'm pretty sure it's *when*," he said, as she paused. The next rock was too far. "You'll never make that one."

"It's not that far," she said, looking from the rock she was on to the one in front of her. She leaped to the rock and landed on the very edge. Her arms windmilled, and she fell backwards.

Jerron caught her before she could hit the water. Her hand smacked him in the eye.

"Sorry," she said with a slight smile. "I guess you were right."

"I was hoping," he said, ignoring the sting as she put her arms around his neck. "I'll get you across dry, but once we get to the swimming hole, you're getting wet."

"It's too cold to get wet," she protested. "It must be fall. The leaves are changing."

"It's not cold. The water is lukewarm. I go there every day to bathe."

"You bathe outside?"

"There aren't any people around. It's a lot easier than hauling water to my cabin. I tried that the first time, and it's not worth it."

"I wasn't meant to live in whatever time we keep ending up in. I miss turning on a faucet and getting water."

"I miss pizza," he said, striding across the water. "Almost everything I miss is food."

"I don't miss my job. Retail isn't fun. I was hoping to start college in the fall. Now, who knows what's going to happen?"

Jerron stepped out of the creek and put Olivia on her feet. He wished he had an excuse to hold her longer. He grinned when she linked her arm with his. His boots squished with each step he took. He usually took them off when he crossed the creek, but he'd been distracted this time.

"I wonder how long I've been gone. It seems like such a long time. I have this horrible recurring nightmare where I wake up in my own bed and I'm an old man."

"I just hope I'm not dead," Olivia said, her lips turning down. "I did fall out of a high window."

"We're not dead," Jerron reassured her. "I'm certain heaven would be better and hell would be a lot worse."

"Maybe we're stuck in the middle until they decide where to put us," Olivia said. Jerron glanced sideways and saw a small smile on her face.

"There it is," Jerron said, motioning ahead. The pond was his favorite place to come. It was deep enough to swim in, and so far, it had been warm.

"Are there any animals in there?" she asked. "I'm not scared of fish, but it might scare me if one touches my leg."

"I haven't seen any."

"How deep is it?"

"It starts out low and goes over my head a bit. I'm going to leave my boots here so they can dry out," he said, sinking to the ground.

"I'm going to go feel the water and see how cold it is," Olivia said, walking to the edge of the water. She kneeled down and stuck her hand in. Jerron wrestled with his boot. It seemed to be suctioned to his foot.

When he finally got them off, he stood and looked at Olivia. His breath froze as he took in the sight. Olivia ran her fingers playfully through the water, completely unaware of the large black and gray wolf standing behind her. Panic, unlike anything Jerron had ever felt, seized him as he tried to weigh his options. He didn't want to scare it into attacking her.

Olivia glanced at him and grinned. "You're right. The water feels nice. What's wrong?" she asked, her smile slipping away. Jerron grabbed a tree branch and walked slowly in their direction. The wolf seemed unconcerned. Olivia stood up and bumped the animal.

"Whoa!" she exclaimed, backing away from the creature. It watched her with its enormous amber eyes. Jerron got closer and put a hand to her elbow. He kept the branch in front of them as they backed up. The wolf turned to the pond and began lapping the water.

"He doesn't seem vicious," Jerron said.

"Should we run?" Olivia asked.

"No, we don't want to tempt him into chasing us. I'm not very knowledgeable about wolves, but I seem to remember hearing that they rarely attack people."

"Yes, but we're in a story where a wolf eats people," Olivia said with a tremble in her voice.

"This one doesn't look hungry."

The wolf glanced up and walked lazily toward them. Jerron pulled on Olivia's arm to encourage her to move a little faster. The wolf didn't seem to be in a hurry, but he was getting closer. Jerron cringed as they bumped into a tree. The animal stopped and studied them.

Olivia held out a trembling hand, and the wolf sniffed it before licking her. Jerron held his breath as it glanced at him and then trotted off into the trees.

"I just got licked by a wolf!" Olivia exclaimed with a shaky laugh. "That was terrifying!"

"Do you want to head home?" he asked.

"No, I don't think he's going to do any harm, do you?"

"I doubt it. He had his chance."

They walked to the water, and Olivia kicked off her shoes. "I'm not going in deep."

"It feels really nice."

"I'm not walking home in a soaked dress," she said. "Besides, I don't go in deep water."

"It's not too deep," Jerron reassured her.

"You said it gets over your head. That's too deep."

"Why do you hate water?"

"I'm not sure. I always have. When I was young, I fell in the water and had to be saved, but I don't remember it. Maybe it traumatized me. I have nightmares about waking up underwater." She lifted her dress to her knees and stepped in.

Jerron trudged into the water and dove under when it was deep enough. It was going to be a soggy walk home. He should have ditched his shirt. He surfaced and wiped his eyes. Olivia stayed in ankle deep water and watched him.

"Sometimes I wish I knew how to swim."

"I could teach you," he offered, making his way to her.

"No," she said, taking a step back. "My parents put me in lessons a few times. I can't make myself try."

"It feels really nice."

"It won't when you're walking home soaked."

"That's probably true. Is that your best wading dress?" he asked, smirking at the long red dress. "I did tell you we were coming here."

"I don't have a best wading dress," she said. "You should see the inside of my wardrobe. Everything is long and almost all of it's red. I don't know if I should blame the real Red, or the mother. Probably the mother. I'm not complaining, though. As Cinderella, I only had those two smelly old dresses. At least these are nice and they don't stink."

"You look good in red," he said, causing her to blush.

"Thanks."

He took her dry hand in his wet one. "Can I tell you something?"

She cocked her head to one side and nodded.

"I think I have a crush."

She raised an eyebrow and giggled. "A crush?"

"Yep," he said, grinning. He couldn't believe he was admitting it to her. It might be more than a crush, but he wouldn't tell her yet. He kissed her hand. "I can't tell you how much I want to kiss you right now. I would if it wouldn't make you disappear."

"And I would let you," she said. "I can't believe Nancy won't send us home. I already feel like I've made progress."

"You're making progress a lot faster than I did. It took meeting you for anything to change." He opened his arms, and she stepped into them. She probably didn't appreciate a wet hug, but she didn't protest. She'd released her hold on the bottom of her dress, so now that was wet as well.

"The wolf is back," Olivia said from against his chest. He turned and peered into the trees. The wolf watched them curiously but didn't come any closer. It had a peculiar expression on its face. If wolves had the ability, Jerron would almost believe it was smiling.

Chapter 10

Olivia placed a basket on the table and loaded it with tasty things her mother had made. There was a heavenly smelling loaf of bread, two apples, a jar of cider, and some cake. Her mother took something to the sick grandmother every day. Olivia wasn't sure why the old woman lived off on her own. It would be a lot easier if she lived with them.

"Red, thank you," her mother said, rubbing her temples. "I feel a headache coming on. I'm going to have to send you to visit Grandmother today."

Olivia's heart started beating double time. Was today the day? She wasn't sure she was ready. "Alright," she said, trying to seem unconcerned. "Can you give me directions?"

"Directions to Grandmother's house?" her mother asked, side eyeing her.

"I haven't been there in a while," Olivia said, covering the basket.

"You've been walking there since you were three! I can't imagine you just forgot the way. Just stick to the trail, and you'll get there the same as always."

Olivia had avoided the trail her mother disappeared down every day. She knew somewhere at the end of it was a big bad wolf. "So, there aren't any turns?"

"For goodness' sake, Red. Turns to where? There's only one way."

Olivia shrugged. "I'm just making sure."

"Well, hurry on your way. She's waiting for you. Don't stop, and stick to the path."

"Of course," Olivia said, wrapping herself in her cape. She pulled the hood over her head and grabbed the basket.

"I'm going to lie down," her mother said, leaving the kitchen. Olivia opened a drawer and pulled out the biggest knife she could find, and she placed it in the basket. She wasn't getting eaten without a fight. She took a resolved breath and left the house. There was no reason to prolong the inevitable, so she hurried down the dirt path.

The trail was long, and Olivia wondered how long she could keep up her pace. She hoped fate was telling Jerron to come after her today. They were supposed to meet later, but she was going to need him soon.

Olivia jumped when a bird squawked nearby. She rolled her eyes and kept walking. The trees were dense and shaded her path, but it was still light. There was no reason to be jumping because of birds.

"Hello," a deep voice said from behind her. Olivia spun around, expecting to see a wolf, but there was a man standing there instead. He was tall with an old-fashioned suit and a top hat. He couldn't be older than twenty. His black mustache curled up at the ends, reminding her of the old cartoons that had a villain tying someone to the railroad tracks.

"I'm in a hurry," Olivia said, turning and rushing down the path.

He came up next to her. "Why are you walking this way? That path is much faster." He pointed, and Olivia glanced at an overgrown path leaving this trail.

"Faster for what?" she asked.

"Getting to your grandmother's house."

Olivia stopped and studied him. "How do you know about my grandmother?"

"I've lived in these woods for years. That path will take fifteen minutes off your journey. I'm surprised you aren't aware of it."

Olivia swallowed and looked into the trees. This wasn't right. Where was the wolf? Was this the wolf in disguise? She wasn't excited to take an unknown path, but if that was where the story was leading her, she better go. This wasn't a day she wanted to repeat.

She turned and walked down the faded trail. The man waved and made no attempt at following her, but that didn't rid her of the uneasy feeling in the pit of her stomach. She picked up her pace and kept looking over her shoulder. There was no sign of the man.

Since Olivia didn't know how far the grandmother's house was, she had no idea how long it would take. It seemed too far for her liking. She wanted to turn around and go to the other path, but she had come a good distance. When she was about to give up, she saw a small cottage up ahead. It was surrounded by flowers and neatly trimmed bushes.

Her pace slowed as she neared the dwelling. Her hands were sweating, and her mouth felt dry. Walking up to the cottage door, she reached inside the basket to make sure her knife was still there. She squared her shoulders and knocked on the door.

"Who is it?" said an incredibly fake grandmother impersonator.

"It's me, Red Riding Hood," Olivia said, rolling her eyes at the ridiculousness of it all.

"Lift the latch, and come in, my dear."

Olivia opened the door and stepped into the cottage. She kept the door open and waited for her eyes to adjust. On one side of the room was a gigantic bed, and inside the bed sat the man from the trail, wearing a nightgown and cap.

"You've got to be joking," Olivia mumbled, as her eyes were drawn to the man's mustache. Did he really believe he was disguised? Olivia kept her hand on the knife.

"Good of you to come," the man said.

"You look worse than I imagined," she said, not going any closer.

"I am very sick," the man said, in a high falsetto voice.

"Grandmother, what big eyes you have," Olivia said, playing along.

"The better to see you, my dear."

"And, Grandmother, what big ears you have," she said, looking at the man's normal sized ears.

"The better to hear you, my dear."

"Strange you've grown a mustache," she couldn't help adding.

The man's eyes narrowed. "It happens as we age sometimes, my dear."

"I'm not going to say it," Olivia said. "You aren't even a wolf." She turned to the door and ran out. Dropping the basket to the ground, she turned around holding her knife in a stabbing position. The man came barreling from the cottage, still in the nightgown, and sped toward her. Olivia screamed as loud as she could, hoping Jerron was nearby.

The man growled and lunged for her. She stepped to the side, and he fell to the ground. Jerron came running from the trees with an enormous ax in his hands. She sighed with relief. She didn't want to stab anyone. The man was back on his feet, and he began circling her. Jerron was getting closer. She kept the knife in the air, hoping it would encourage the man to stay back.

Before Jerron could reach her, the wolf from the day before lunged out of the trees and jumped on the man. Jerron lowered his ax and pulled Olivia away. The man yelled as the gigantic wolf growled into his face.

"Quick, into the cottage," Olivia said, grabbing Jerron by the hand. They ran inside and slammed the door. Jerron bolted it, and they shared a concerned look.

"That was different," Jerron finally said.

"Why was it a man?" Olivia asked. "That made it terrifying." She peeked out the window. "He's gone. The wolf is just sitting there."

Jerron scanned the room. "Shouldn't there be a grandmother in a closet or something?"

"Right," Olivia said, rushing to the only door in the room it could be. She pulled on the doorknob and couldn't open it. "Grandmother? Are you in there?"

"Yes!" said a feeble voice. "I can't open the door!"

"Stand back," Jerron said. He grabbed the doorknob and slammed his weight into the door. It didn't open. He plowed into it harder, causing it to pop open and break the frame.

A petite, sickly woman came out and wrapped her arms around Olivia. "I'm so glad you're safe, my dear," she said. "That wolf was a crafty one."

"Wolf?" Olivia asked.

"Yes. And a talking wolf at that. I've seen a lot in my time, but nothing like that."

Olivia shared a confused look with Jerron.

"What did you bring me today?" she asked, climbing into her bed. She seemed recovered from the entire ordeal. Jerron retrieved the basket and handed it to the grandmother.

"We have to be going now," Olivia said. "My mother is going to worry. It took me longer than usual to get here."

"Tell your mother hello," the old woman said, pulling the cake from the basket. "And don't talk to strangers."

Jerron and Olivia left the house and hurried toward the better used path.

Olivia patted the wolf's head. "Thanks for your help," she said, as they passed him. His eyes followed, but he made no move to go with them.

"I think this story is done," Jerron said.

"This one was messed up," Olivia said with a shiver. "Why was the wolf good and that frightening man acting the wolf's part?"

"No idea. I've never had anything happen like that before."

"Perhaps, that's because you haven't been here long enough," the wolf-man said, stepping in front of them. His clothes were torn, and he had blood all over his shirt and a deep scratch across his cheek. He peeled off his fake mustache and tossed it to the ground. "The longer you stay, the worse it will be. Happiness does not exist. Make your own fun and ignore the rules."

"Who are you?" Olivia demanded.

"No one and everyone," he said with a grin. "Some days, I exist, and some days, I don't."

"What do you want?" Jerron asked.

"Who can tell? Not you. Not me. Perhaps the witch, but she won't. Oh, no, she won't." He laughed maniacally. "She won't tell you anything because she's a witch. She has her own agenda. I want to kill her agenda, and I will. Don't worry, I will." The man squinted off into the trees. "Is that her? Witch!" he yelled. "You won't escape me this time!" He darted off into the woods. Olivia searched the trees, but there wasn't anyone there.

"Let's get out of here," Jerron said, grabbing Olivia's hand and pulling her along at a quick pace. "We need to put distance between us and that guy." Jerron had never had a story go wrong when he wasn't the cause of it. He hoped that didn't mean they had to redo the day.

Jerron had gone out to chop wood today, when he had a desperate desire to walk through the woods. He had been around long enough to know he shouldn't ignore his instincts, so he grabbed his ax and headed into the trees. Something told him today was the day, so he didn't waste time.

After walking aimlessly for an hour, he heard an ear-piercing scream and went running. He never imagined he would be relieved to see a wolf, but he had been today. Its behavior made little sense, but he was grateful it had been there.

Once they had put a respectful distance between themselves and the man, Jerron stopped. "I have an uneasy feeling about that man back there."

"Not surprising," Olivia said, catching her breath. "If stories can change without us causing it, how will we know what to do?"

"I've been in stories I wasn't familiar with before. I felt tugs and pulls that took me in the right direction. Today, I had an undeniable impression to walk in the woods."

"I'm going to be more nervous now. I was expecting a wolf, not a creepy guy."

"Hopefully, it was a one time thing."

"What now?" she asked, looking up at him through her eyelashes.

"First, we need a plan. If we are in a story and something gets too dangerous, you kiss me immediately. I've never tried to get out of a story early, so I can't swear it will work, but we'll try."

"What if we aren't in the same stories again?" she asked, studying at the ground.

He put a finger under her chin and lifted it gently until she looked up. "I'm not going to think about that. It's going to work out. I feel it." He wrapped his arms around her, and she rested her head on his shoulder. "Nancy isn't being as picky as she once was. I used to redo days all the time. I've only had to redo two or three since you came."

"Maybe she senses you trying harder."

"That might be it," he said. "I wasn't very cooperative before."

"What changed?" she asked, pulling back and gazing into his eyes.

"I used to try so I could go home," he said, running a hand over her cheek. "Now I try so that we can go home. My heart is committed now, not just my head."

Olivia smiled as Jerron leaned in and kissed her. He held her tight, hoping to keep her there a little longer. Jerron's head started spinning, and he sighed. Still not good enough.

Olivia opened her eyes in a panic. She was underwater! She flailed her arms around and tried to kick her legs. She could see surprisingly well, but everything felt wrong. She held her breath and tried to pull herself upwards. Where was the surface? She couldn't tell if she was trying to go up or down. Her heart couldn't take this. It beat rapidly, and she feared it would stop.

Someone grabbed her arms and steadied her. "Marina! Stop!" commanded a raven haired mermaid. The woman had a tail! Olivia's mouth opened in shock, and it surprised her to find she was alright. How was she breathing underwater? Looking down, she saw her own mermaid tail.

"What?" she sputtered in confusion.

"What were you doing?" the other mermaid asked her.

"I need to go up," she said with a trembling voice. It amazed her she could hear underwater.

"Up where?"

"To the surface."

The mermaid gave her a funny look. "Isn't that why you're always getting into trouble? I wouldn't risk it. Father is not in a good mood today."

"I need to go up!" Olivia said, still afraid her heart might stop. She moved her arms around to keep herself from tipping sideways. A fish swam by causing her to shriek and swat it away.

"What are you doing?" the mermaid asked.

"I can't stay upright!" Olivia exclaimed, flapping her tail haphazardly. How was the other woman staying upright without trying? "I can't stay down here!"

The mermaid put one hand on her hip. "Fine, but don't say I didn't warn you."

"I need help! Can you take me up?"

The woman's eyes widened as she pointed to herself. "Me? You want me to take you up there? I'm not taking on Father's wrath. You're on your own."

"Please," Olivia begged, grabbing the girl's arm. "I can't swim."

The mermaid moved her lips from side to side and seemed confused. "You can't swim? That makes no sense."

"I can't explain. Something's wrong with me, and I need to go up."

"Normally, I would ignore you, but you were acting really weird when I came down. Come on." She grabbed Olivia's arm and pulled her rapidly through the water. Olivia was too terrified to take in all the colorful fish they passed. After a few minutes, she could see light up above.

As her head broke the surface, Olivia inhaled a deep breath, even though she didn't need to. That was all in her head. She flapped her arms and swung her tail, trying to stay up.

The other mermaid tilted her head as she studied her. "What's wrong with you, Marina?"

"Help me to that rock," she said. The mermaid shook her head but towed Olivia to the rock. She grabbed hold and pulled herself up.

"I don't know what's gotten into you, but this is dangerous. The beach isn't far, and you can't risk anyone seeing you."

Olivia tried to stay up on the slippery rock and push her wet hair out of her face at the same time. She had never felt anything so unnatural in her life. Goosebumps rippled over her arms, and she shivered.

"You go, I'll be fine," she said, not believing it.

"I can't leave you here like this. You aren't acting stable at all. Did you hit your head?"

"No, I'm fine. Go. It's okay."

"Alright, but if Father asks, I'm going to have to tell him where you are, and then I'm going to get in trouble." She turned and disappeared beneath the surface.

Olivia glanced at the shore and couldn't decide what to do. It wasn't far, but it might as well be in a different country. If she got there, what would she do? She had a tail! A gross fishy tail! She pulled herself farther onto the rock and draped over it, lying on her stomach. Tears ran over her face as she ignored the sun on her back. She was stuck.

Jerron was a prince again, which was preferable to a lonely woodcutter. He wasn't sure which prince, but the memories that came to him were of a spoiled life of luxury. Not that it was uncommon as a prince. The first thing he had done was eat a large breakfast. It was good to eat something that wasn't his own cooking.

He spent the morning walking around the castle trying to figure out what story he was in. He was still clueless. The castle had a view of a prosperous little town on one side, and the ocean on the other. He could get used to this place. He wondered how Olivia was doing.

There was a man named Martin that liked to show up and tell him what to do, and his memories told him to only take the man with a grain of salt. He'd tried to question him about some things to get any hints as to what the story was, but he got nothing.

"Your Highness," Martin said, popping out in front of him as he strolled down a white marble hallway. "Have you decided what you would like to do next week? Should I make arrangements to go out on the ship? If so, I need to know soon so I can finalize plans."

"Where would we go?"

"Nowhere in particular. We would just be on the ship having a good time, as usual. Of course, we would have to listen to all the silly tales about mermaids and other nonsense."

"Mermaids?" Jerron asked, feeling uneasy.

The gray-haired man shook his head. "No need to frown. You know the sailors all love to spin yarns about mermaids.

It's ridiculous that some of them claim to have actually seen them. I suppose the life of a sailor can get dull, and they have to entertain themselves somehow."

"I've got to go," Jerron said, making his way to the palace doors. If Olivia was a mermaid, she was probably having a panic attack. She'd mentioned more than once her fear of water.

"Where are you going?" Martin called from behind him.

"I'll be back soon," Jerron said, ignoring the question. As soon as he left the palace, he sprinted down the steps and ran in the direction of the beach. He scanned the calm waters and hoped for a sign.

He cupped his hands and brought them around his mouth. "Olivia!" he yelled. "Olivia!" Nothing. He ran down the beach, calling her name. The ocean was vast. His chances of finding her weren't good. As he was about to give up, he heard something. Looking out over the ocean, his eyes stopped on a rock. Someone was sitting on top, waving at him.

"Olivia," he whispered, as he made large strides toward the water. He paused to throw off his boots and shirt. Jerron stepped into the small waves and walked until the water was deep enough to swim. He plunged into the water and swam to her. He reached the rock and put a hand on it to hold himself steady.

Olivia looked down at him, and he frowned at her red splotchy face. How long had she been out here crying? She wiped her eyes. "You came," she sniffed.

"As soon as I realized what was happening."

"I can't do this," she said. "I was so far under the water."

"I'm sorry."

"I've never been that scared in my life!"

"How did you get up here?"

"Another mermaid brought me. I really don't know how I can do this," she said, new tears filling her eyes. "It was so deep. I can't go back down there. I can't even swim as a mermaid."

"Come here, and I'll swim us to shallow water," he said, holding out his free hand. She took it, and he helped her slip into the water.

ele

Olivia tried not to panic as Jerron helped her back into the water. She held onto his hand and the rock. Why did water scare her so much? This was unreasonable. She knew she could breathe underwater, and she was still terrified.

"I need you to be calm and not freak out," he said. "If you do, you might pull me under. Do you think you can do that?"

"I'll try," she said.

"Okay, I need you to relax and float against my arm."

"I don't know how to float."

"Just relax, and don't get tense."

Olivia closed her eyes and rested her head against Jerron's arm. She felt herself floating and forced herself to stay calm.

"Okay, I'm going to swim. Just keep doing what you're doing." He floated to his back and started backstroking toward the shore. Olivia did her best to stay relaxed.

"I'm going to stand now," Jerron said. "Put your arms around my neck and don't panic." Olivia's heart pounded as she gripped Jerron's neck, and he shifted. He stood up, holding her around the waist. The water was to his chest.

"I feel ridiculous," Olivia admitted. "I have a tail, and I can't swim."

"What do we do now?" he asked.

Olivia bit her lip. "No idea. I don't see how I can do this. I can't go back if I can't even put my face in the water."

"I could try to teach you to swim."

"Have you ever tried to swim with a tail?"

"No, but we can probably figure it out."

"I don't think I can force myself to go back."

"We were wondering if we could end a story early. Do you want to try?"

Olivia's lip quivered. She was turning out to be a wimp. She closed her eyes and nodded, pressing her forehead to his.

"I'll try my best to find you fast," he said. She felt his warm breath on her lips. She wished things could be different. Moving closer, she pressed her lips to his. For a moment, she forgot she was surrounded by water. It wasn't long before the spinning started.

Chapter 11

Olivia sat up in bed and studied her new bedroom. She must be a princess. The tiara on the table was a dead giveaway. The room was spacious and full of collectible nick-nacks. There were shelves of them. She rubbed her hand over the soft bed.

She'd never been a princess before, so she wasn't sure what would be expected of her. She curled back into a ball and snuggled under the heavy comforter. She wanted to stay like this until memories of waking up under the ocean disappeared. If anyone was allowed to stay in bed, it should be a princess. She yawned and enjoyed the comfort of the bed. It had been a long time since she'd been this cozy.

Her eyes flew open as she heard the creak of the door. She stared at the wall, too scared to roll over and see who had entered. The door closed softly, and she heard it lock. Foot-steps came closer, and she made a fist. Someone touched her shoulder, and she spun around and punched as hard as she could. She made contact with the person's face.

"Ouch!" Jerron exclaimed, stumbling back. He put a hand to his eye.

"Jerron!" She hopped off the bed and threw her arms around him. "I'm so sorry, you scared me to death!"

"I should have knocked," he said, returning the hug. "I thought I better slip in fast before someone saw me. I'm just glad you were really the princesses. I was guessing."

"Wow, you grow facial hair fast," she said, running her hand over his two inch beard.

"It's almost as impressive as your hair," he said, grabbing a handful of her hair and holding it out to her. She gasped. It was black. "It looks good."

"I guess it's better than a tail. That experience didn't cure my fear of water." She stepped back and frowned. He was going to have a black eye. "Sorry about your eye."

"I'm sure I deserve it."

She studied his leather pants and tunic. He didn't look like a prince. "Who are you supposed to be?"

He sighed and sank down onto the bed. "Not who I want to be. Nancy's magic is starting to get messed up. If you're Snow White, I should be the prince."

"I'm Snow White?"

"Yes."

"And you aren't the prince? Does that mean I have to kiss someone else?"

"You better not," he said with a small grin. "I'm the huntsman."

"Oh," Olivia said, narrowing her eyes. "Have you talked to the queen yet?"

"Yes. She already commanded me to kill you and bring her your heart."

"That's morbid."

"Yeah. Should I kiss you now?"

"That might not be a good idea. What if we keep changing and ending up in worse places? Or what if we can't find each other one time?"

He tilted his head and watched her. "So, we play it out?"

"Maybe not all of it. I'm not excited to bite into a poisonous apple. We can end it before that."

"The queen isn't even that pretty. I mean, she's alright, but if she bans every woman that's more beautiful than she is, it's going to be an empty kingdom. Not to brag or anything, but I might even be prettier than she is."

Olivia grinned. "I wouldn't doubt it."

Jerron winked. "I'll wait outside your door. Get dressed, and I'll show you to the kitchen. After you eat, we can make a plan."

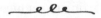

Olivia wandered around the grounds of the castle, waiting for Jerron. They were supposed to meet in a few minutes.

"Well, what do we have here?" asked a man from behind her. Olivia turned around to face a prince. He was tall with walnut brown eyes and messy brown hair. With a gasp of recognition she took a step back. He was the crazy man from Little Red Riding Hood.

"I like the hair, but it makes you appear a bit washed out," he said, leaning against the castle wall. "You could use some sun. Do you want to go for a walk?"

"I'm busy right now," Olivia said, taking another step back.

He laughed and grabbed her arm. "Too busy for me? But I'm a prince. Everyone loves the prince."

"Not everyone," Jerron said, coming around the corner. He had a bow with an arrow pointing at the man. "Let her go."

"Why are you here?" he asked, dropping Olivia's arm and crossing his own. "Get out of my story."

"You're the one in our story," Olivia said, positioning herself behind Jerron.

"I take whatever story I want," he said, narrowing his eyes. "I want this one. That means you need to play your little role and then leave. I've been watching this one," he said, pointing at Olivia. "She's the one that's going to break my spell and finally free me from this prison."

"You're a real person?" Olivia asked.

"Of course I am. Can't you tell how solid I am compared to the other people? I used to be called Terrence, or Terry, but I'm beginning to forget that guy."

Olivia wasn't sure Terry was playing with a full deck. Even dressed as a prince, he gave off a chilling presence.

"You can go wherever you want?" Jerron asked.

Terry's eyes glistened. "I can. I can do whatever I want in this place. Terry doesn't follow the rules anymore, and the rules no longer bind me. Isn't that right Nancy?"

Olivia scanned the grounds. Nancy was nowhere to be seen.

"Nancy! Tell them how you're not my keeper anymore!" he yelled. "Tell them I'm beating you at your own game!" He leaned forward and whispered, "She has no power over me. She fears me."

Olivia wouldn't be surprised. There was something wrong with this man. She wondered if he had always been like this, or if this place had made him crazy.

"Well, the time for the prince hasn't come," Jerron said, not lowering the bow. "I guess we'll meet you later."

"Not you huntsman," Terry said with a grin. "You only get to be in the first part of the story. I'll see Snow later." He winked and sauntered away.

"That guy is scary," Olivia said, as they walked into the woods near the castle.

"He is," Jerron agreed. "I was already nervous to let you go running off into the woods. Now, I'm terrified. You need to stay away from him."

"I'll try."

"I don't know what to do about the next part of the story," Jerron admitted. "I'm not a hunter, and I'm supposed to bring the queen a heart. Who calls these kids' stories? I really don't want to kill a deer, and I can't ever imagine trying to find its heart."

"You shouldn't go back to the queen. You could come with me."

"Then, she might realize you're not dead and come after you faster. Or we might have to repeat."

"How often did you repeat before we met?"

Jerron swung his bow over his shoulder. "In the beginning, all the time. Once I caught on, it was less frequent. Now, it rarely happens, even when I think it will. Of course, all my days as the woodcutter were the same. I could have repeated them and not noticed."

"Should I go running off into the woods now?" Olivia asked, turning to him. She wished he could come. She wasn't looking forward to finding the seven dwarfs and becoming their maid.

"Probably," he said with a sigh. "I'll try to find you as soon as I deal with the queen. I don't want to stick around once she realizes you're still alive. I don't remember the story well, but I seem to remember things don't go too well for the huntsman."

"What if you can't find me? If Terry ends up kissing me, I won't be happy."

He ran a finger tenderly over her cheek. "Neither will I. I'll find you."

Olivia nodded. "Be careful." She turned and ran into the woods. Dragging out a goodbye wouldn't make it easier.

Jerron stood before the queen and offered her a box. Inside the box was the heart of whatever the butcher had given him. She rose from her gilded throne and floated over to him, taking the small box.

She peeked inside and laughed. "It's about time. Snow White will be a thorn in my side no longer!"

Jerron remained impassive as he waited to be dismissed. The queen returned to the throne with the box clenched in her hands. She smiled as she opened the box again.

"You've done well," she said, gazing at him. "What would you have as your reward?"

"I need no reward," Jerron said.

"You needn't look so serious," she said. "Be happy. You've done me a glorious service. You have rid the world of one of the worst creatures to crawl the earth."

Jerron tried not to roll his eyes. Everything was always so dramatic. "Am I dismissed, Your Highness?"

"If you don't want to celebrate with me, there are plenty who will." She put the box on the throne and walked toward him, pulling her long brown hair over her boney shoulder. "You should be happy. You've pleased the queen." She ran a finger over his arm, and Jerron stepped back.

"I've got things to attend to," he said, as she frowned at him.

"Fine," she said, tossing her hair back over her shoulder. "But I want you to meet me here again tomorrow. I'll send for you."

"Do you know Terry?" Jerron asked. He couldn't help thinking they would make the perfect pair.

"Prince Terrence?"

"Yes."

She tapped her lip with her long fingernail. "I haven't thought about him in a while. He's a bit cracked. They meant him for Snow—hm. If Snow was supposed to have him, then I should instead. Anything meant for that girl should be mine."

"I agree," Jerron said.

"You may leave. I'll see you back here tomorrow."

"Of course," he said, bowing and leaving the room. He made his way swiftly through the halls and out of the castle. The sooner he found Olivia, the better.

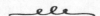

Olivia gave up on running. If no one was chasing her, it seemed pointless. The last woods she'd been in had been pleasant to walk through, but these were draped in spooky shadows. She'd jumped at nothing more times than she wanted to admit. It was daylight, but there were no birds singing or animals stepping over the forest floor. The silence left an eerie feeling inside that she couldn't shake.

Breakfast seemed far away, but the only food she had seen were apples, and she wasn't testing that. Not in this story. Olivia spun around at the sound of a snapping twig. Nothing. She took a shaky breath and decided there might be more reason to run than she thought. Who would have guessed there would be so much running in fairy tales?

Olivia sprinted through the trees and wished for more than the first time that she had better shoes. She hadn't had a comfortable pair since she began this journey. Her long blue skirt slapped against her legs. She turned the run into a speed walk. Glancing over her shoulder, she missed a root in her path and tripped. The ground came fast, and she caught herself on her elbows.

"What is the point of this?" she called out. "If you can hear me, Nancy, tell me that!" Getting to her feet, she inspected her elbows. They were scratched, but not bleeding.

Olivia froze. She had the feeling she was being watched. Turning slowly, she faced the wolf from the previous story. His amber eyes studied her, and he took a few steps in her direction. He angled his head forward.

"How did you get here?" Olivia asked. The wolf almost seemed to motion into the trees. "You want me to follow you?" The wolf nodded as he walked further into the woods. Olivia followed at a distance. This might be a mistake. How many fairy tales had a big good wolf? She couldn't think of any.

Every few minutes, the wolf would look back to make sure she was following. He walked at an easy pace, and Olivia had a hard time not getting too close. He might seem friendly, but looks could be deceiving.

Olivia saw something through the trees. It was a cottage. Butterflies filled her stomach as she neared the dwelling. It was small and didn't give off an inviting vibe. She paused and inspected it. The roof sagged in places, and the windows looked like they'd never seen a cleaning rag. Vines grew up the sides, and weeds grew all over the place.

The wolf motioned to the cottage with his head, and Olivia blew out a long breath.

"I guess you want me to go in there?"

The wolf nodded again.

"It doesn't look like they are seeking company," she said, going up to the door.

She knocked firmly and waited. When no one answered, she glanced at the wolf. He motioned forward again.

"That's called breaking and entering," she mumbled, trying the doorknob. It was unlocked. "Just because you live in the middle of nowhere doesn't mean you should leave your house unlocked."

Walking cautiously inside, she opened the door wide to let in light. Once her eyes adjusted to the dim place, a sloppy sitting room appeared before her. Chairs were scattered in no particular order, and dishes were shoved under some of them. Garbage littered the floor, and nothing had been dusted in ages.

The wolf pushed his head in and glanced around the room. "I am not cleaning this," Olivia said, shaking her head. "It's disgusting." She wasn't sure what the wolf was thinking, but she assumed he might agree.

He turned and ran his head under her hand. She rubbed near his ears, and he closed his eyes. "Do you have a name?"

He didn't answer. She didn't expect him to, but you could never tell in a place like this.

"I'm going to call you Finn. Is that alright?"

He gazed up at her with shining eyes.

"Should we inspect the rest of the house?"

Finn didn't protest, so she went exploring.

There wasn't a lot to the place. There was a filthy bedroom with seven beds. Seven regular sized beds. She was expecting them to be small. There was a kitchen that she only stayed in for a minute. It reeked of spoiled milk. How was she going to stay here?

"Well, I guess that's it," she said to Finn, as she returned to the sitting room. "This place is gross. If I remember right, Snow White cleaned the cottage and made food, then fell asleep. I'm not doing it, though. I wonder if they'll kick me out. I'll make some cookies, but I'm not cleaning, and I'm not falling asleep."

Finn followed her into the kitchen and wrinkled his nose.

"I hear you," Olivia said, scanning the room for supplies. "I'm surprised they haven't given themselves a disease or something."

She searched the cupboards for a mixing bowl and couldn't find a single clean dish. Sighing, she returned to the sink and pumped the water. The water was chilly, but at least she didn't have to haul it in from outside. It looked like she would be doing dishes after all.

"If I sing, will a bunch of animals come in and help?" she asked, as she pulled the dishes from the counter into the sink. Finn cocked his head and watched her. "I didn't think so. Lucky for you because I can't sing that well."

Once Olivia cleaned the dishes on the counters, she did the ones on the table and floor. She wasn't sure where they belonged, but since the cupboards were empty, she put them wherever she guessed they should go. She couldn't cook in a mess, so she scrubbed the table and counters. Finn curled up in the corner and watched.

"I can't believe I'm doing this," she admitted. "They should clean up their own messes." Once all the surfaces were clean, she swept the floor. There was no reason to have an almost clean kitchen. She drew the line at mopping. "Does it smell better, or am I just used to the stink?" She looked at Finn, but he was asleep. How could he sleep in a strange house? She knew she couldn't.

Making cookies proved to be a bigger challenge than she expected. All the ingredients were in canisters that were un-marked, and their oven was confusing. She searched in vain for chocolate chips, but once again, only found raisins. She added oatmeal instead and was happy with the aroma filling the small kitchen. Her stomach growled as she pulled out the first batch. She waited two minutes to let them cool and then popped one into her mouth. It was hot, but it was good.

Waiting for the cookies to bake was boring, so she picked the garbage up off the sitting room floor and did the other dishes she found scattered around. When the baking was done, she found the cleanest chair and sat in it. She was exhausted. She couldn't gauge how long she'd been here, but it felt like four hours at least. Her eyes stung, but she didn't close them. She wouldn't fall asleep and lose her advantage.

Olivia's eyes flew open, and she jumped to her feet. Seven frowning men surrounded her. How had she fallen asleep? She scanned the room for Finn, but he was nowhere to be seen.

"Who are you?" a man with red hair asked. "What are you doing here?"

Olivia studied the men, hoping to see a friendly face. She had expected them to appear a lot different. They were short, but only for men. None of them was more than an inch shorter than she was. She also hadn't expected them to be so well built. They all looked like bodybuilders, except for one.

"I'm sorry," she managed. "I got lost in the woods, and I saw your cottage."

"So, you thought you would rob us?" a man with a brown greasy beard asked.

"Rob you? If I was going to rob you, why would I clean your kitchen and fall asleep?"

"You cleaned our kitchen?" the redheaded man asked. "Why would you do that? What's wrong with you?"

"No idea," Olivia admitted.

"What's that smell?" the non-muscly man asked.

"I made cookies."

His eyes lit up. "Cookies? I had a cookie once."

"You did not," said greasy beard.

"I did! You don't know everything I do."

"What if they're poisonous?" someone asked.

"I'll eat one first," she said.

"Sounds fair."

"So, who are you?" greasy beard asked.

"My name is Snow White."

"Snow White? Like the princess?"

"Yes."

"Why would a princess sneak into our house and bake?"

"My stepmother is not a pleasant woman. She tried to have me killed, so I ran away." Seven sets of eyes stared at her, and then one by one, the men laughed. She glared at them. "It's nice to know you think my death would be funny."

"Why would the queen have you killed?" asked the man with red hair.

"She's jealous, and I assume she wants to remain queen."

"I suppose that makes sense," he said, rubbing his chin. "Now, what do we do with her?" he asked his brothers.

"Let's test the cookies before we decide," said another man.

The men all nodded and raced into the kitchen. Olivia sank back into the chair. Their fighting voices carried into the room. It sounded like furniture breaking. Her neck ached from sleeping in the chair. She messaged it with one hand and sigh. She hoped this was a fast story.

Jerron hurried through the woods, scanning the ground for any sign that Olivia had come this way. Stories usually guided him to where he needed to be, but he was breaking the rules.

The huntsman wasn't supposed to after Snow White. It might be impossible to find her. No feelings told him which way to go, and he was hopelessly lost.

He thought about calling for Nancy, but that had never helped him. She had to be monitoring him somehow. He imagined her sitting behind a desk, watching them through a crystal ball.

Jerron would comb through these woods forever if he had to. He needed to find Olivia before the evil queen got to her, or worse, Prince Terrence. He didn't like to think about Terry. The moon was casting eerie shadows over the woods, and Jerron was getting tired.

Walking over to a large tree, Jerron sat down and decided to sleep for a while. He didn't enjoy sleeping outside, but he'd gotten used to it back when he was Robin Hood. With luck, a plan would come to him at night. If not, he was in for another day of walking around aimlessly. Hopefully, this wouldn't count as messing up the story, even though he was.

Just as he drifted off, something touched his hand. His eyes popped open, and he grabbed his bow. An enormous wolf stared down at him. He stood up and took a few steps away. The wolf grabbed his tunic in his mouth and pulled him. Was this the wolf from before? It wasn't growling or being aggressive.

"Where are you taking me?" he asked.

The wolf released his shirt and walked forward.

"Can you take me to Olivia?"

The wolf turned and studied him, his eyes glowing in the dark. Jerron felt oddly calm. It looked like he was going to follow a wolf all night instead of sleeping.

Sooner than he expected, they entered a clearing with a rundown cottage. A light shone from the window. He didn't want to get too close. "Is Olivia in there?"

The wolf trotted over to a tree and sat down. Jerron joined him. It appeared he would be sleeping in the woods, after all. At least now he knew where Olivia was. He settled near the wolf and prepared himself for a long night.

Chapter 12

"If you don't stop fighting, I swear I'm going to lose it!" Olivia yelled at breakfast the next morning. Seven faces turned to her. She sighed and pushed a long piece of black hair behind her ear. "Is that all you do? Fight?"

"Of course not," Earl said. He was the one with red hair. "We mine most of the time. We only take the time to fight when we're relaxing."

"Well, stop. You're driving me insane," Olivia said, stabbing her pancake with a fork. "I've worked with five-year-olds that were easier." The men had agreed to let Olivia stay with them if she made their meals. She agreed, after warning them about her cooking skills.

"It was Roco that started it," Earl said, pointing to his skinny brother. "It's always the little ones. They think they have something to prove."

"Take it back," Roco said, holding a pancake in the air in a threatening manner.

"Do not throw that or I will make you eat it!" Olivia threatened.

Roco tossed the pancake back onto his plate. "I'm just as tall as you all are," Roco pouted, leaning back in his chair.

"Tall, yes. Big, no," said Jurry, the man with the greasy beard. "You could be if you weren't such a lie about. We work hard all day while you sit in the sun complaining."

"I work plenty hard. I just don't got the muscles you all do because I'm the youngest. It'll happen."

"It'll happen when you stop being lazy," Jurry said.

"This is the best food I ever ate," said Noll, the blond brother. The others nodded in agreement. Olivia took a bite of her pancake and shook her head. They must be hard up if this was the best. The outsides were burned, and the inside was still gooey. If Olivia wasn't so hungry, she would have skipped it.

"I'm not sure we should leave the princess here alone," said Jurry. "What if the queen finds her?"

"She thinks I'm dead, so I should be safe until she learns otherwise."

"I seen a wolf outside this morning," said Earl. "He didn't look menacing, though."

"He's not," Olivia said. "I call him Finn. He's friendly. He actually helped me when I was lost."

"Neat," said Roco. "A tame wolf. That could be handy."

"Hurry up, boys," Earl said, standing. "It's time to get to work."

"Not until you put your dishes in the sink," Olivia said. "I'm happy to cook for you, but I'm not cleaning up messes like yesterday all the time. That was ridiculous. You're grown men. Take some pride in your home."

"What does that mean?" Roco asked, scratching his head.

Olivia rolled her eyes. "Just clean up after yourselves. Do you really enjoy living in a pigsty?"

"We clean up in the spring," Noll said. "It's called spring cleaning."

"You have to clean more than that. You're going to make yourselves sick, living the way you do."

"Princesses are bossy," Roco said, taking his plate to the sink.

Olivia smiled. "Sometimes." The others cleaned up their plates, then they all left for work.

Olivia could only tell Roco, Jurry, Noll, and Earl apart. Mert, Levy, and Toad were triplets, and they talked little. They looked exactly the same. She doubted she would ever figure them out.

Placing her dishes in the sink, she glanced out the window, hoping to see Finn. The wolf was nowhere in sight. She sighed and started the dishes. She should have brought a spare dress. This one was a mess, and it was a shame because it had been nice. She wanted to wash it, but she had nothing else to wear.

Jerron waited for about twenty minutes after the men left the cottage before he dared approach. The wolf followed him to the door, and he knocked. Footsteps clicked up to the door, and it opened a crack.

"Jerron!" Olivia said, pulling the door open and smiling. "You found me! That was fast," she said, giving him a hug.

"The queen is crazy. I didn't want to hang around. Thankfully, the wolf led me here."

"His name's Finn," Olivia said, rubbing Finn's head. "He brought me here as well. Do you want to come in? Or I can come out. It's cramped in there. It smells better than it did yesterday, though."

"I hate to beg, but do you have anything I can eat?"

"Oh, sure. Come in. There are some leftover pancakes. They don't taste good, but they're better than starving." She led him through a small room and into a kitchen.

"I thought everything would be small," he said, sitting at the table. "The men I saw leaving didn't look that small, though."

"No, they aren't. They're all about as tall as I am."

"They appeared strong too."

"It's kind of funny," Olivia said, grabbing the plate with the leftover food. "I was expecting them to be little old guys, but I doubt any of them are over forty. Let me try to warm these up for you," she said, looking suspiciously at the stove.

"I don't need them warm," he said, grabbing one off the plate and taking a big bite. He was starving, but he still almost gagged. The middle wasn't as solid as it should be. He grimaced. "Starving might actually be preferable."

Her mouth turned up at the corners. "Sorry, I'm not really getting any better at cooking. I wasn't good before I came here, and these stoves are all so strange."

"It's fine," he said, trying to smile. They were really gross.

Olivia wiped off the stove. "They said I could stay here, and they seem decent enough, but man. They fight a lot, and they are so messy!"

Jerron took another bite, then sat the pancake down. He couldn't eat this even to be polite. "Can I teach you to make pancakes?" he asked.

Olivia's cheeks turned a lovely shade of pink. "I know, I'm terrible."

"It's alright, but I can help you. Pancakes are easy. I'll teach you some tricks."

"Alright."

They spent the morning making pancakes and cleaning up. It all felt so normal, and being with Olivia made things seem more stable. It had been a long time since anything had been consistent in his life, and going through stories with Olivia was comforting. He hadn't realized how much he missed a human connection until she had come.

"I didn't want to clean their mess," Olivia said, "but I couldn't cook in here until I cleaned it. It smelled terrible and had to be unsanitary. I'm planning on making them clean after dinner. They need to get into some good habits before I leave."

"It smells a little peculiar," Jerron said, brushing flour off his pants.

"The floor needs to be scrubbed, and their room is still a mess. They can do that themselves."

"Where did you sleep last night? This cabin's pretty small."

"On the floor in the sitting room," Olivia said, putting the broom in the corner.

Jerron frowned. "They made you sleep on the floor?"

"That was my choice. I bet the bedding has never been washed. I cleaned a spot on the floor and slept there. Today I'm going to mop, so it won't be as dirty tonight."

"Did you have a blanket?"

"No, I'm not using their gross stuff."

"It was cold last night. I slept under a tree."

Olivia tilted her head and studied him. "I guess we should have brought some things with us."

"I'll take the garbage," Jerron offered, grabbing the can in the corner. He whistled as he walked out of the cottage. Once he was outside, he looked around. Where would garbage even go? It wasn't like they had a garbage truck coming by once a week. In all the time he'd been in this world, he'd never had to take out any trash. When he lived alone, he burned it.

Something crashed into the back of him, and the can flew out of his hands, garbage littering the ground. Before he saw what hit him, someone knocked him to the ground and sat on him.

"Who are you, and why are you here?" growled a man's voice.

"Jurry!" Olivia exclaimed, running from the cottage. "What are you doing? Get off him!"

"He's a thief! He was taking our garbage!"

"He was helping me," Olivia said, coming closer. Jerron rolled over and pushed the man off.

"Well, who is he?" the man asked, jumping to his feet. Jerron stood up and glared at the short man.

"He's the queen's huntsman, but he helped me escape."

"Helped you escape and then came after you?"

Jerron brushed the dirt off his clothes. "I came after her to make sure she was alright."

"Likely story," Jurry said, crossing his arms. "You can't just trust people, Snow."

"I've known him for a while," Olivia said. "He wouldn't hurt me."

"Well, I don't trust him. And now he knows where you are, he could tell the queen."

"He had to leave so the queen wouldn't find out he helped me escape. She wouldn't forgive that."

"That's for certain," Jurry said, scratching his beard. "The queen has been nothing but bad for the kingdom. That's why we prefer to keep to ourselves. We don't want her attention on us."

"I thought you said you wouldn't be back until evening?" Olivia said.

"We decided someone should come check on you. Roco wanted to come, but he just likes to do all the simple things."

"I'm fine. Nothing to worry about."

"That remains to be seen. I still don't trust you," he said, pointing at Jerron. "Once my brothers get back, we'll decide how to deal with you. Don't go running off. We will find you."

Jerron nodded and tried not to seem amused. He also took a step back because Jurry smelled as bad as the cottage. Jurry stomped off down a well-worn path. Before he was out of sight, he turned and gave Jerron one last warning look.

"Friendly guy," Jerron said, scooping up garbage and putting it back into the can.

"They're a little rough, but I think they're good," Olivia said, helping him. "It's better than being in the ocean. Sorry I freaked out the way I did. I just couldn't pull off the mermaid thing."

"It's alright. I'm surprised Nancy even put you into that story. She obviously knows what we're doing at all times, so she should have heard you say you were terrified of the water."

"Of course I was aware of that," Nancy said, appearing in front of them.

"Whoa!" Jerron exclaimed, taking a step back. "I didn't know you could do that."

"I'm a fairy godmother," she said, rolling her eyes. "I can appear wherever I want."

"You don't look like a fairy godmother," Jerron sneered, taking in the woman's business suit.

"If you would prefer I appear in a tutu, that's usually fine. Today, I have a meeting."

"So, you made Olivia a mermaid when you knew she was terrified of water? That seems low, even for you."

"I don't understand why you keep picturing me as the enemy, Jerron. I'm only looking after your own best interests."

Olivia cocked her head. "How was putting me in the middle of the ocean my best interests?"

"I was thinking of Jerron when I did that."

"You put Olivia in a traumatizing situation for me?" Jerron asked. This woman was unbelievable.

"Yes. I've gotten to know you fairly well. You like to be comfortable. I put you in a nice castle with everything you could want. As soon as you realized the tale you were in, you turned your back on the comfort and ran to find Olivia. It was beautiful, Jerron."

"So, you wanted to see me sacrifice comfort?"

"Yes—for someone. You were willing to leave the story immediately for her. You are finally making progress, don't you see?"

"So, why don't you send him home?" Olivia asked, putting her hands on her hips.

"It isn't time. You both have more to learn, though Olivia has progressed faster than anyone I've ever seen. I bet you'll both be home before the year is out."

"Why can't you send us now?" Jerron asked.

"I could, but I won't. I don't want you to go home and immediately fall back into your old habits. We want to make sure it sticks."

"Are you spying on us all the time?" Olivia asked. "That's unsettling."

"No. There isn't time to focus on only two people. I've got others to check up on. I have been a little more diligent about watching you because of a complication. I won't bother you with that."

"Wait, what complication?" Jerron asked.

"Nothing for you to worry about," Nancy said, nervously straightening her suit jacket.

"Do you mean Terry?" Olivia asked.

Nancy glanced quickly between them. "He introduced himself to you?"

"Yes," Jerron said. "Is he like us? From the real world?"

"This is a real world, in its own way, but yes, Terry is from your world."

"Can't you keep him out of our stories?"

Nancy shook her head. "Terry has gone rogue, and I can't figure out how. It should be impossible. He's jumping to whatever story he wants and ruining them. There are thousands of stories, and he has figured out a way to go anywhere. I'm worried that he followed you here. He's never bothered the same people twice."

"Can't you send him home?" Jerron asked. "I get that you're trying to fix people, but he might not be fixable."

"I'm almost certain he isn't, but I can't send him back. Who knows what magic he has turned to? I can't seem to do anything about it, which is irritating. I'm afraid something inside of him is broken. He seemed perfectly normal for such a long time."

"You must have broken him," Jerron said. "You pushed him too far. Can't you see you might be doing more damage than good?"

"I can't be blamed for Terry. I've had hundreds of successes. He is the only one who cracked."

"When did he crack? What happened?" Olivia asked.

"Nothing big," Nancy said. "He was in a story and decided he wanted to stay there. He begged me to leave him, but I couldn't."

"Why?"

"Because he was fascinated with someone that wasn't for him. If he stayed there, it would have been a hollow life. I'm not sure what he did, but he disappeared for a time. When he reappeared, it was to cause havoc in every story he entered. I don't understand how he's manipulating the stories. Jerron was supposed to be the prince this time."

Jerron rubbed his chin. "Can we capture him?"

"I'm not sure, as I don't understand what he's doing. If you could render him unconscious, I could send him back. Whether he could come here again, I can't say."

"If we capture him, you send us home," Jerron said.

"I can't do that."

"Won't."

Nancy shrugged. "I won't."

"Fine. Come back if you change your mind," he said.

"One day, you will understand why I've done all of this."

"We'll see."

"I say we give him a chance," Earl said, leaning back in his chair.

"He looks shifty to me," said Roco.

"Roco should know," said one triplet. Olivia wasn't sure which. "Roco's a bit shifty himself."

"I'm not shifty," Roco protested.

"That's true," said Earl. "Roco's lazy. He doesn't have enough motivation to be shifty." All the brothers laughed, and Olivia rolled her eyes. Jerron sat on the floor in the corner, where everyone could monitor him.

"Remember when Roco hid all morning in the woodpile, just so Mama couldn't have him make his bed?" one triplet asked. "He was so covered in bug bites when we finally found him, we could barely tell it was him!" More laughter followed, and Roco scowled.

"I'm sure lots of kids hide from chores," Olivia said, feeling bad for the man.

"Kids, yes, but he was dang near twenty-three!" he said, slapping his knee.

Roco's brows knit together. "Making a bed is a waste of time, and I don't see none of you doin' it now that Mama ain't around."

"I don't think any of you are cleaning at all," Olivia said. "Don't you worry about germs? And the smell of this place is horrid."

"What good comes from cleaning?" Roco asked. "Sure, it might look nice, but it's just gonna get messed up again anyhow."

"Not if you clean up after yourselves. You are adults, acting like children."

"Everyone treats us like children," Jurry grumbled. "That's why we stay away from everyone. They tease us for being short." He rubbed his beard. Olivia wondered if the beard made him feel more manly.

"You aren't that short," Olivia said.

"We tried to fit into the town, but it's hard when you're the size of a girl."

"You are short, not small. You guys are stronger than most of the tall men I know."

"You have to be strong to work in a mine," Jurry said. "Unless you're Roco."

Roco stuck out his tongue and crossed his arms.

"We wasn't this strong when we went to town," said a triplet. "People might respect us more now."

Earl scratched his head. "I'm not willing to test it."

"There are other things you could do to make people accept you better," Jerron said from his place on the floor. Everyone turned and looked at him in surprise, as if they forgot he was there.

"Nobody asked you," said Jurry.

"What things?" Noll asked. "I'm getting sick of only being around you all for company."

"Hygiene," Jerron said.

"Hi what now?" asked Noll.

"It means being clean," Olivia explained. "People don't tend to hang around with you when you're dirty and you smell."

Jurry laughed. "Are you saying we need to take baths? We already had our biyearly bath a month ago."

"You should take one every day," Olivia said. "Especially since you do hard labor that makes you sweat."

"Every day?" Roco laughed. "That's the dumbest thing I ever heard. Who gets dirty every day?"

"I'm just trying to help," Olivia said. "You should try it. You might find you like it."

"Do you take one every day?"

"I try to," Olivia said. "Of course, I haven't today because I don't know where I could do it." She didn't add that she hadn't the day before, either, since yesterday had been crazy.

"There's a stream not too far from here," Noll said. "That's where we go. Just south of the cottage."

"I bet women like a man that smells good," Jerron said, winking at Olivia.

"That's something to think about," Roco said. "I wouldn't mind meeting an amiable woman."

"Problem is, she would want someone who knew how to work," Earl said. "How would you support a family if you were to trick some woman into falling for you?"

"We got plenty of gold from the mine."

"But you never mine it."

"I would for the right woman."

"I'll believe that when cows can fly and horses spit nails," Jurry said with a grin.

"I'd believe that cows can fly before I'd believe that Roco could do a full day's mining," said a triplet. Olivia really needed to figure out a way to tell those three apart if she was going to be here for long.

"The mine shares go seven ways," Roco said, smiling. "It doesn't matter who works the hardest, it's all split even."

"Still, no woman wants a lazy lie about," Jurry said. "It might be good for us to find a woman for Roco. She might whip him into shape."

"Jurry used to have a woman that liked him," Roco said. "Then, he scared her away."

"Aw, shush," Jurry growled.

"Her name was Meena."

"How did you scare her away?" Olivia couldn't help but ask.

Roco grinned. "He acted like an ornery cuss till she stopped coming round."

"Sad thing is, she'd take him back in a heartbeat if he asked," said Earl.

Jurry glared at his brothers. "You're all jealous 'cause no gals ever liked you."

"So, do I get to stay?" Jerron asked, getting back onto topic. "I don't mean in the house. I'll sleep outside."

"I suppose," Jurry said, as the others nodded. "But you best not cause us any trouble."

"I won't."

"And you have to help protect the princess. If the evil queen stays in power, more than a few people will suffer."

"Of course," Jerron said, standing.

"I was going to make you all help with the dinner dishes, but I'll do them if you all go down to the stream and bathe."

"I can't decide what's worse," Roco said, scratching his head.

"You all scratch your heads a lot. That's probably from having greasy hair," Olivia told them.

"Itching hair from not washing?" Noll asked. "That's probably just a myth they tell princesses or something."

"We'll go wash," said Jurry. "Don't expect it on the regular, though." They all shuffled out of the house.

"You watch yourself," Earl said to Jerron. "I see how you look at Snow. She's too good for you. Tell that to yourself every time you get any funny ideas."

Chapter 13

The next week flew by. The brothers spent most of their time mining, and as soon as they left for the day, Jerron and Olivia would do the chores around the house and then spend the rest of the day going on walks around the woods. Jerron had slipped into a nearby town and gotten them both a change of clothes and blankets. It made sleeping on the floor a lot more tolerable for Olivia. She almost didn't mind the hard surface.

Today, Jerron was out cutting wood. It was one of his contributions for being allowed to share meals with the brothers. Olivia was curled up near the fire, reading a book. It was cooler than normal, and it had been a long time since she'd read a book. Of course, the only book to be found was a fairy tale. It was one she wasn't familiar with, but she found herself enjoying it regardless of the ridiculous situations the characters found themselves in.

Thunder jolted Olivia out of her reading stupor, and she jumped up and scurried outside to grab the clothing on the line. Olivia had set up a system where everyone helped clean up after dinner, but she had still taken on most of the cleaning. She resented it, but at the same time, she realized if she didn't do her part, she was a freeloader. It wasn't like there was really a lot to do around here.

Olivia glanced up at the overcast sky as she shoved the clothes into a basket. She couldn't hear the ax, so Jerron must have finished and moved onto another task. There was a small barn with a few animals, and Earl had Jerron taking care of them. Olivia raced to the house, basket in hand, as the first drops of rain splattered against her cheek. She opened the door and dropped the basket to the floor.

Before she could close the door, hoofbeats sounded in the woods. They were coming closer. She gently closed the door and latched it. Who would be coming this way? She pushed back her panic and creeped to the window. It couldn't be the evil queen. She wouldn't be coming at such a speed, let alone on horseback.

Kneeling on the floor by the window, she peeked out the very corner. A shiny black horse carrying a rider galloped into the yard and pulled up near the door. The man straightened his crown and studied the cottage. Olivia ducked down and took a deep breath. It was Terry. Crawling quickly to the door, she stood and bolted it. Where was Jerron?

There was only one door to the cottage, so the only other way to get out would be through a window. A pounding on the door caused her to jump. She willed her heart to quiet down and waited, hoping the man would give up and go away. More pounding.

"Snow?" Terry called, as he kept pounding. "Snow, it's me. The prince." Olivia rolled her eyes and focused on the door. "I know you're in there. No reason to ignore me. Nobody ignores a prince." He pounded harder, and Olivia panicked at the way the door was bending. It couldn't take much more.

Olivia walked carefully through the house, doing her best not to make any sound. She entered the bedroom and gazed hopefully out the window. No Jerron. She grabbed the window and pulled. It slid open with a terrible squeak. She didn't wait to see if it was loud enough to alert Terry. She was through the window in a flash, running down a dirt path.

Soon it would be a mud path. The rain was coming down hard now, and Olivia ignored it as it pelted her in the face. Jerron had to be around here somewhere. She passed the pile of chopped logs and kept moving.

"Snow!" Terry yelled from behind. "Stop! Where are you going?"

Olivia didn't turn to see how close he was. She turned and darted into the trees, hoping they were thick enough to hide her, and that the muddy footprints she was leaving wouldn't be obvious.

A branch whipped her cheek, and she skidded, almost falling. Regaining her balance, she creeped around a large tree and pressed herself against it. She prayed Terry hadn't seen her. She couldn't keep up the fast pace. Pushing her hair out of her eyes, she willed her breathing to quiet. With the way she was breathing, Terry would be able to hear her from space.

"Snow?" his voice beckoned. "Where are you? I know you're here!"

Olivia shivered and bit her lip. He sounded too close for comfort.

"Why are you running from me? I can help you. You need me to figure out this world. I don't obey the rules anymore, and you don't need to, either."

Terror filled Olivia as she tried to decide whether or not to run. He might be close enough to grab her if she tried. Terry rounded the tree and stood a few feet in front of her. He smiled, and she froze. His bangs clung to his forehead and his crown sat crooked.

"Hello," he said.

Olivia didn't respond.

He wiped at the rain running down his face. "It's like I was saying, don't follow the rules. It isn't fun, but when you do as I do, life is full of surprises for everyone. Would you like to join me?"

"No, thank you," Olivia said, rubbing the goosebumps on her arms.

"You want to keep following Nancy's stupid rules?" he growled. "I've been here for eternity. I used to cooperate, but it never ends! If you follow her rules, you will be her puppet forever!"

"I'm going to keep trying," Olivia said, wishing she was back at the fireplace with her book.

"Then, you will be here forever, always thinking there is hope when there is none. Every time you think you've succeeded, you will find you've failed. Well, Nancy is going to be sorry she ever chose me for her amusement." Terry laughed maniacally, and Olivia thought about running again.

"She might let you go," Olivia said. "Perhaps, you should ask her."

"Ask her? I've begged. I've pleaded. I'm done with that. Now, I've discovered how to go where I want. I'm going to ruin her stories to the best of my abilities. Eventually, I'll find her and finish her. Just imagine all the people who will be indebted to me then."

"There has to be a better way to get home," Olivia said, wondering why she was trying to reason with someone who wasn't completely right in their mind. Something inside of her wondered if he could be right, but she ignored it.

He sneered. "I don't want to go home anymore. Now that I follow my own rules, I like it here. Once Nancy is out of the way, I will be the one in control around here. That's why you should join me now. You don't want me as an enemy."

"Why would you want me to join you? You don't even know me."

"But you're real." He reached his hand out and touched Olivia's cheek. She flinched and pulled back. "It's been a long time since I've met anyone real. It shocked me when I saw you before. You and the huntsman. You both seemed to glow, which told me you were real."

"So, you want us to join you and overthrow Nancy?"

"Not both of you. Only you. Competition isn't my thing, and the huntsman is a good-looking man. I don't need him turning your head. I'm giving you the opportunity to be my queen. Who can pass on that?"

"Me," Olivia said, moving around the tree and walking back to the path. It was slow going with the mud trying to steal her shoes with every step.

"You might want to rethink that," Terry said, walking a few steps behind. "You do not want to make me angry."

"I'd rather try Nancy's method than yours."

He raised a brow. "Really? How can anyone win with her methods? Nancy wants everyone to believe in some type of happiness, yet she puts us here with people that aren't real. If we fall in love with someone that isn't real, then what? We start to believe in happiness, only to have it pulled away. You think I'm crazy, but Nancy is the crazy one."

Olivia stopped. Terry was right in some ways. How did Nancy's world work for anyone? If she wanted them to believe in love and put them with a bunch of fake people, how did that benefit anyone?

"Are you beginning to understand?" he asked.

"We don't really know that the other people aren't real," she finally said. "Even if they aren't, I'm not going with your plan." She started walking again.

"I don't think they started out fake. In my opinion, they all slowly lost themselves here until they didn't even know who they were."

Olivia shivered at the thought.

"I'll give you three days to change your mind," he said.

Olivia turned to respond, but he was gone.

"Olivia!" Jerron yelled into the wind. He ignored the rain and scanned the trees around the cottage frantically. He had come in from milking the cow to find no sign of Olivia and an open window. A large black horse was grazing innocently in the rain, but he couldn't see anyone to claim it.

He hoped it wasn't the queen. He wasn't ready for that. The time he had spent here with Olivia had been wonderful. It was the best week he'd had since coming here. He ran around to the back just in time to see Olivia come flying out of the trees, turning to glance over her shoulder.

"Olivia!" he said, rushing toward her.

"Jerron!" she called, flinging herself at him. She was drenched and covered in mud from her knees down. He hugged her and led her to the cottage. They entered and sank down in front of the fire.

"What happened?" he asked, as she shivered. "The queen?"

"No," she said, glancing at the door. "It was Terry."

"What does that guy want? I wish he would stop showing up."

"From what he said, he wants to kill Nancy and take over. He was trying to convince me to join him."

"I hope Nancy's happy," Jerron said. "She probably drove him crazy. You can't force people to be the way you want them to. Why doesn't she get that?"

"I wonder how many people she's tried to help."

"One is too many. Aren't fairy godmothers supposed to help people with what they want? Did he hurt you?" he asked, scanning her face. "You have a big red welt on your cheek."

"It was just a tree branch. He scares me, though. There's something in his eyes that I can't explain, but it freaks me out."

"So, what do we do about it? He knows where we are. Should we leave?"

"I have a feeling he can follow us. He said when he saw us in the last story, we seemed to glow, and he knew we were real. He found us again on purpose."

"That complicates things. We could jump through a bunch of stories to try to confuse him, but I worry about not being able to find you fast enough."

"I'm not sure what we should do."

The door opened, and the brothers came filing in. They were all dripping and talking at once. Jerron had never seen people that could talk as much as this group. Talk and not listen.

"Whoa, what happened to you?" Earl asked, studying Olivia. She quickly explained what happened, and to Jerron's surprise, they were all quiet and listening. She left out some details that wouldn't make sense to them.

"We need to catch that prince," Noll said. "We can't have anyone taking Snow from us."

"And from now on, Jerron sleeps inside," Jurry said. "Right in front of the door."

"With his ax," Mert agreed.

"And he needs to stay with Snow at all times," Levy added.

Jerron nodded. That would make him feel better, and he preferred sleeping on the floor to the dirt. He tried not to be squeamish about bugs crawling across his face at night, but that was a hard thing to get used to.

"I can stick around too," Roco offered. "I can keep watch on the back."

"You're just trying to be lazy," Toad said. Jerron had learned to tell the triplets apart. They all held their mouths differently when they spoke, and Toad had a small scar at the corner of his eye.

"Let's just accept the fact that I'm always going to be lazy and let me be who I am."

"We have accepted it," Earl said. "But that doesn't mean we'll stop bothering you about it."

"So, now we're on the watch for an evil queen and a crazy prince," Jurry said, rubbing his beard. "I don't like it."

"Jerron and I can leave," Olivia offered. "We don't want you to feel you're in danger."

"I'm not worried about us," Jurry said. "We can take care of ourselves. Taking care of you is a priority. You are the princess, after all."

Roco nodded. "And even if you aren't the best cook, yer a lot better than any of us."

"And the place smells a lot better since you came," Noll said. "And so does Jurry."

They all laughed as Jurry slugged his brother on the arm.

"You didn't smell that good yourself," Jurry mumbled.

"Nothin wrong with a foul smell every now and again," Roco said. "I don't want to get too clean, or people might expect it."

A noise startled Olivia from a deep sleep. She froze. It had been three days since her talk with Terry, and she had been on edge. Something about that man gave her nightmares. Sitting up, she scanned the room. The fire cast dancing shadows around the room, but she couldn't see anything that would be threatening.

The doorknob turned slightly and then stilled. Olivia untangled herself from her blanket and grabbed the metal shovel that was used to clean the fireplace. Tiptoeing near the door, she pressed herself against the wall, gripping the shovel in one hand. The knob turned slowly, and the door creaked open.

A shadowy figure stepped in, and Olivia acted immediately. "Aaaaaah!" she yelled, as she whacked the man in the stomach with the shovel.

"Oof!" the man exclaimed, bending in the middle. Olivia jumped on his back, knocking him to the floor.

"Help!" she yelled, as she used all of her weight to try to keep the man down. He muttered something, and an army of running footsteps came toward the room. All seven brothers came bursting in, and the room filled with light as Jurry held up a lantern.

"Olivia, what the heck?" Jerron complained from beneath her. "Are you trying to kill me?"

"Jerron?" Olivia exclaimed, jumping to her feet. Jerron slowly stood, one hand on his stomach. "I thought . . . You scared me."

"False alarm," Earl said, lowering a club he'd been holding in his hands. The brothers all grumbled and returned to bed.

"I'm so sorry!" Olivia said, dropping the shovel to the floor. "I heard the doorknob, and it was turning so slowly, I was sure you were Terry."

"Didn't you realize I wasn't asleep in front of the door?" he asked, sinking down into a chair.

"I didn't even think," Olivia said. "I just woke up and panicked. Are you going to be okay?"

"I'll be fine," he said. "Probably just a few bruised ribs."

"Why did you turn the knob and stop and do it so slowly?"

"I saw an owl and got distracted," he said.

"Well, what were you doing outside?" Olivia said, tears threatening to fall. What if she broke his ribs or something? His black eye had only gone away a few days ago. He might begin avoiding her.

"I drank a lot of water before bed—I just had to step outside."

"Oh," Olivia said, feeling absolutely ridiculous. "I'm really sorry."

"It's alright," he said, holding out his hand. She took his hand, and he pulled her onto his lap. "It makes me feel better knowing you aren't defenseless. You can hit pretty hard."

She shifted around and leaned her head on his shoulder.

He gazed down at her. The shadows from the fire jumped over his face.

"I still feel bad."

Jerron brushed a hand across her cheek. "I wish I could kiss you without causing us to disappear."

Olivia's heart sped up. Did he mean it? "I wish you could too."

"Do you?" he asked, raising an eyebrow.

"Every time I see you," she admitted.

Jerron sighed, wrapping his arms around her. Olivia closed her eyes and snuggled into his neck. He placed a kiss on her cheek and rested his head on hers.

Birds singing outside pulled Jerron from a restless sleep. He was going to be stiff from spending the night sitting on a chair, holding Olivia. He carefully slid her onto the seat and stood. She mumbled something but didn't wake. He rotated his torso and listened to his spine pop. His back felt better, but the twisting hurt his ribs.

He yawned and opened the front door. It was early. It was also time to talk to Nancy again. He hoped she would come. He walked to the trees and lifted his shirt to inspect his ribs. A five inch black and purple bruise stared back at him. It was going to hurt for a while.

Once he got far enough from the cottage, he called for Nancy. She didn't appear. "Come on, Nancy! I need to talk! I'm ready to go home. Nancy?" He kicked at the ground. Why was the woman so stubborn? "I've changed. Can't you see? I've fallen in love, and I want you to send us home. I *believe* Olivia, and I can be happy. Isn't that what I'm supposed to learn?"

Jerron slumped back against a tree. Either, Nancy couldn't hear him or she was ignoring him. What did it take to please the woman?

"Frustrating woman, that Nancy," Terry said, coming out from behind a tree.

Jerron's stomach jumped, but he appeared calm. "What do you want?" he asked, refusing to let the man make him uneasy.

"I'm just here to sympathize with you. Nancy is really the criminal around here. Why does everyone let her get away with it? How long have you been here?"

"I don't know. A couple years."

"I've been keeping track," Terry said. "I've been here for over five years. Five years of Nancy playing with my life. I doubt she ever plans to let people go. Are you going to stand for that?"

"I see little choice."

"I've made a choice. I'll let you join me in overthrowing her. You and Snow—Olivia—whoever she is. I wasn't sure if I should let you in at first, but I don't think Olivia will join me without you."

"Nancy has magic. I doubt you'll be able to do much against her."

"I've learned a thing of two," Terry said. His eyes turned black, and he twisted his hands through the air, causing smoke to appear and swirl around itself.

Jerron's eyes felt like saucers. "You've learned magic?"

"Yes," he said, his mouth turning up. "And I'm planning something unexpected for Nancy. If you help me, I'll be sure you get home. You and Olivia."

Jerron paused. He didn't know how to react. There was no way he was joining up with Terry. He wasn't stable, and he was as creepy as Olivia thought. He also didn't want to make him mad. Jerron wasn't a fan of Nancy, but he didn't believe she was evil. Just misguided in her charitable efforts.

"Why the wolf?" he finally asked.

"What?"

"Why were you the wolf in Little Red Riding Hood?"

Terry grinned. "I always choose the best part."

Jerron's eyes narrowed. "I'll stay around and see what happens."

"It's your choice, of course," Terry said, his mouth set in a firm line. "Let me warn you, as a friend. I will not play nice with those who oppose me. I never have. There could be a book about all the people who opposed me over the years and regretted it."

Jerron shifted. "Thanks for the advice."

"I thought I was lucky when I found you and Olivia, but it turns out you might both turn into complications."

Jerron crossed his arms. "Not if you leave us alone. Let us navigate this our own way."

"I might," he said with a grin that didn't reach his eyes. "But then again, I might not. I suppose we will see. Take care, huntsman. I doubt this will be the last time we meet."

He spun in a circle and disappeared in a cloud of smoke. Jerron coughed and waved the smoke with his hand. They needed to get out of here. Out of *Snow White*, and out of Nancy's world.

Chapter 14

Olivia scrubbed her dress in the steam. Having two dresses was better than one, but it was hard to clean them every time they got dirty. If she didn't wash them every day, she worried about smelling. It was usually easier to wash them in the kitchen sink, but it had backed up, and Jerron was trying to fix it. He wasn't anything close to a plumber, so it wasn't going well.

Roco and Toad sat on rocks nearby. They were her protectors today. Toad was whittling something from wood, and Roco was throwing rocks in the water. Ever since Terry's appearance, there were always two men assigned to go with her if she left the house.

The dress wasn't coming clean. Jerron taught her to make a pie the day before, and she spilled cherry juice all over her front. If she couldn't get the stain out, she would have to wear it this way. She couldn't live in one dress—at least not comfortably.

A noise in the woods caused Olivia to gaze across the trees. An old woman carrying a basket came limping into view. She was hunched over and wore a brown cape. Olivia let out a slow breath. This must be it. She wasn't ready. She liked it here. The time she spent with Jerron every day was special, and changing tales might ruin that.

"Evil queen at five o'clock," Olivia said. As soon as she said it, she felt ridiculous. She didn't even know what that meant.

"That's not the evil queen," Roco said with a laugh. "The evil queen is young and beautiful. That old hag is ninety, at least."

"She's magic," Olivia said, lowering her voice so the woman wouldn't hear. "She can change her appearance."

Toad stood up and dropped his project. "What do you want, old woman?" he asked with a blaring shout.

"Who, me?" the woman asked in a feeble voice. "I'm just out for a walk in this lovely autumn weather. Now, why don't you and your brother go back to your cottage and let me talk to your friend?"

"Alright," Roco said, standing. "Come on, Toad." Olivia watched with an open mouth as Toad and Roco abandoned her. She couldn't blame them. The queen was obviously using magic. They wouldn't leave her on purpose.

"Hello, dear," the queen said, smiling a toothless smile.

Olivia stared at the woman. She felt like she'd swallowed a rock. She didn't want to do this.

"It's polite to greet your elders," the woman croaked.

"Just give me the freaking apple and be on your way," Olivia growled, as she fought the tears that wanted to spill. What was wrong with her? She knew this was coming.

The queen's eyes widened, and she reached inside her basket. "How perceptive of you to know I've got apples." She pulled out a shiny red apple and held it in front of her. "Beautiful, isn't it?"

"It's so beautiful *you* should eat it," Olivia tried.

She laughed. "Me? No teeth."

"So, why carry around apples? That seems a little silly."

"I like to share with others. Here, take it."

Olivia grabbed the apple and ground her teeth. Why now?

The woman grinned. "Take a bite. They're delicious."

"How would you know?" Olivia demanded.

"I make them into juice."

"I'm going to take it in the house and share it with my friends," she said, pushing a stray hair from her face.

The queen looked like she was going to argue, and then changed her mind. "I suppose sharing could be a good thing." Her unnatural smile curdled Olivia's stomach. "It only takes one bite after all."

"One bite for what?" Olivia challenged.

"To fall in love with my apples."

"I'm sure that's true. I'm going to take it in now and try it."

"Wonderful." She turned and hobbled back into the woods. She stopped for a moment to glance over her shoulder. "Make sure you eat it soon. You don't want it to lose its flavor."

Olivia glared down at the fruit. She left her dress sitting near the stream and started for the cottage. She swallowed a lump in her throat. No crying. What good would it do? It wasn't like she would never see Jerron again, but what were the chances they would get to spend time together like this? Was Nancy trying to teach her to believe in happiness or to experience a heavy heart?

Opening the front door, Olivia peeked inside. No one was in the front room. She wandered into the kitchen and smiled as she watched Jerron fight with the sink. Olivia loved his determination. She would've given up by now. The apple clutched in her hand reminded her she had nothing to smile about.

Jerron turned and grinned at her. "Hey. Did you get the stain out?"

"No," she squeaked.

His grin faded, and he washed off his hands. "What's wrong?"

Olivia held up the apple, and tears sprang to her eyes. "I guess it's time."

"No," Jerron said, hurrying to her. She placed the apple on the counter and buried her face in his chest. He enveloped her in a hug and ran his hand over her hair.

"Sorry, I don't know what's wrong with me," she said, sniffling. "I knew it was coming, so I don't understand why I'm being such a baby about it."

"It's been nice here," Jerron said. "I'll find you, though, and I'll do it fast. As soon as you wake up, find the nearest town and stand on the busiest street. I'll find you."

"What if there isn't a town?"

"Then, find the tallest hill and meet me at the top."

Olivia shivered. "I don't want to bite the apple."

"Don't. There's no reason."

"No reason?" Jurry's voice boomed. "That's the best looking apple I've ever seen!"

Olivia pulled away from Jerron in time to see Jurry take a large bite of the apple.

"No!" she yelled a second too late. Jurry fell to the ground. Olivia watched the apple drop and roll away. Her eyes widened in panic. "What do we do?" she asked Jerron. "This is my fault! I should have just bitten the darn thing!"

Jerron dropped to his knees and rolled the man over. "He's not breathing."

"That's to be expected. What should we do?"

"I guess you could try to kiss him?" Jerron said, rubbing the back of his neck.

"Gross," Olivia said, wiping her eyes. "He still has breakfast in his beard. Besides, you're the only person I've ever kissed, and I want to keep it that way."

Jerron grinned briefly. "You've never kissed anyone else?"

She rolled her eyes. "No. Don't tease me. We need to find the others and get rid of that apple."

"You burn the apple, and I'll go get the brothers."

Olivia grabbed the apple and took it into the front room. The fire was out, so she quickly lit it and tossed the poisoned fruit in. Green flames sprang up, devouring the apple, and then settled into nothing.

She returned to the kitchen to watch Jurry. Poor guy. What could they do? They had to do something. Perhaps, going to bed would be their best bet. The day would probably have a do over, and she could make things better.

After what seemed like hours, the door to the house banged open, and the kitchen quickly filled with Jerron and the brothers. For once, nobody seemed to know what to say.

Earl kneeled down and put his fingers to Jurry's neck. "No pulse," he said. "He's still warm."

"It's a spell from the evil queen," Olivia told them. "It can be broken, but only by a kiss."

"So, kiss him already," Noll said.

"It needs to be done by someone that loves him."

"I'm not doing it," Earl said, taking a step back.

"Me either," Toad said, crossing his arms. "Out of all the brothers, he's not ever been my favorite."

Olivia shook her head. "It needs to be someone that's *in* love with him. Not a family member."

"That's a relief," Earl muttered.

Roco scratched his head. "What about Meena?"

"Even Meena has standards," Earl said. "What are the chances she wants to kiss a mostly dead Jurry?"

"She might," Mert said. "She's always been peculiar."

"Can someone go fetch her?" Jerron asked. "We should hurry."

"I'll go," Earl volunteered. "I'm the fastest." He sped out the door without looking back.

Jerron was feeling claustrophobic. There were too many people pacing around the small cottage. He was leaning against the counter with his arms around Olivia. She seemed to have a permanent crease in her forehead.

"It isn't your fault," he said in a low voice so only she could hear.

"It kinda is," she said. "I hope Nancy gives us a do over if this doesn't work. If she does, you kiss me first thing in the morning."

"Yes, ma'am," Jerron said, kissing her cheek. It had thrilled him to hear her confession about not wanting to kiss anyone but him. He'd assumed she liked him, but he wasn't sure if she liked him as much as he liked her. Now, he realized he more than liked her. He'd admitted that to himself a while ago, and to anyone that might have been listening to his rant to Nancy in the woods.

He heard the door open, and everyone froze. Earl and a woman entered. The woman was a good three inches shorter than Earl and she had bright red, frizzy hair. She was plump with rosy cheeks and bright green eyes.

"Oh, my poor Jurry!" she exclaimed, falling to her knees. "Why did I ever let you chase me away?" She put her hands to his face and glanced up at Earl. "He's warm. I thought you said he was dead?"

"He's magically dead." Earl said, shrugging.

"What is magically dead?"

"The evil queen poisoned him," Olivia said. Meena's eyes caught Olivia's. "The only way to break the spell is true love's kiss."

"Well, I can handle that," Meena said. Jerron smiled at the woman's determined nod. "How long of a kiss are we talking? I don't want to overdo it and look like a scarlet woman, but I don't want to underdo it, either."

"I'm not sure," Olivia said. "A few seconds should be fine."

"Alright, Meena," the woman muttered to herself. "You can do this." She pushed up her sleeves and placed her hands on the floor next to his head and stared down at him. Puckering her lips in an exaggerated manner, she leaned forward. The room was silent as everyone held their breath. If there was an award for the loudest kiss, Meena would get the award.

Jerron held back a chuckle. Jurry's eyes popped open, and he sat up. "What just happened?" he asked, as his brothers all cheered. Jerron could feel Olivia's relief as she relaxed against him.

"You ate a poisonous apple, and I saved you!" Meena said, clapping her hands.

"How could you save me?" Jurry asked, knitting his brows.

"With true love's kiss!" she squealed. "You owe me now, Mr. Jurry! I want to go courting and I want it now! I've been terribly patient with you." She jumped to her feet and grabbed his hands, pulling him up.

He scratched his beard and tilted his head. "I don't know what to say about any of this."

"Say nothing, just come with me!" Meena said, pulling him out the door. All the brothers cheered and laughed.

"It's about time," Roco said. "Picture all the extra room we'll have if they get married and Jurry moves out."

"You have a lot of money," Jerron said. "Why don't you build a bigger cottage?"

Earl scratched his chin. "We never thought about that before. What do you guys think?"

"Let's do it," Noll said. "We can even add a room for Snow."

"I can't stay," Olivia said. "In fact, it's time for me to go."

"What? No!" Roco protested.

Mert shook his head. "If you go, the queen might get you."

"I'm going to go somewhere she can't."

"What about the kingdom?" Toad asked. "You can't leave it to the queen."

Olivia looked up at Jerron. "I didn't think about that."

"Let's go for a walk," he said, leading her to the door. "We'll be back," he said over his shoulder. They walked out into the crisp breeze and wandered toward the woods.

"We don't want to fight the queen," Jerron said. "I'm afraid if we don't leave, we're going to have to redo today."

Olivia frowned. "But we can't leave everyone at the mercy of the queen. These guys are our friends."

"We wouldn't be leaving them in an unpleasant situation," Jerron said, unsure how to explain. "I don't think they're real."

"It's hard for me to accept that," she said. "If they aren't real, what are they?"

"NPCs?"

"What?"

"You're not a gamer, I take it."

"No. I don't care what they are. If I leave them like this, I'll feel guilty forever."

Jerron blew out a breath and ran his fingers through his hair. "What do you want to do? Chase the queen?"

"I don't know."

"Fancy meeting you again," said a feeble voice. An old hag hobbled over to them. "I see you didn't eat the apple."

"How can you see that?" Olivia asked.

"I just sense it," she said. "Can I offer you another?"

"No thanks," Olivia said. Finn came leaping out of the woods and stood in front of Olivia and Jerron. He bared his teeth and growled at the queen.

"Down, boy," the queen commanded.

Finn continued growling and moved in closer.

"It looks like he can see through your disguise," Jerron said.

"Leave us," she said, gazing into Finn's eyes. He was undeterred. The woman took a step back. Finn wasn't small, and his teeth were impressive.

"Your magic doesn't work on him," Olivia said.

A cloud of purple smoke swirled around the queen and her hag disguise disappeared. Now young and less horrifying, she pushed her neat hair over her shoulder and scowled at them. "You force my hand," she said. "The poison would have been quick. Now, we must do things the hard way."

"Yes, we must," said Roco, joining them. He held a large club in his hands, and his brothers followed him. All of them held a crude wooden weapon.

The queen laughed. "The men from the woods. I've heard of you. Now, you want to save your precious princess? You really believe you can defeat me?"

"I know we can," Roco said. "Get her!" The queen's eyes widened, and she turned and ran, holding up her billowing skirts. The brothers chased after her with Finn at their side.

"Do we follow?" Olivia asked.

Jerron shook his head. "No. They'll take care of it."

Olivia's heart was heavy as she closed the door to the cottage for the last time. She had enjoyed her time here, and now, she was going back to the unknown. That was what scared her the most. What if she couldn't find Jerron? He grabbed her hand, and they walked soberly away.

When the brothers had returned home, they said the evil queen was no more. They didn't give any details, and Olivia hadn't asked for any. Saying goodbye had been hard. Finn was curled up near the house and didn't seem to have an interest in following them.

"I wonder what comes next," she said.

Jerron glanced sideways at her. "If you could choose, what story would you pick?"

"I've actually thought about it a lot when I can't sleep at night."

"Oh, yeah?"

"I'm not sure there is some grand adventure I would prefer, but there is a lot I really don't want to do. I worry about landing in one that I'm not familiar with. Has that ever happened?"

"A few times. When I tried, it wasn't hard to go with the flow and figure them out. There was one weird one with a girl that wore donkey fur. It was a little weird, but once I realized she was the main character, I figured it out."

"*The Little Mermaid* would be the worst, but hopefully, we dealt with that one. I wouldn't put it past Nancy to put us there again, but I hope she doesn't."

"I should have taught you to swim. I know you're against it, but it might help with your fear."

"It might be fun to do *Beauty and the Beast*, but only if you were the beast. If it was someone else, it might be terrifying."

"With my luck lately, I'd be an object inside the castle that's bolted to the wall."

Olivia laughed. "I'd still fall in love with you, even if you were a candlestick." Jerron stopped abruptly and turned to her. Olivia swallowed. Had she said that out loud?

Jerron's eyes searched hers, and he placed his hand on her cheek. "Does that mean you've fallen in love with me now?"

Heat crawled up Olivia's neck, but she forced herself to keep eye contact. "Yes," she whispered.

"And I love you," he said. "I'll see you somewhere?"

She nodded and leaned in. She wished the kisses lasted longer. Her knees felt wobbly as he pressed his lips to hers. She held him tight and hoped to keep him with her. Almost as soon as it began, the spinning in her head started. Olivia could almost understand Terry's hate for Nancy.

Chapter 15

J erron slammed into the ground and sat up in confusion. Everything was dark and his head was still spinning. Every time a story changed, Jerron woke up. Nothing like this had ever happened before.

"Jerron?"

"Olivia? Are you alright?" he asked, crawling toward her voice. He stopped when he bumped into her.

"Yes—What happened?"

"I don't know." He grabbed her hand, and they both jumped as lightning lit the sky.

"We're outside?" she asked in amazement. "Where's the moon?"

Jerron squinted into the sky. "I don't know. Everything feels wrong."

A light flickered on and off and then stayed on. Jerron squinted as he studied his surroundings. They were in a large white room. There was no furniture and no door.

"We aren't outside," she said, getting to her feet. "How was there lightning?" Glancing down at him, she frowned. "Why are you smiling like that?"

"Sorry," he said, standing. He hadn't realized he was smiling. Her blue dress and white apron had a lot of volume, and only coming to her knees made it funny. Her white tights and black shoes added to his grin. "I was admiring your dress. How does it poof out like that?"

She looked down and smiled. She pushed the dress against her legs, and when she released it, it sprang back out. "I feel ridiculous, but it might explain the confusion."

He tilted his head as he studied her. "How?"

"*Alice in Wonderland*. Nothing in that story makes sense."

"Why are we together? Who am I supposed to be?" he asked, looking down at his tux.

"James Bond?"

He straightened his bow tie and winked. "Am I pulling it off?"

"Perfectly," she said, with a slight blush.

"I don't remember James Bond in *Alice in Wonderland*," he said. "I read the book once in middle school, and I saw the movie when I was little, but I think I would have remembered."

The lights blinked again, and they were in a grassy meadow by a stream. "Wow, that was odd," Olivia said. "It's like the story is glitching or something."

"Should we try calling for Nancy?" he asked.

"Does it ever help?"

"Not really."

Jerron reached into his pocket and pulled out a gold pocket watch. He flipped it open and studied the face. A sense of panic overcame him. "I'm late!" he said. "Dang it. I'm the white rabbit."

Olivia giggled. "You don't look like a white rabbit."

He sighed. "I have an immense desire to run and get some place."

Olivia grinned mischievously. "I guess that means I'll get to chase you."

Jerron winked. "Sounds fun. I don't have rabbit ears, do I?"

"Nope."

"Well, let's get this party started."

___ele___

Olivia watched in disbelief as Jerron jumped down a rabbit hole. She peered down into the dark hole and tried to see anything. The hole was large and went down at a slope. Sitting at the top of the hole, she stuck her legs inside and tried not to picture snakes at the bottom, waiting to bite her.

"There aren't any snakes in *Alice*," she muttered. She lowered herself into the hole and slid at a faster speed than was comforting. She closed her eyes and lowered her head, trying to ignore the dirt falling on her face. When she came out at the bottom, she sprang to her feet and spit dirt.

Her hair was probably dirt colored now, but there wasn't anything to do about that. She dusted off her dress and glared at Jerron, who was standing in front of her, laughing. He brushed dirt from her head with a wide smile on his face.

"Why are you still clean?" she asked. His tux was spotless.

"Bunny powers, I guess."

Olivia cocked her head. "Bunny powers?"

"It's a thing."

"Sure it is," she said, looking down a long hallway that boasted several doors. "I guess we choose a door?"

"I'm up for it," Jerron said, wandering forward with Olivia at his side. Each door was a different pastel color.

"I assume we want that door down there," she said, pointing to a small door at the end of the hall. It stood a foot high and was made of wood.

Jerron ran his hand through his hair and blew out a loud breath. "And we're going to fit through it how? I really don't remember the story very well."

"Alice always had to eat something to change sizes. Look for something we can eat."

"Look where?" Jerron asked. "This hallway is empty."

They came up to the door, and Olivia kneeled beside it. She turned the handle. "It's locked. If I remember correctly, Alice grows really big, then cries huge tears. She eats or drinks something and shrinks and floats on her tears through the keyhole."

A clunking sound caused them both to turn. A table sat behind them, and on the table were goopy brown things that said, 'EAT ME' on top.

Olivia wrinkled her nose. "I'm not sure I can eat that thing."

"I won't even say what it resembles," Jerron said, poking the glob with a finger.

"It was supposed to be candy or something."

Jerron cringed. "It's definitely something."

"Where's the key? Growing and shrinking sounds like a waste of time, and even if I make myself enormous, I can't make myself cry on demand, so I won't be able to make a sea of tears. It would be better to only shrink once and go through the door."

"No key," Jerron said, sitting on the floor and leaning back on his elbows. "Let me try something." Pulling his foot back, he kicked it into the small door. The sound of breaking wood reached their ears, but it didn't open. Jerron kicked it two more times, and on the third time, the door broke from the hinges. He grabbed it and threw it behind them.

"Great," Olivia said, eyeing the brown atrocity on the table. "Now we just have to eat that."

"Or we could go through a different door," he said, standing.

"We should probably go the right way."

Jerron pulled the brown thing off the table and smelled it. "No odor. That's a good sign, right?"

"Possibly."

"Come on. At the same time."

Olivia picked up a piece of the gooey brown mush and nodded. She swallowed hard. She wasn't brave when it came to trying new food, and this didn't look palatable.

"No puking," Jerron said with a wink. "Ready? One, two, three." He popped the entire thing in his mouth and Olivia nibbled on a corner. They both shrunk down, small enough to fit through the door.

"That was crazy," said Olivia. She look up at the huge table. It was as big as a mountain.

Jerron tilted his head. "That tasted a bit like dirt, but not as bad as it could have been."

"You know what dirt tastes like?" Olivia asked, as they walked through the door.

"It's just one of those things you know. Childhood memory maybe? Instinct? It's like play dough. Does anyone not know what it tastes like? Or crayons? You just know."

"Wow," Olivia said, looking around. They were on a dirt path, surrounded by trees. Checkered blue and yellow trees. The grass was purple, and small animals in clothing were running all around. Her eyes couldn't focus on anything. Nothing appeared stable and almost seemed to bounce.

"Too much of this, and I might puke," Jerron said, stepping over a mouse in a raincoat. "I wonder what's wrong? We should call for Nancy. This place is broken."

With every step, Olivia feared falling. The ground wasn't visibly moving, but it felt like it was coming up and meeting her foot too early. If they weren't careful, they might end up injured.

"Nancy!" Olivia called. She didn't really figure the woman would answer, but it might be worth a try. "Nancy! We need you!"

"Nancy!" said a cheerful voice from a tree. "Who needs Nancy?"

"Cheshire Cat?" Jerron asked, peering into the branches. All that could be seen was a smile. It didn't look like a cat's smile. It seemed more human.

"Curiouser and curiouser," Olivia muttered, folding her arms and glaring into the tree.

"That's the spirit of it," said the mouth. A chill ran down her spine, but she kept her angry stance. It was unsettling to see a talking mouth.

"Are you going to appear?" Jerron asked.

"I might," said the mouth, "But then again, I might not. I don't even know what I'm going to do! It's delicious!"

"Do you know Nancy?" Olivia demanded.

"Everyone does. You, me, all the others. Nancy, Nancy, it's all about Nancy."

"He's crazy," Jerron said. "Let's move on."

"Not crazy! MAD! Everyone here is mad, don't you see? All these animals are mad. I'm mad, you're mad, and that is why we belong here. I love it here. Nothing needs to make sense. It's more fun to be mad with friends."

Olivia grabbed Jerron's hand, and pulled him away. Her stomach was swaying with the strange world.

"I'm coming," the mouth said, lowering itself from the checkered tree.

"Don't come on our account," Jerron said.

"Please. You want to find Nancy, and I know where she is!" The mouth started humming a fast tune and slowly became visible.

"Terry!" Olivia exclaimed, looking down at the man. He had fake cat ears and was on his hands and knees.

He licked his hand and smiled. "Not today. Today, I'm a cat. I won't let you ruin that. You ruined the last story. This one's my favorite. I stay here most of the time."

"We have to go," Jerron said. "We're late." He glanced at the pocket watch and then snapped it shut.

Terry crawled down the path. "Without me, you won't find Nancy."

"Is she here?" Olivia asked.

"Of course she is. I brought her here, and here, she will stay. Isn't it marvelous? Ever since I captured her, everything has been wonky. Even more so than usual. I like it. This place never makes sense on the best of days, and now, even I can't predict it."

Dread filled Olivia as they followed the bouncing path. Terry had never seemed normal, but this was worse.

Terry was moving faster than one would expect a grown man on his hands and knees to go. He was keeping up, and they were walking at a brisk pace. Olivia wondered what he had been like before he came here. If Nancy had driven him mad, she had a lot to answer for.

Making a decision, Olivia grabbed Jerron's arm and stopped him. He looked at her with a raised eyebrow. She went to her toes and kissed him. She pulled back, but they were still there.

Terry cackled. "Doesn't work here, doesn't work now. You are stuck until I say, and now is not the time. Nancy has no power, you have no power. I'm the only one."

Olivia pursed her lips and looked at Jerron. He just shrugged. The thought of running came to her, but with the unsteadiness of the place, they would probably fall. She didn't know what Terry could do, either.

"If you're going to spout nonsense, you could at least make it rhyme," Jerron said, moving faster down the path. He kept hold of Olivia's hand. She was getting motion sick.

"That's a good idea," Terry said. "I'll work on it. Now, where do you want to go? I'm feeling generous, so I'll let you choose. Tea party or Queen of Hearts?"

"Tea party," Jerron said. "I've had my fill of evil queens this year."

"Good choice," Terry said, bounding down the path. "It's nearby, and the Mad Hatter makes a wonderful tea. He should. The man has been stuck at that tea party forever."

"Stuck?" Olivia asked.

"Stuck. The Hatter, the March Hare, and the Dormouse wronged Time, and they are stuck forever. It's convenient for me because I can always find a party. Follow me," he called, frolicking down the path.

"Why are we following him?" Olivia asked Jerron under her breath.

"No clue. I've been debating knocking him out and making a run for it, but if he really has Nancy, we need to find her. She's probably the only one that can fix this. And we don't know how much magic he has."

"Here we are!" Terry called over his shoulder. They followed him through some trees and around a cottage. In the backyard was a large table covered in every pastry and dessert Olivia could think of.

"Well, at least we won't starve."

Jerron studied the three characters at the table. There was an old man sitting at the head of the table, noisily slurping his tea. His gray hair stuck out in all directions. A large rabbit sat in another chair. It had a rabbit's head, but his body was almost human. He had hands to hold his teacup and biscuit. A mouse in a suit sat on the table nibbling a cookie.

Terry grinned and jumped on to a chair. "The Hatter isn't himself since I borrowed his hat for *Little Red Riding Hood*. Wolves don't wear top hats, but I couldn't find a better disguise."

"I wish you would stay away," the Hatter said to Terry. "You always ruin the mood."

"But I've brought friends," he said, gesturing at Olivia and Jerron.

"Well, what do you know," said the Hare. "We might tolerate you for that."

"But only if we like your friends," the Hatter said, pointing a spoon in his direction.

Olivia sank onto a chair, not waiting to be invited. Jerron followed her example. His head was tired from the moving landscape. Thankfully, things didn't seem to move here and his stomach was settling.

"Well, their manners are lacking," said the Hare. "Didn't even wait for an invitation."

"Will it matter?" Olivia asked. "You're going to be rude to us whatever we do, and I'm starving." She reached out and grabbed a muffin and began eating it.

"I like a woman who understands what she wants and takes it," the Hatter said with a wide grin.

"As do I," Terry said, licking milk from a cup. He was taking this role a bit too seriously.

Jerron grabbed a plain biscuit and took a bite. If his stomach could handle it, he might try something else.

"Are you ever going to bring my hat back?" the Hatter asked Terry.

"I told you I lost it. You're a hatter. Make a new one."

"I would, but you know we can't do anything but have tea parties. My head feels naked without it. The least you could do is bring me another one. You are the one always bragging about your magic."

"I'll try to remember," Terry said. "Can't promise, though. I have a lot in motion."

"I have some in the house. Can't you go in and get one?" the man asked.

"Not now," Terry said.

Olivia rolled her eyes. "Where are they? I'll go get one."

"Thanks, dear," the Hatter said, clapping his hands. "If you go in the back door, there is a room to the right. It's full of hats." Olivia nodded and hurried to the house.

"You couldn't just go in and get the man a hat?" Jerron asked Terry. "That's pretty lame, especially if you keep inviting yourself to his party."

"I don't know if you've noticed, but I'm the villain. I can't do too many favors for people."

"It's not even a favor. You stole his hat."

"Villain, remember?"

"Still. If you party with them, doesn't that make them your people? Even villains should look out for their friends."

"Agreed," the Hatter said. "You come eat all of our food and don't even say thank you. You could make an effort."

Olivia came out of the cottage with a gigantic pile of hats in her arms.

The Hatter's eyes lit up, and he clasped his hands together. "Oh, my sweet hats! I've missed you!" Olivia placed the hats in front of the man and returned to her seat. The Hatter lovingly studied all the hats, rubbing the fabric of each one.

Jerron forced himself to eat until he was full. Who knew when they would get to eat again? Olivia seemed to enjoy the food. Her stomach must be more stable than his.

"I have an idea!" the Hatter exclaimed. "We should have a hat party!" He walked around the table, plunking hats onto everyone's head. "You get this one," he said to Jerron, placing a brown leather hat on his head. "It's a casual hat since you aren't dressed for a party."

Olivia smiled at him and studied his tux. He was the only one that looked like he was going to party. Jerron smiled back as the Hatter dropped an enormous hat on her head. It fell over her eyes. She pushed it up and reached for another dessert. She was going to make herself sick.

The Hatter, Hare, and Terry all started dancing around the table, singing. What was in the tea? Jerron and Olivia hadn't touched it, and the others were all acting drunk. Jerron glanced at his pocket watch. He wasn't sure what he was late for, or if he was late for anything at all, but it was nagging at him.

Terry curled up under the table and fell asleep, snoring loudly. The Hatter and Hare were still dancing around. Jerron weighed his options. They should leave Terry. He could probably find them at will, but they didn't understand his game, and they needed to find Nancy.

"Let's go," he said, getting up. Olivia was up in an instant. They walked away without anyone paying any attention. "We need to find Nancy."

"How do we do that?"

"No idea. I'm hoping it just happens naturally."

"I'm just glad everything stopped being out of focus."

"It makes it easier," he agreed, as they started down a dusty path. The trees weren't checkered anymore. They were still the wrong color, but it made them easier to look at.

They walked in a silence that almost felt peaceful, considering the strange circumstances. Jerron felt more confident the further away they left Terry. It was possible he wouldn't come after them. He knew that was wishful thinking.

"Now's your chance," Olivia mumbled to herself.

"What?"

"Just giving myself advice," Olivia said with a sly smile.

"What kind of advice?"

"I was just thinking. We can't disappear when we kiss anymore. We should take advantage of that in case it changes."

Jerron stopped, and he grinned. "I can't believe I didn't think of that."

Olivia put her arms around his neck and leaned in. He didn't know why his heart was pounding so hard. It wasn't like they hadn't kissed before. It had never lasted long before the spinning came, though.

Wrapping his arms around her waist, he kissed her. His head started spinning, but it was completely different this time. This time, she wasn't going anywhere. He felt free. How had he spent so many years not believing in love? He understood now why so many people were willing to fight for it.

Chapter 16

Olivia tried to stop smiling as she strolled arm in arm with Jerron. They should move faster, but suddenly, things were more magical. She shook her head. This place wasn't a good kind of enchanted. Nothing here made sense, and they needed to leave. She couldn't start imagining this place was a good place to be. Nothing good would come from that.

"Did you hear that?" Jerron asked, stopping.

"What?" Olivia whispered, her ears perking up. A noise in the trees caused them to take a step back.

"Who's there?" Jerron called.

Two short, round, identical men stumbled out of the woods. Both were dressed in red school boy uniforms with propeller hats on their heads.

"I'm Tweedle-Dee, and this here is my brother Tweedle-Dum," said the one on the right.

"I'm not in the mood for this," Jerron said, so only Olivia could hear.

The two brothers placed their arms over each other's shoulders and held out their free hands as they walked toward them. "Now, let's shake, shall we?" Tweedle-Dee said.

Not knowing whose hand to take first, Olivia grabbed each one's hand with one of her own. The two brothers immediately started dancing around in circles, taking Olivia with them. Why did everyone here have to be crazy? Olivia tried to break free, but they had a good grip.

"Okay, that's enough," Jerron said from the sidelines. The twirling stopped, and Olivia broke away. Jerron was standing a few feet away with his hands in his pockets and a slight smile. Olivia could only imagine how funny that had appeared. Everything she did had to look funny in this dress. She wished it was longer and less puffy.

"We have to be on our way," Jerron said. "Do you know how we can get out of the woods?"

"Sure, sure," said one brother. Olivia had already forgotten which was which.

"So . . ."

"So, we are going to tell you a tale," one said, puffing out his chest.

Jerron stared down at the man. "We don't have time."

"Everyone has time for a story."

"We really don't," Olivia said. "Can you point us out of here?"

"You see, there was this walrus," he began.

Olivia rolled her eyes. "Come on, Jerron." She wasn't sticking around to be polite.

One man shoved his brother. "Hey! What's in your pocket?"

"My pocket? Nothing's in my pocket," the other one said, stepping back.

"Oh, there is something in there. No secrets! No secrets!" He reached over and tried to stick his hand in the other's pocket.

"No, no! You stay away!"

"Is that my rattle? Is that my rattle?"

"Mine, not yours!"

"Aren't you both a little old for a rattle?" Jerron asked.

They both turned and stared at him. "Never too old!"

Jerron raised an eyebrow and shook his head.

"We must have a battle!" yelled one of them.

"A battle, indeed! To the death!"

"But we battled to the death last week."

Olivia felt tired. "Oh brother. Why are we even here?"

"Let's go," Jerron said, grabbing her hand. They hurried down the path and out of sight of the fighting twins.

"I've never liked this story, but I like it less being in it," Olivia said. "And I really like it less with Terry."

"Once we find Nancy, we need to save her and make her let him go. He needs to get out of here before he completely loses his mind."

"I'm not sure he hasn't."

"I guess we don't know what he was like before he came here."

"Losing my mind?" Terry said, appearing behind them. Olivia let out a little yelp and Jerron spun around. Terry was dressed in a fancy red robe with a golden crown on his head. Red hearts were embroidered on his cuffs. "Whatever could you be talking about? No matter. It's time for you to meet my wife. How are you at Croquet?"

Olivia bit her lip. Now, he was changing characters? And since when did he have an accent? "I don't play."

"I'm Terrance the King of Hearts. And you are?" he asked.

"You know who we are," Jerron growled.

"Shall we go? My wife loves Croquet. She's playing with the dutchess right now, but you know the dutchess. She's more concerned with her baby than actually playing. Come, I'll take you there."

They reluctantly followed King Terry. She wondered if they would ever get out of here. She couldn't imagine living here forever. If they had to get stuck somewhere, she would prefer Snow White. She had wonderful memories there.

"I'm tired of the woods," Olivia said. "Why do all stories seem to have a huge amount of walking through the woods?"

"I never thought about it," Jerron said. "You're right, though. Almost every story I've been in has had woods."

"There's the castle," Terry said, gesturing ahead. "Beautiful, isn't it?"

Olivia refused to be mesmerized by a castle. "If you've seen one, you've seen them all."

Terry led them up to the castle and around the back. Olivia didn't add that this castle was much smaller than the one in *Cinderella*. There was no reason to provoke Terry. When they rounded the castle, a large grassy area met them.

There was no doubt who the queen was, with her large crown and shimmering red dress. The biggest surprise was that she was pretty. She had a long slender neck, and her black hair fell in gentle waves around her shoulders. When she walked, it was graceful and light.

Another woman, who must be the duchess, stood to the side, holding a crying baby that was wrapped in a blanket. She appeared too old to have a baby, with her gray hair and wrinkles around her mouth and eyes.

"Who have you brought me?" the queen asked, floating over to them.

"Some lost travelers," Terry said. "I thought you might want to meet them."

She smiled, a far off look in her eyes. "Yes, how lovely. Do you play?" she asked, holding up a mallet.

Olivia was happy to see it wasn't a flamingo. She shook her head. "I never have."

"Neither have I," Jerron said.

"It's easy enough," she said in a soft, light voice. "I'll explain."

Olivia tried to listen as the queen recited the rules of the game, but it was hard to pay attention. She felt like she was being put to sleep. How could a person make their voice so even?

"Do you understand?" the queen asked.

"Yep," Jerron said, picking up a mallet.

"It's more fun if there is a prize or a punishment. Shall we think of some?"

Olivia's head came up sharply. She shouldn't have been surprised.

"I'm not up for this right now," Olivia said, wondering if you were allowed to say that to a queen.

"I'll play for her," said the duchess. "If she holds my baby."

"I can do that," Olivia said, taking the baby.

"The winner gets to name their prize," the queen said. "Those who do not win lose their head." Her expression didn't change.

"Sounds reasonable," Terry said.

The baby fussed, so Olivia bounced her arms.

"Are you going to play, my love?" the queen asked Terry.

"No, my sweet. I'll be cheering for you." He blew her a kiss, and she smiled. Olivia and Terry stood off to the side. Olivia would bet he didn't want to let her out of his sight. He probably didn't want to have to find them again.

Olivia didn't mind sports, but this one was boring. Playing would have been better than watching. Jerron was good, but the queen and the duchess were better.

The baby cried again, and Olivia looked down. She moved the blanket from its face and let out a small squeal. She wasn't holding a baby. It was a piglet!

"Shhh," Terry said. "Just keep bouncing the wretched animal."

"It's a pig!"

"Don't let the duchess hear you. She's a little crazy. She imagines it's a baby, and it's best to not tell her otherwise."

Olivia steadied her breath. It was nothing to freak out about. It was a cute little thing. At least it wasn't a snake.

"Are you going to take us to Nancy?" she asked Terry.

"Nancy? I don't believe I'm acquainted with anyone by that name."

"Seriously? What kind of game are you playing? You need to take us to her. I don't want to stay in this place forever."

"You're quite confusing," Terry said, holding up a hand and staring at his perfectly manicured nails.

"I suppose you don't remember crawling around like a cat earlier today?"

"Crawling? Me? Preposterous. You possess a wonderful imagination. Kings don't crawl. It's not dignified."

Olivia could feel a vein in her forehead throbbing. This man was infuriating. "Please take us to Nancy." She wasn't above begging.

"I'm sorry, I can't help you. If I ever meet a Nancy, I will tell her you're looking for her."

"I really want to hurt you right now," Olivia mumbled under her breath.

"That's all I can handle," the duchess said, taking the piglet from Olivia. "Why don't you trade places with me?"

"No thanks," Olivia said.

"I'll go," said Terry, taking up a mallet.

The duchess cuddled the piglet. "The queen cares about this game too much. It gets boring day after day. I wish she would stop chopping heads so she would have more people to play with."

Olivia willed Jerron to play better. She liked his head. "Do you, by chance, know a woman named Nancy?"

"Nancy, hm," the duchess said, tilting her head. "Does she have silver hair and a fancy dress?"

"Possibly. She has silver hair, but I don't know what she would be wearing."

"There was a woman last week that played with the queen. She lost, of course, as everyone does."

"Did she lose her head?"

"No. They made a different deal. I believe she had a type of magic, but the king had blocked it. If she won, she got to go free. If she lost, they put her up in a tower and she could never leave."

"Can you tell me where the tower is?"

"What tower?"

Olivia fought the urge to roll her eyes. "The tower you were telling me about."

"I don't believe I was telling you about a tower. I believe you were complimenting my baby."

Olivia moved her jaw back and forth in frustration. "The woman who had magic. Where is the tower the king put her in?"

"Why in the world would the king put someone in a tower? You've been out in the sun too long. Can I get you some water?"

"No," Olivia said, grinding her teeth. If she ever got home, she was staying away from everything that had anything to do with this story.

"You seem a bit distressed. Are you worried about your man? It does look like he's going to lose. Perhaps, the queen will be lenient and let him keep his head. She might send him to the north tower like the woman last week."

Olivia pursed her lips together. "Jerron, we need to go!" she said, leaving the duchess.

"He can't leave," the queen said. "If he leaves, it will count as a forfeit, and he loses his head."

"He can't lose his head. We don't have time for that. We're in a hurry."

"Queen's rules," Terry said. "There's no way around them."

"Oh my," the queen said, taking a step back. Her eyes were focused on something behind Olivia. Jerron smiled. A growl sounded behind her, and Finn leaped in front of her. He bared his teeth at the queen. Jerron moved over to Olivia.

"I hate that wolf," Terry said, stepping in front of the queen. "How does he keep finding me?"

"You let us leave, and we won't let him eat you," Olivia said. She hoped they would buy her bluff. Maybe if they thought she could command Finn, they would cooperate. "Go into the castle. Now."

The queen turned and ran to the castle with the duchess at her heels.

"Go with them," Jerron told Terry.

"It isn't fair," he growled. "This wolf is not natural! Magic doesn't work against him, and he does whatever he wants! I will figure out a way to defeat him." He turned and stomped toward the castle.

"Which way is north?" Olivia asked. "The duchess said something about a magical woman with gray hair in a northern tower. It could be Nancy."

"I have no sense of direction here," Jerron said.

"Hey, Finn," Olivia said, scratching the wolf behind the ears. "Do you know where Nancy is?" He rubbed his head into Olivia and then ran. Olivia took off after him and hoped Jerron would follow. They had to find Nancy. Finn might be their best chance.

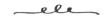

Jerron's legs were burning when Finn finally stopped in front of a tall tower. The wolf curled up on the ground and watched them. The tower was thin and made of stone. He bent over and rested his hands on his knees. Olivia dropped to her knees, trying to catch her breath.

"Now what?" Jerron asked.

Olivia grinned. "You need to call out and ask Nancy to lower her hair."

"I am not climbing Nancy's hair," Jerron said.

"That always sounded so painful."

He stood and examined the tower closer. It had a balcony and a door at the top. He was in pretty good shape, but he couldn't imagine climbing this. There were hand holds between the rocks, but they were thin. Climbing had never been his thing.

"Nancy!" he yelled. "Nancy!"

Olivia sighed with disappointment. "Her mouth might be covered. I'm going to walk around and see if there's another way in." She walked slowly around the tower while Jerron kept his gaze focused on the door.

"There's another door!" Olivia called. Jerron ran around to meet her and examined the large wooden door. "It's locked," she said.

"I can't kick this in," he said. "It seems pretty solid."

"You might need this," said a man's voice. Jerron turned to see Earl, standing there with his messy red hair and an ax in his hand.

"Earl?" Olivia squeaked, giving the man a hug. "How did you get here?"

"No idea," he said, handing the ax to Jerron. "I followed your wolf and ended up here. I've been hiding in the woods trying to figure things out when I heard Jerron yelling."

"Great timing," Jerron said, hitting the lock with the ax. The door splintered, and the lock broke. "That wasn't too bad," he said, tossing the ax to the floor. He pulled the door open and entered.

"Come on, Jer," Earl said, picking up the ax and following him. "You don't leave the weapon. We could be walking into danger."

"I guess I'm not thinking," he said, glad to have the man with them.

"I'll keep watch," Olivia called behind them. "I don't want Terry sneaking up on us."

A spiral staircase filled the walls of the tower. Jerron and Earl walked up cautiously. They could find anything up there, and with the noise the ax made, they had warned anyone who may be there that they were coming.

At the top, they found a small room. There was nothing in it except a small pile of blankets against one wall—with Nancy on top.

"Is she dead?" Earl asked.

"I hope not," Jerron said, rushing to her side. He dropped to his knees and rolled the woman over. "She's alive," he said, as he watched her breath. "She isn't conscious, though." Jerron scooped her up, and they descended the stairs. He liked to think he was in good shape, but they wouldn't get far if he had to carry her.

"Is she alive?" Olivia asked, as they exited the tower.

"Yes, but I don't know what we're going to do with her. She's too heavy to carry for long."

Finn wandered over to them and grabbed the hem of Olivia's dress. He pulled her gently, and they all followed. The wolf stopped when they came to a small spring. Jerron laid Nancy on the ground, and Olivia took off her white apron. She dipped it in the cool water and rubbed it on Nancy's face.

"What?" Nancy said with a groan. Her eyes fluttered and opened. "Olivia? Jerron? What's happening?"

"We just saved you from Terry's tower," Olivia explained.

"Yes," she said, sitting up and putting a hand to her head. "Terry. Why did I ever choose that man?"

Jerron had something to say about why she chose anyone, but now wasn't the time. "Can you get us out of here? Terry isn't far away."

"I'm not sure. He shouldn't be able to do the things he does. I've spent hundreds of years in my line of work, and I've seen nothing like Terry. He shouldn't have been able to block my magic, and he shouldn't be able to move through stories."

"Can you try something? Everything here is messed up," Jerron said.

"We are in *Alice in Wonderland*," Nancy said. "What can you expect?"

"It's more than that. Things aren't stable. Things weren't in focus."

"I suppose that's to be expected. Terry is messing with the flow of things. The story is probably trying to resist and failing. Help me up."

Jerron grabbed her hands and pulled her to her feet. She smoothed down her wrinkly dress and patted her messy hair. Finn circled her, and she patted him on the head.

"You shouldn't be here, puppy," she said. "I bet you're helping, though. You shouldn't be here, either," she said to Earl. "This is all very peculiar." She pulled a wand out of her pocket.

"I can't believe Terry didn't take that from you," Olivia said.

"He doesn't know I have a wand. Most people don't. The only ones that see it are the ones that are in *Cinderella*, and only Cinderella sees it." She swung the wand in a circle, and a stream of color followed it. "It appears it still works. I'll send you back first," she said to Earl.

"Thanks for helping us," Olivia told him. "We would have been helpless without you."

"I'm happy to help you again, Snow. You were good to us."

Nancy swished her wand, and Earl disappeared. "Now for the rest of us," she said.

Jerron rubbed his chin. "Will it do any good? Terry follows us. I'm guessing he'll be right behind us."

"That is a problem," Nancy said, tapping her wand against her cheek.

"Can't you send him home?" Olivia asked.

"I don't think I can. Not without him in front of me anyway."

"He doesn't want to go home anymore," Jerron said. "He wants to rule this world, and if we don't stop him, he's going to succeed."

Nancy frowned. "It's a fine mess I've made of things."

"I hope it teaches you to not mess with people's lives."

"Oh pish," she said. "I've made some beautiful stories over the years. You don't stop something so glorious because of a failure. I'll be more careful in the future. I never should have taken Terry. I knew he wasn't exactly stable when I chose him, but I thought he still deserved a try."

"You took someone that wasn't stable?" Jerron asked. "I thought this place made him the way he is."

"Terry was a stage actor. He only played dismal roles. I suggested he take some that were a little more upbeat, but he refused. When I first brought him here, he was brilliant at playing the parts. He seemed to thrive for the first year or two. After that, everything went downhill."

"I don't see why you don't understand that it's not your place to force people into your mold."

"I'm surprised you are fighting me on this. You found Olivia. If Terry hadn't interfered, you both would have gone home after the last story."

"Really?" Olivia asked.

Jerron's frown deepened. "Just because some people find happiness doesn't mean it's your responsibility."

"How do you know what the responsibility of a fairy god-mother is?"

Jerron had no response to that.

"If we're going to argue, can we do it somewhere else?" Olivia asked. "I can't help worrying about Terry while we stand here."

Nancy swished her wand, and they were immediately in a serene meadow.

"Can't you send us home?" Jerron asked. "If we're ready, what's the point of keeping us here?"

"I could send you home," she said. "But do you really want to leave this world like this? It's going to be a pitiful place if Terry wins."

"You're in a better position to fight him," Jerron said. "What can we do? We don't have magic."

"I do, and he still caught me. Terry won't be taken down easily. He needs to be tricked. I can't do it alone. Will you help me?"

Jerron sighed. He wanted to go home. He wanted to sit on a sofa with a cheeseburger and a good movie, and he didn't want to move for a week. Of course, he wanted Olivia to be with him as well.

"We'll help," Olivia said, as Jerron nodded. What were they getting themselves into?

Chapter 17

Terry's reach was spreading. Olivia and Jerron had gone back to *Snow White* and the cottage and were waiting for Terry to make an appearance. It had been a week, and so far, there was no sign of him. At least, no sign of him physically. The story was beginning to glitch, just like in *Alice in Wonderland*.

Nancy worried that whatever Terry was doing was ripping the world in unnatural ways. Sometimes, everything felt jumpy, and other times, it would get dark. Everyone was being careful as they walked because there was no telling when the ground would jump up and trip them. It was getting common to see red grass or purple trees.

Nancy's self-proclaimed perfect world was being turned upside down, and she was not pleased. She stayed in the shadows, waiting for Terry to show his face. She was getting more agitated by the day. Olivia had sympathy for the woman, but she had brought this on herself.

All the brothers were staying closer to the cottage, watching for anything strange. All the brothers except Jurry. Ever since he started courting Meena, he had been harder to keep track of. All of his brothers were excited for him and let his absences go unnoticed.

"Roco's hurt!" Earl called, bursting into the kitchen. Olivia jumped from her spot at the sink, and she dropped the cup she was washing.

"What happened?" she asked, drying her hands on a towel.

"Nobody saw. His head is bleeding, and he's unconscious. He must have fallen. The others are bringing him."

The front door creaked, and Olivia rushed into the front room to see Toad and Levy carrying Roco. Earl, Noll, and Mert followed behind. Roco's head was drooping to one side, and blood ran down his face.

Olivia frowned. "Put him in his bed. I'll get some towels. Earl, go find Jerron. Noll, go outside and call for Nancy. Maybe she can help."

Noll's eyes became wide. "But she's scary!"

Olivia glanced up sharply. She didn't know what her face looked like, but Noll bowed his head and nodded, scurrying from the house. Olivia grabbed some towels from the kitchen drawer and got one wet.

Blood wasn't on the top of Olivia's list of things she liked to deal with, but she could keep a level head when it was needed. Placing a dry towel to Roco's head, she applied pressure to stop the bleeding. Blood soaked through the towel and got on her hands. "Just breath," she reminded herself, switching out the towel for a clean one.

"What's going on?" Jerron asked, entering the room. He quickly assessed the room and moved near Olivia. He took another towel and placed it on the one she was holding. "I've got it," he said. "Go wash your hands, then bring me a needle and thread."

Olivia cocked her head and studied him as she released her hold. What would he do with a needle and thread?

"I wanted to be an EMT when I was younger," he said. "I did a program in high school to get started."

"Have you ever done stitches?"

Jerron sighed. "No, but I've seen it done a few times. Someone has to do it. Do you want to?"

"No," Olivia said, leaving the room and washing the blood from her hands in the kitchen.

Noll entered, his lips in a tight line. "She didn't answer."

"Can you get a needle and thread and take them into the bedroom? Jerron's going to sew Roco's head."

"Sure," Noll said, rummaging through a messy drawer. Olivia hoped the thread was sanitary.

"I'll heat the needle," Noll said. "Just to make sure he doesn't get an infection."

"Good idea." Olivia was glad she'd taught him something.

"Do you think he'll be alright?" he asked, as he strolled over to the stove.

"I'm not sure how bad it is. It sounds like Jerron knows a bit about medical things."

"Well, that's a relief."

"After you heat the needle, take it to Jerron. I'm going to see if I can find Nancy."

Olivia hurried outside and looked around. Things were more mellow today than the day before. Everything was the right color. "Nancy!" Olivia called. "Nancy, we need help!" The only answer was a bird perched on the roof.

"I don't suppose you know where Nancy is?" She felt ridiculous as soon as she talked to the bird, but wasn't that Snow White's thing? The bird flew away, and Olivia sighed.

"Ah, Snow! You're back!" Terry's voice said cheerfully behind her. They had been waiting for this, but now was not a good time.

She turned and glared at the fake prince. He swung off his black horse and straightened his crown. "I worried when you disappeared."

"I don't have time for this."

"Time for what?" he asked.

"Time for you."

"Well, that's a bit harsh," Terry said, shaking his head. "Your stepmother is going to come for you. I'll stay near, just to make sure you're safe."

Olivia studied the man. He was so strange. One second, he wanted to take Nancy down, and the next, he was playing his parts. He must not know the queen was dead.

"I can't stay and chat," she said. "My friend is hurt."

"The huntsman?" Terry asked with sparkling eyes.

Olivia glared. "No."

"Too bad," Terry said. "Well, be careful, and know that I'm looking out for you."

"Thanks," she said, entering the cottage. She didn't have time to waste on Prince Terrance today.

Jerron's eyes were burning. Sleep had been hard to come by. He had spent most of his time next to Roco, who remained unconscious for three days. They had gotten some water into him today, but it hadn't been easy. Things had been quiet. All the brothers helped without complaining. Terry hadn't shown up again, but neither had Nancy.

Roco groaned and touched his head. His eyes fluttered, and he grimaced as they opened. "What's going on?" he mumbled.

"You hit your head," Jerron told him. "You've been unconscious for three days."

"Three days?" he mumbled. "I feel like a horse ran me over."

"Let me get you some water," Jerron said, reaching for the cup on the nightstand. He put it up to the man's mouth and gave him a small drink.

Mert poked his head in and grinned. He turned and yelled, "Hey, everyone! Roco's awake!"

"Do you have to yell?" Roco complained, covering his ears. Within half a minute, the room was flooded with all of Roco's brothers and Olivia.

"How are you feeling?" Olivia asked.

"I've been worse," Roco said. "But not in a long time. I'll live. I'm pretty hungry, though."

"I'll get something," Mert said, rushing away.

"You can always count on Roco to do something that gets him out of working," Earl said, running his hand through his red hair. "This seems a little extreme, though. Even for you."

"I'd rather work than feel like this," Roco said, touching the bandage on his head.

"Not to ruin a favorable moment, but I saw a prince on a horse when I was out working today," Toad said. "He looked like he was trying to hide, so I pretended to not see him."

"I figured he was around here somewhere," Olivia said. "Now that Roco's awake, we should probably try to capture him."

Mert returned with a bowl of soup that had been waiting on the stove, and Jerron helped Roco sit up so he could eat.

"I'm surprised I don't need to use the outhouse," Roco said, taking a spoonful of broth. "Three days is a long time to hold it." Olivia rubbed her arm and gazed out the window, and Jerron grinned.

Jurry crossed his arms and frowned. "You can't hold it for three days."

"But I did. Right?"

"We never talk about this," Jurry said. "There are things you don't want to know, and things we don't want to speak of." All the brothers nodded.

Jerron held back a chuckle as he watched Roco's eyes widen. His face turned the color of Earl's hair. "Well, that's what brothers are for, I suppose."

"Now we know Terry is still around, we should put our plan into action," Olivia said, taking the attention away from Roco.

"Do we go ahead without Nancy?" Jerron asked. "I thought she would be around bossing us."

Olivia bit her lip. "I think we should. Who can say what she's up to? She said she would stay close, and she hasn't. Or if she is, she's staying in hiding. It would have been nice if she came and helped when we called for her."

Jerron rubbed his chin. "Can we pull it off without her? We don't have the magic we need to do some of the plan."

"That's true. I forgot about that."

"Yelling for her doesn't seem to work."

"We should probably try again."

"I don't want you out there," Jerron said. "I don't trust Terry. He might pretend to be Prince Charming, but at the end of the day, he's the biggest villain around right now."

"He gives me the creeps."

Earl crossed his arms. "I don't get why you don't let us handle the man. He sounds like a pansy to me. Hiding off in the woods and such."

"I'm not sure he's in the best frame of mind," Olivia said. "That makes him more dangerous. You can't predict what a person like that might do."

"Can I get more soup?" Roco asked. "If I'm going to be any help, I need to get my strength back."

"Let's give it three days," Jerron said, taking Roco's bowl. "If we haven't found Nancy by then, we'll do it ourselves."

———ееее———

Olivia was tired of being cooped up in the house. Part of the plan was to keep Olivia out of sight for a few days. The brothers went about their chores with solemn expressions so Terry would think something was wrong if he was spying on the cottage. She pounded on the bread dough she was kneading and tried to push a piece of hair from her face with her arm. Her hands were too sticky.

"Why the sour expression?" Nancy asked, appearing beside her.

Olivia jumped. "You scared me!"

"Sorry. I didn't want to risk Terrance seeing me. He's been circling this area like a vulture. You've learned to make something besides cookies?" she asked, gesturing at the bread dough. "You've made your fair share of cookies since coming here."

"How do you know that?" Olivia asked.

"I know most everything that happens, or I did until Terry went rogue. I also do my research. Cookies were the only thing you really made before coming here. That's why I always make sure you have a healthy supply of raisins in each reality."

Olivia glared at Nancy. "You couldn't give me a supply of chocolate chips?"

Nancy blinked twice. "Who would choose chocolate over raisins?"

"There are so many things wrong with you. You must not have researched me very well. I would never put a raisin in a cookie."

"Why not?"

Olivia shook her head. "It's not important. Where have you been? We've called for you several times."

"I can't pop in every time someone calls me. I have so many people to check on."

"We thought we were going to put this plan into action a lot sooner. You made it sound like we were short on time." Nancy sat on a chair and arranged her frilly pink dress. "We are short on time. That doesn't mean I could neglect all the others. Anything could have happened in the time Terry had me locked up. Now that I know everyone is taken care of, we can proceed."

Olivia pulled the sticky dough from her hands and tried to stick it back in the bowl. "Are things glitching everywhere?"

"Yes. It's really a mess. All the stories are in chaos. This story is actually doing far better than some. I might need to give up on *Alice in Wonderland* forever. That place was always a wild card, and now there is no sense to be found."

"I've been staying in the house so Terry will sense something's wrong."

"Wonderful. Are we ready then?"

"Yes."

"You look nervous."

"I am," Olivia said, giving up on the dough.

"No reason to be nervous," Nancy said, pulling her wand from her pocket. She waved it and pointed at the bread dough. It immediately became two steaming loaves of bread.

"I could use a wand," Olivia said, washing her hands.

"Solving things with a wand isn't really ideal. It's better to use your mind and your muscles. If everything is solved by magic, you become weak and lazy."

She was one to talk. Wasn't that how she solved problems?

Jerron stepped into the kitchen and stopped when he saw Nancy. "It's about time you showed up."

"I'm a very busy person."

"Wow," he said, inspecting the bread. "That looks great."

Olivia bit the inside of her cheek. "Nancy helped."

"It's time," Nancy said. She stood and waved her wand, and a flawless glass coffin appeared next to the table.

Olivia breathed in through her nose. "I can only imagine the fingerprints."

"We don't have to do it like this," Jerron said. "We can come up with another plan."

"This will be best," Nancy said. "I know Terry. He either fumes and wants to kill me, or he is in character. He switches back and forth, but he's been in character for this story. Our best bet is to follow it."

"Can I have a minute?" Olivia asked. She hurried to the other room and ran a brush through her hair. If she was going to be in that coffin with everyone gawking at her, she wanted to look decent. It was still strange to see the long black hair. She returned to the kitchen. "Alright. I'm ready."

"Lie down against the pillow," Nancy said, pointing at a delicate pink pillow. Why a dead person would need a pillow was beyond Olivia. She climbed up and laid down, her eyes pleading with Jerron. Olivia hoped they were telling him to not let this get messed up. She arranged her hair over her shoulders, placed her hands on her stomach, and tried to relax.

"Lovely," Nancy said, placing a bouquet of purple irises in her hands. "You still seem tense. You don't need to worry. It will be like a peaceful sleep. If Terry is watching as closely as I think he is, you'll only be in there for a few hours at most."

"What if he changes his mind and leaves or doesn't come?"

"Then, I will break the spell. Now, let me rub this on your lips," she said, pulling out a small vial. "Make sure you don't lick them. As soon as Terry kisses you, he'll fall into a deep sleep." She rubbed something from the vial onto Olivia's lips, and she immediately had to force herself not to lick them.

"I still don't like the idea of Terry kissing you," Jerron said.

"At least I'll be unconscious," Olivia muttered.

"Alright, here we go," Nancy said, swishing her wand. Olivia closed her eyes and hoped when she woke up, all of this was over.

The fingerprints were real. Jerron shook his head as he tried to rub them off without smearing the water on the glass. They had carried the coffin outside and placed it near the cottage. All the brothers had touched it like kids at a toy store. Having fingerprints all over it ruined the illusion they were trying to make.

"Are you sure she's alright?" Noll asked, touching the glass again.

"You all need to stop touching," Jerron scolded, as he scrubbed the prints. Nancy hadn't come out. They didn't want Terry to know she was here.

"Does she seem pale?" Earl asked.

"Much too pale," Jurry growled.

Jerron blocked Toad so he couldn't tap the glass. "She's fine."

"Of course she is," Roco said. "Her lips are still nice and red."

Jerron stared at Olivia. He knew she was fine, but there was still a sense of eeriness to it all. She did seem pale, but he would trust Nancy. He didn't really have a choice at this point.

Levy scratched his head. "Should we be crying? To make it more realistic?"

"I don't even know how to cry," Jurry said.

"You don't need to cry," Jerron assured them. Tears on the coffin wouldn't be any more attractive than fingerprints.

Mert trampled over and tossed a bouquet on top of the coffin. Jerron bit his tongue to stop himself from cursing at the man. He'd pulled the flowers out by the roots and the dirt littered the coffin. He didn't know why keeping it clean was so important to him.

"Look at the mess you made!" Earl said, picking up the flowers and brushing the dirt off. He ripped the roots from the flowers and placed them down. Now, there were more fingerprints and smeared dirt. The flowers weren't as nice as they could be, now that they had been ripped apart at the stems. He resisted the urge to cut them nicely.

"Hark! What do I see?" Prince Terrance said, riding into the yard. Jerron rolled his eyes as the man hopped from his horse and dramatically ran to the coffin. "Oh my! What a beautiful maiden! But what is this? She is the maiden I have met in this wood before!"

Jurry snorted, and Jerron shot him a warning look.

"What has happened to her? She isn't dead, is she? Perhaps, sleeping? I refuse to believe she is no more! I have dreamt of her these many days."

"She ate a poisoned apple," Roco volunteered.

"Poisoned? Who would poison such a charming creature?"

"It was the evil queen," Earl said in a monotone voice. "But fear not, we have slane her." Jerron shook his head. Between Terry and Earl, they couldn't sound more scripted if they tried.

Terry dropped to one knee. He made a fist and pressed it to his forehead. "What a substantial loss to this world! Is there nothing I can do?"

"It has been said that true love's kiss can heal all," Toad said, adding his own bland addition.

Mert shrugged his shoulders. "But where will we find one who can perform such a kiss?"

Noll shook his head, and at least managed to appear sad. "The princess did not know many. It will not be a simple task."

Jerron wanted to run. If Terry was buying this, he was an idiot.

"I shall do it!" Terry said, springing to his feet. "I love the princess and have from the first time I laid eyes on her."

"Oh joy," said Levy. "Please bring our princess back to us."

Jerron wondered if he was doing a better job at keeping his face passive than Jurry was. Jurry was watching his brothers like they were a bunch of fools.

Terry gestured to the coffin. "Can we lift the lid, my good fellows?"

Earl and Noll helped Terry remove the casket lid and put it off to the side. Mert's flowers fell to the ground.

"I hope I am worthy," Terry said, dramatically leaning over Olivia.

"Worthy?" Jurry snorted under his breath. "Not likely." If Terry heard him, he didn't react.

Jerron wanted to close his eyes or look away. The thought of Terry kissing Olivia turned his stomach. Still, if he didn't, it would ruin the plan, and then what? Jurry looked ready to hit someone and the others all leaned in with bated breath.

"What a vision she is," Terry whispered. "When I awaken her, we will ride off to my kingdom and be married. You are all welcome to come, of course."

"Just kiss her already!" Jurry complained.

"Of course," Terry said. He leaned further down and pressed his lips to Olivia's. He pulled back and glanced at her. "Did it work?" A second later, Terry fell to the ground. His crown rolled away, and the man began snoring.

"It worked!" Earl said, jumping up and down. All the brothers clapped each other on the back and danced around.

Nancy came bounding from the cottage. "We did it! We stopped him!"

"Great," Jerron said, looking down at Olivia. "But why is she still asleep?"

"Don't be silly," Nancy said, smiling at him. "Terry wasn't in love with Olivia any more than she was in love with him. It's a true love's kiss. Not an enemy's kiss. I would have thought you knew that by now."

"Alright—so what now? I can't kiss her, or I'll end up like Terry."

"Yes, yes," Nancy said, pulling out her wand. She swished it around Olivia's face. "Now it's safe."

"Are you sure?"

"Of course I'm sure."

Jerron leaned over and kissed Olivia.

Her eyes fluttered and opened. "Jerron?" She sat up in alarm. "Did you kiss me? Are you poisoned?"

"No, I'm fine," he said, gesturing to the fallen prince. "Terry not so much."

She glanced down at Terry and shuddered. "So, he kissed me?"

"Yep."

"And so did you?"

"He had to," Nancy said. Her smile was big enough to break her cheeks. "It had to be true love's kiss, you know. Anything else won't work."

Jerron scooped Olivia off the cool glass coffin and spun her around. She giggled, and everyone clapped.

"Now, do you see why I do what I do?" Nancy asked.

Jerron gently put Olivia on her feet and placed a protective arm around her. "I see what you think you are doing, but I still don't agree with it. Look what happened to Terry. That's not ideal."

"But he is the exception," Nancy argued. "I've had no one else fail so badly."

"But others have failed?" Jerron asked.

"Yes, unfortunately."

Jerron's eyes narrowed. "And what happened to them? Did you send them home?"

"We will not talk about that now."

"So, do we get to go home?" Olivia asked.

"Soon," Nancy said. "First, I believe you need at least one more memory, just to be sure."

"What do you mean?" Jerron asked, frowning. Nancy smiled and waved her wand. Jerron felt dizzy, then he felt himself falling.

Chapter 18

Olivia woke up in a bumpy carriage. She sat on a golden upholstered seat, and her teeth hit together with each bounce. What was going on? She grasped the seat and hoped for the best. Was anyone driving this thing? Thoughts raced through her head as she tried to decide what to do. She could stay here and hope someone had control, or she could jump.

Holding on to the window and peering out, she watched the scenery fly by at neck breaking speed. The carriage raced through a meadow of weeds and then splashed through some shallow water. They tipped up onto two wheels, and Olivia screamed, sitting back on her seat. It righted itself, but it didn't feel like it was in any more control.

Taking a deep breath, she grabbed a handle on the carriage door and threw it open. There was a chance she wouldn't survive, but if she stayed here, she had less chance. Grabbing her long green dress so she wouldn't trip, she jumped from the runaway carriage.

The ground came fast, and Olivia didn't stop. She rolled painfully. When she stopped, she was lying in an inch of muddy water. She tried to steady her breathing and not focus on the pain. She sat up and held her wrist. It was probably broken. She watched the carriage fly away.

Now what? She pulled back her skirt and examined her scraped knees. What was Nancy thinking? Olivia had thought they could go home once they caught Terry. This didn't seem fair. She got unsteadily to her feet and pushed her dripping blonde locks from her shoulder.

She took a step and cringed. Everything hurt. Something sparkled on the ground to her right. She trudged through the wet mud and leaned down and scooped up a diamond tiara. Had she been wearing it? Probably. Who else would be out here? There weren't any roads or trails. She must be a princess again.

"Nancy!" she yelled. "Nancy, you have a problem! Let us go! We helped you!" There was no answer. She didn't really expect one. She gazed around the soggy meadow, and her eyes stopped on a hill. On top of the hill was a castle. She sighed with relief. It was far off, but at least she knew where to go.

Plopping the tiara on her head, she sloshed through the muddy mess. She must live up there. Hopefully, the horses pulling the carriage were okay. She hadn't seen anyone driving, so there was also the lost driver to worry about. She needed to hurry and warn the castle so they could send out a search party.

Jerron was mad. Nancy wasn't playing fair. He should be back home. Olivia should be back home. He'd played the game, and he should have been sent back. Now, he was a prince again, with an overly protective mother that couldn't seem to give him any space.

He had no idea what story he'd been thrown in. All he knew was that his mood was sour and not getting any better. He didn't even care what the story was. All he cared about was finding Olivia and Nancy. When he found Nancy, she was going to have to explain herself.

This kingdom seemed strange. The castle was located far away from any of the people. There was nothing to see when he looked out the castle windows. No houses, no town. How did a person rule from far away? He wouldn't think about that. He didn't care, and it didn't matter. How was he going to find Olivia if there wasn't a town?

Yanking open the castle door, he stormed outside into the sun. At the bottom of the steps, staring up at him, was Olivia. "What happened to you?" he asked, rushing toward her. She was covered in mud, and her face was scraped.

"I jumped out of a runaway carriage," she said, sinking into him as he wrapped his arms around her. She flinched and cradled her wrist. "I think my wrist is sprained or broken."

"Come on. Let's get you inside."

"Why did Nancy do this? Can't she ever be satisfied?"

Jerron put a hand to her back as they ascended the stairs. "I'm not sure she can. She thinks she's doing this service for people, but I think she's doing it to entertain herself. Or to make herself feel more important."

They entered the castle, and Jerron pushed the heavy door shut.

"Who do we have here?" the queen asked, floating over to Jerron.

"Um . . ." Jerron still didn't know the story or what to call her. He glanced at Olivia, and she shrugged. "Her name is Olivia. Princess Olivia," he said, looking at the tiara.

"Princess?" the queen asked, raising an elegant eyebrow. She fluffed her silver curls and frowned as she inspected Olivia. "She doesn't look like a princess to me. And look. She's an absolute mess!"

"I don't know what happened to my carriage driver," Olivia said. "I had to jump into the mud."

"Interesting story," the queen said. "I suppose you aren't really here to catch yourself a prince?"

"She's obviously a princess," Jerron said, rolling his eyes. "She has a crown. Sure, she's dirty, but she jumped from a moving carriage, for goodness' sake."

"A crown does not a princess make," his new mother said. "But we will see."

"She's hurt. I'm going to take her to see the physician," Jerron said.

"Very well. And while you do that, I will come up with a test."

"What kind of test?" Jerron asked.

"A princess test, of course."

"Right."

"There are lots of girls who want to marry a prince, Jerron," she said, patting his cheek. "You can't let them trick you. You appear stressed. Don't worry about it. Mother will take care of it."

Jerron led Olivia down a long hallway. "I wonder what a princess test is. I still haven't figured out what's going on in this story. How about you?"

"No idea," Olivia said. "I don't know anything about who I'm supposed to be, or where I've come from. I'm not even sure I'm supposed to be a princess. The tiara was on the ground after I jumped, and I figured it was probably mine."

"I wonder why I get memories of the character I play and you don't."

"You said you didn't at first. Maybe I didn't reach that point."

"I guess. I do know we have a decent physician. Who knows what that really counts for in this place? Are you hurt anywhere else?"

"My wrist is the only thing that's really bad. Everything else is just scrapes. My head doesn't feel great, either."

"Do you think the kissing thing works again?"

"I have no idea, but now that I'm finished jumping from the carriage, I'm not in the mood to end up in another story. Who can guess what it would be?"

"That's true. Hopefully, the worst part is over. I mean, it hasn't been bad for me, except for the annoying mother."

"Where is the town? I imagined a town would be surrounding a castle."

"The closest one is miles away. It's a little strange. There aren't a lot of staff members, either. The queen might be a little off."

Olivia tilted her head. "You think?"

Jerron smiled. "She's very protective. She doesn't want to share me."

"I get that," Olivia said. "I don't really want to share you, either."

He laughed. "Don't tell her that. She wouldn't take it well." They stopped in front of a door, and Jerron knocked.

A middle-aged man with dark hair and a goatee opened it. "Prince Jerron," he said, bowing. "How may I help you?" He looked quizzically at Olivia but was polite enough to not ask.

"This is Princess Olivia," he said. "She had to jump from a moving carriage, and she hurt her wrist. Would you mind examining it?"

"Of course," the man said. "Please come in."

It was always a strange sensation, having memories jump into your head that weren't really yours. He felt like he knew this man, even though he'd never met him. They entered the room, and he had them sit on a stiff floral sofa. This wasn't like any doctor's office Jerron had seen. It was more like an old ladies' parlor. He counted five doilies.

The doctor kneeled by the sofa and examined Olivia's wrist. "Does this hurt?"

Olivia jerked away and cradled her hand.

"I'll assume that means yes." She nodded. Jerron paced the room. The more he dwelled on it, the more angry he became. Olivia was hurt because of Nancy. If it wasn't for her, they wouldn't be here.

"It's broken," the doctor finally said. "It seems to be a simple break, so it will probably heal well, if you're careful. I can wrap it now, or I can do it after you've had time to bathe."

"Can I do that?" she asked Jerron.

"Yes. I can have someone draw you a bath."

She smiled slightly. "Draw me a bath?"

"I'm pretty sure that's what I'm supposed to say," he said with a grin.

The doctor raised a questioning eyebrow. "Does your mother know about your visitor?"

"She does."

"And she's agreeable about it?"

"Not really. She's devising a princess test as we speak."

The doctor laughed. "I imagine she is."

"Does she do that often?" Olivia asked.

"She's been known to make tests for everything," the doctor said. "When Princess Graciella visited, she had her take a test to make sure she was smart enough. The poor thing failed miserably."

Jerron smiled at the amusement on Olivia's face. "She doesn't want me to get married."

"You just can't get a break. In *Cinderella*, all your father wanted was for you to get married."

"Yeah, it gives variety to life, I guess."

The doctor was looking at both of them like they were crazy. Jerron didn't really care. Following rules didn't seem to help, so why try?

Olivia studied herself in a full-length mirror. It was the first time she had seen herself in a mirror this big since she came here. Taking a shower had been painful, but it was nice to be clean. She had a big scratch across her cheek and one on her forehead.

Jerron had secured her a long blue dress that wasn't dirty or full of holes. It wasn't overly frilly, but still appeared fancy. She wished the sleeves were longer to cover up some of her scrapes. Her hair was wet from being washed and hung limply over her shoulder. There wasn't a brush in the room, so she wasn't sure what to do about it.

A knock sounded at the door, and she opened it to find a teenage girl in a gray servant's dress. "I've come to help you with your hair," she said. It was odd having a stranger fix her hair, but she let the girl work on it. She would normally try to befriend the girl, but she was tired and sore, and with luck, she wouldn't be here long. The girl put her hair into a complicated updo and then left.

She quickly found the doctor and had her wrist wrapped, then she wandered the castle halls searching for Jerron. After what seemed like an eternity, he found her.

"What are you doing?" he asked.

"Looking for you."

"I went to your room, and you weren't there. Are you ready to eat?"

Olivia nodded. "Yes, I'm starving."

Jerron grinned and pointed at her head. "That's some fancy hair you've got there."

"Yes, I feel ridiculous."

"It's nice."

"Thanks."

"I'm sorry the queen has to eat with us."

She cringed. "That's fine. Have you figured out what story we're in?"

"No. I can't even guess."

"I'm guessing there isn't a Disney version of it. Even though I usually avoid fairy tales, my sister gets me to watch them at least once."

Jerron led her to a large dining room with an enormous table. The queen sat at the head and she smiled a wide, fake smile when they entered. Jerron helped Olivia sit, and she tried to not act nervous.

The food was incredible, but it was hard to enjoy it with the queen watching her eat. Every time they made eye contact, the queen would smile.

A plump woman came in and whispered something to the queen, then the queen turned to Olivia. "You look tired, my dear," she said. "Are you ready to retire? I've made sure you have wonderful sleeping conditions so you can rest peacefully."

"I am tired," Olivia admitted.

"Wonderful. Ninna will take you to your room."

Olivia followed the woman. When they entered the bedroom, Olivia's eyes opened wide. An enormous pile of mattresses stood stacked one on top of another, almost to the high ceiling.

"The queen had extra mattresses added to make sure you sleep well," said Ninna.

"How am I supposed to get up there?" Olivia asked.

"I suppose you'll have to climb," the woman said. "Pleasant dreams."

The woman left and Olivia stared at the mattress tower. There was no way she was getting up there with her hurt wrist. Even if she could, she would probably fall off in the night and die.

She had a vague memory of a poster for a play at her high school that had a picture of a mountain of mattresses. It was too bad she didn't go see it. Then, she might understand what she was up against. She didn't know what the queen's game was. She wasn't climbing that thing. There was a sofa against the far wall. That would do. She grabbed a robe to use as a blanket.

<hr/>

"You don't need to test the princess," Jerron told the queen, as they stood in the hallway outside his room. "What's the point?"

"To see if she's really a princess."

He sighed. "Why do you even care?"

"You can only marry a princess."

"Who said anything about getting married? Just because I help a princess doesn't mean I'm trying to marry her."

"You are so naïve, Jerron," the queen said, smoothing out her skirt. "A filthy woman shows up on the doorstep, and you believe she's a princess because she has a tiara. She probably scuffed herself up and came here to trick you into helping her so she can marry you. All girls want to marry a prince. Believe me, I know."

"It's not like that, *Mother*."

"Well, it won't matter. By tomorrow morning, we will have learned she isn't a genuine princess."

"And how will we know that?"

"Princesses are delicate. Soft."

Jerron hid a smile. The queen didn't take him as delicate or soft. "Where are you going with this?"

"I've put a pea under the princess's mattress. On top of that mattress are twelve more mattresses."

Jerron smacked himself in the forehead. "*The Princess and the Pea*. I should have guessed." He didn't know the story personally, but he'd heard references over the years. "So, you want to see if she can feel the pea under all the mattresses?"

"Yes. If she is a real princess, she will feel it for sure."

"Come on. She's already exhausted. You should let her have a good sleep."

The queen scoffed. "Tomorrow night she can rest—if she's a real princess, that is. If she's an imposter, I'll throw her from the castle."

Jerron yawned. "Alright, fine. I'm going to turn in."

"Don't think about warning her."

"What are you talking about?"

"I see the way you watch her."

"Goodnight," Jerron said, going into his room. He was tired and not in the mood to fight with his fictional mother.

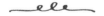

Olivia wanted to yell the next morning as the girl from the day before fixed her hair. She felt terrible. She was sore from her fall yesterday, and sleeping on the narrow sofa hadn't helped.

Her wrist had throbbed all night, and now, her back hurt. She hoped this story was short. If she changed stories, her wrist would be better.

"You must hurry," the girl told Olivia. "You overslept, and the queen and prince are waiting for you."

"Thank you," Olivia said, standing. She made her way to the dining room. She'd seen her reflection, and it wasn't pretty. Bags rested under her eyes that were worthy of someone much older.

"Oh, there you are," the queen smiled.

Jerron winked and pulled a chair out for her. She sank into it. "How did you sleep?" he asked.

"I've slept better," she said. "I had a hard time getting comfortable."

"A hard time?" the queen asked, pursing her lips. "Why was that?"

"My wrist hurt," she said, holding up her arm.

The queen smiled in triumph. "She slept poorly because of a previous injury," she said to Jerron.

"My back is killing me too," she said. "I'm not sure why." She didn't want to admit to sleeping on the sofa. She didn't want to offend the queen after she went through all the trouble of having those mattresses stacked in such a ridiculous manner.

Jerron grinned and turned his own triumphant smile on the queen. "Her back hurts. Almost like she spent the night sleeping on a pea."

"A pea?" Olivia asked with a small smile. "I don't think a pea would cause back pain."

He winked at her. "Not unless you are a delicate princess." Olivia narrowed her eyes and tried to figure out what they were talking about.

"*The Princess and the Pea*," Jerron said. "So, she's a genuine princess, Mother."

The Princess and the Pea? Olivia remembered hearing that before, but she didn't know what it meant.

The queen blotted her mouth daintily with a napkin and stood. "Excuse me for a moment." She quickly left the room.

"How did you get on top of the mattresses?" Jerron asked.

"I didn't. I slept on the sofa."

Jerron laughed. "So, you didn't even sleep on the pea?"

"Why would I sleep on a pea?"

"That's the story. *The Princess and the Pea*."

"I've heard the name, but I don't know the story."

"A princess is supposed to be so delicate she can feel the pea under all the mattresses."

Olivia giggled. "That's ridiculous."

"Well, I believe you passed, complaining about your back pain. I don't really trust the queen, though. I think the story is over." Jerron got up from his chair and helped Olivia stand. "Are you ready?"

"To switch stories? I wish we could just stay in one place if we could be together."

Jerron grinned and ran a finger over her cheek. "I love you."

Her heart pounded in her chest. "I love you too," she said, leaning into him. His lips met hers, and she immediately felt the room spin. He loved her. Everything would be okay. She could only imagine where she would be when she woke up.

Chapter 19

Olivia's eyes seemed glued shut. She tried to force them open, but she felt so weak. The light waiting to greet her was harsh against her eyelids. Everything was still sore from the day before. She'd been expecting to feel better once the story changed. Her wrist was still throbbing. A beeping sounded in her ears, and she tried to ignore it. The more she tried, the more annoying it became.

She'd had dreams she couldn't open her eyes before, but she was almost positive she was awake. Raising her hand to shade her eyes, she pried them open. It only took a moment to recognize it as a hospital. An IV ran into her hand, and there were wires running to other machines she didn't recognize.

Panic overtook her as she glanced around the room and found that she was alone. The bed she was on had a button with a picture of a nurse on it. Reaching out an unsteady hand, she pushed the button. In less than a minute, a middle-aged woman in scrubs came rushing into the room.

"You're awake!" she exclaimed with a wide smile. "How do you feel? Can you talk?"

"I'm a bit sore," she croaked. Her voice sounded raspy, and her throat was dry.

"That's not surprising," the nurse said, sending a quick text from her phone. "You fell out a window, and you've been in a coma for over a week."

"A week?" Olivia croaked, her brows knitted together. "It was much longer than that."

"I believe it's been nine days. I texted the doctor, and he should be here any moment. He can explain more to you."

Nine days. Could that really be true? Was it all a dream? A lump formed in her throat at the thought of Jerron not existing. It had to be real. She could remember it in a way she'd never remembered a dream.

"She's awake!" a middle-aged doctor said, entering the room. "Can you tell me your name?"

"Olivia."

"Wonderful. I'm Dr. Peters. We need to do some tests and take some vitals to see how you're doing. Cara, will you get her some ice chips?"

The nurse smiled. "Of course."

Emily rushed into the room. "Olivia? You're awake! Are you alright?"

"I will be. The nurse said I've only been here for nine days. Is that true?"

"That sounds right," Emily said, sitting on a chair near her bed. "I've spent almost all of my time by your side." Olivia took in Emily's exhausted appearance. She wasn't wearing any makeup, and her clothes were ridiculously wrinkled.

The doctor listened to her heartbeat and pushed on some places on her arm. "How is your wrist?" he asked, holding up her hand. It was in a bright pink cast. It matched a cast on her foot.

"It's okay. I broke it yesterday when I jumped out of a carriage," she said to Emily.

Emily looked up at the doctor in concern.

"It's common to be disoriented after waking up from a coma," he reassured them. "You broke your wrist and your foot when you fell from your apartment. You had a bunch of bumps and bruises, but we were all surprised at how few injuries you had from falling so far."

"Can I sit up?"

"Yes," Dr. Peters said, raising her bed. Nurse Cara came back with a styrofoam cup full of ice and put it on a table next to her. Olivia took a piece and put it in her parched mouth. Swallowing was hard, but the coolness of the ice was refreshing.

"Is there a man here at the hospital that just woke up from a coma?" she asked hopefully. She didn't want to give up on love now that she knew it existed. How would she go on if Jerron was only a dream?

"No, not recently," the doctor said, checking her blood pressure.

"You've really been sitting here with me every day?" Olivia asked Emily.

"Yes. Mom and Dad stay for part of the day as well. Not as much as they should, of course, but that's not surprising."

Olivia put a hand to her head. "And I've just been lying here?"

"What else would you do in a coma?"

Olivia frowned. "It just doesn't make sense. I was gone for so much longer than nine days, and I wasn't here. I can't explain it."

"Head injuries can cause a lot of confusion," the doctor said, pressing on her arm.

"It wasn't confusing. I mean, it was, but not like head injury confusion. Em, do you remember the woman I was talking to at the bridal shop?"

Emily nodded.

"Well, she wasn't just a regular person. She's magic, a fairy godmother. She's responsible for all of this."

"Okay—How is she responsible?"

"She made me fall out the window."

Emily raised an eyebrow. "You leaned out to get Toby."

"Yes, and she made me fall. I've been stuck in some weird fairy tale world. She said it was her goal to make people like me believe in happily ever afters." Olivia wasn't sure why she kept talking. Emily looked at her like she was crazy. The doctor's expression remained neutral, but that was probably part of his training.

"It sounds like a crazy dream," Emily finally said.

"It wasn't a dream. I don't know how it happened, or why it was so much longer for me there than here. Now, I need to find Jerron."

"Jerron?" the doctor asked, his head popping up.

"Yes."

"Who is Jerron?" Emily asked.

"He's my happily ever after. I have to find him. We always find each other. I sound crazy."

Emily shook her head. "You don't sound like you, that's for sure."

"Is there anyone in this hospital named Jerron?" she asked the doctor.

The doctor adjusted her IV. "We aren't allowed to give out personal information."

Olivia sighed. What if they were right? What if she had just had a crazy nine day dream? How could a dream that long fit into nine days?

"I should call Mom," Emily said. "Excuse me a minute." She stepped out of the room and Olivia sniffed, holding back her tears. She was too tired to cry, and what good would it do?

ele

Jerron couldn't figure out what was happening. He hadn't woken up in a new story, or if he had, it was the worst one ever. No plot, and no characters. Everything was red. The ground, the sky, his clothes. Everything. There was nothing ahead of him, or behind him, except the red.

He had been walking, hoping to come to a place, any place, but so far nothing. The only sound was his shoes smacking against the ground. He couldn't tell if he was inside or outside. He had the horrible feeling he was lost forever. The thought made him want to scream.

Calling out for Olivia or Nancy had produced no results. His voice had echoed around and given him a headache. Giving up was tempting, but if Olivia was lost in this, he needed to find her.

"You might as well sit down and wait," Nancy said, appearing in a red dress in front of him.

He jumped and then scowled. "Wait for what? Where am I?"

Nancy tilted her silver head and shrugged. "It seems to be some sort of limbo."

"Seems to be? Don't you know?"

"I can't know everything. People who know everything are insufferable."

Jerron pursed his lips. "Why didn't you send us back after we trapped Terry? That wasn't fair."

"I had to make sure you were ready."

"We were. That last story didn't make us any more ready. Where's Olivia?"

Nancy glanced around. "She's not here."

"I figured that much."

"Everything is up to Olivia now. She needs to find you."

Jerron ran his fingers through his hair in frustration. "How is she going to find me if she isn't here?"

"I guess we will see. Olivia's a creative girl. She'll figure something out."

"How is she going to figure it out? This doesn't seem to be the place people stumble into."

Nancy nodded. "I'm sure it's not. I've never seen it until now."

"I thought you were in control of everything."

"Not everything. Not this place."

"But you came here. You must know something."

"I can sense where you are. I was as surprised as you to be here."

Jerron fixed his eyes on her. "Can't you take me to one of the stories? Then, I have some chance of finding her."

"Sorry, I don't see how. This place does strange things to my magic. I can only take myself out."

"Do you still think this was a good idea? Messing with our lives?"

Nancy smiled. "Of course I do. Don't you?"

"No!"

"If I hadn't brought you here, you wouldn't have met Olivia. Think about that."

Jerron paused. That was true, but it was still wrong. How many years had he lost because of this woman? Still. He wanted Olivia to be in his life forever. He never would have given love a chance if Nancy hadn't brought him here. That didn't make her right, though.

Nancy beamed. "I've learned a lot from you as well."

"Oh?"

"You were so stubborn. That's what gave me the idea of putting you with another person. You never connected well to any of the stories until I brought you and Olivia to the same one. It made me reevaluate my methods. From now on, I'll put two of my beneficiaries in each story. If they don't connect, I'll switch it up."

Jerron shook his head. He could talk himself blue in the face, and Nancy wasn't ever going to listen. "What are you going to do when someone teaches you a lesson someday? I'm sure you won't take it as well as you might think."

Nancy laughed. "What lesson would someone need to teach me?"

"I can think of a few. You brag about your successes, but what about Terry? What's going to happen to him?"

"He can't be sent back. He's too much of a danger now. I fear he would wake up and magic himself back. He's a dangerous one."

"Only because you brought him here."

"I regret that, but he isn't a danger anymore."

Jerron narrowed his eyes. "What will you do with him?"

"The dwarves have helped me move the glass coffin to a tower where no one will disturb it. We've placed Terry inside."

Jerron cringed at the thought of Terry sleeping in the coffin Olivia had been in. It sounded unsettling. "I hope nobody ever climbs the tower and finds him. That might give them nightmares."

Nancy dusted off her dress. "He's a good-looking man, if you can get past his personality."

"What happens if someone comes and breaks his spell?"

"The only way to break the spell is by me, or true love's kiss. I don't see either of those things happening."

"Just don't call on me if it happens," Jerron said.

"I won't. Your story is almost at a close. I'm not one hundred percent sure why you ended up here and not in your own world. I assume it's because you need a little more humility."

"Are you going to tell me anything helpful? If you aren't, I'd rather go back to wandering around alone, feeling sorry for myself."

Nancy rolled her eyes. "That sounds like a wonderful use of time."

"I figure it won't last long. There doesn't appear to be any food or water here, so I'll probably be dead in a few days anyway."

"You can't die in these kinds of places. It's almost like being dead, but you are very much alive. You don't need food here or even sleep. That could be an enjoyable thing."

Jerron laughed and spread his arms out. "Enjoyable? It's red. It's red here, it's red there. Everywhere is red, and there is nothing else! How is that supposed to be something to celebrate?"

"Settle down, Jerron. You're starting to sound unhinged. You don't want to end up like Terry, right at the finish line."

"Please leave," Jerron begged. He couldn't handle this conversation for any longer. If Nancy had anything important to say, he would listen, but otherwise, she was wasting his time.

"Alright, I'll go. I want you to take this," she said, handing him a carved wooden wolf. "Toad carved it for Olivia." He took it and placed it in his red pocket. "I also want you to take this." She handed him a silver sword.

Where had she been hiding that? "Why do I need a sword? To cut through the redness?"

Nancy huffed. "You are very disagreeable today. I hope your mood improves. Places of limbo are often unsteady and almost always have some type of beast inside them."

Jerron glanced around at the redness. At least a beast would give him something else to look at.

———⁓ℓℓ⁓———

"So, you cycled through all of those fairy tales and then woke up?" Emily asked, twisting a lock of brown hair around her finger.

Olivia nodded. "Yes. I realize it sounds crazy, and I know I wouldn't ever believe anyone who told me that story, but it was so real."

"I'm afraid if you keep talking about stuff like this, the hospital won't ever let you go. They're going to think you're crazy."

"Do you think I'm crazy? Mom and Dad did when they came yesterday."

Emily studied her. "I don't think you're crazy. You just had a really realistic dream while you were out."

Olivia frowned as she picked at her cast. "It's really frustrating, Em. You know how I've perceived love, and now, it's all changed. If it wasn't real, I fell in love with a dream. How can a dream make my heart hurt so much?"

Emily sat next to Olivia and put her arm around her.

Olivia rested her head on her sister's shoulder and sniffled. "When I woke up yesterday, I was so sure it was real. After sleeping last night, it still feels real, but more faded. I can still see Jerron's face so well."

Emily rubbed her arm. "I'm sorry. I don't have any good sisterly advice. The memories of a dream usually fade quickly. Hopefully, the heartache will as well."

Olivia's lip trembled. "I wanted to come home so badly, and now, I wish I could go back."

"Don't say that. It makes me nervous."

"I wish you could have seen Finn. You would have loved him. He was a huge gray wolf with amber eyes. I thought he was bad at first, but he ended up helping us more than once."

"I do love wolves," Emily agreed. "And a large, friendly one would be neat to see."

"One brother from *Snow White* was whittling a wolf. I kind of think he was doing it for me. If we hadn't left, he probably would have given it to me. I should learn to whittle while I'm stuck here."

"I doubt your wrist is up for it."

"Probably not."

"Do you want to stand for a while?"

Olivia sighed. The doctor wanted her to stand for a few minutes every hour and try to walk on her crutches for at least a few steps. She could do more than they were allowing her, but she would get what she could. "Sure," she said. She needed to stop talking about her *dream*. It was only going to cause trouble.

Chapter 20

Time had no meaning here. Jerron couldn't tell if he'd been here for one day or five. Not needing to sleep was messing with him. He'd tried to sleep, just to let his mind rest, but he was wide awake.

Jerron sat on the ground and waited. He'd done enough wandering, and the sword was getting heavy. He laid it across his lap and studied the hilt. It wasn't anything special. It had some intricate swirls that made it less comfortable to hold, but aside from that, it was just a regular sword. He thought about leaving it behind, but he didn't want to regret it later.

The ground rumbled, and Jerron's ears perked up. It was the first sound he'd heard since coming here that hadn't come from him or Nancy. He stood and gripped the sword in his right hand. He wished he knew how to use it.

In the distance, he could see something dark coming toward him. At least it wasn't red. He would probably see red every time he closed his eyes for the rest of his life. He looked from the sword to the dark shape. It was getting bigger by the moment. If his heart beat any harder, it was going to burst.

The creature came closer, and Jerron started stepping backward. It looked like a really round dragon without wings. It had large, pointed teeth and big, empty eyes. Thankfully, it wasn't moving very fast. He might be able to outrun it. Turning, he dropped the sword and bolted off into the redness, hoping the creature wouldn't be interested enough to follow him.

Olivia was tired of the hospital. The food was fair, and Emily stayed with her most of the time, but she'd been awake for a week with nothing to do. Dr. Peters said she could go home in a few days if she kept improving. She stopped talking about her dream too. Emily was right. She didn't want them keeping her here, thinking she was out of her mind.

"I'm tired of playing Uno," she told Emily. "I never thought I would say that. We need a new game."

"I could buy something later," Emily said, putting the cards in her purse. "Any requests?"

"No. I'm just so bored. I don't get how they can have so many channels and all that's ever on is game shows, sports, and that stupid pig cartoon. How did that ever catch on? No plot and horrible illustrations. Kids must like it, though, because they show episode after episode. If I ever have kids, that show is banned from my house."

Emily laughed. "It is pretty bad."

There was a commotion in the hall, and something rolled into the room and under the bed. A woman with messy red hair poked her head in. "I'm sorry, I dropped something. Can I just grab it?"

"Sure," Olivia said.

"Hi, Maggie," Emily said.

"Oh, Emily, hi. This must be your sister," the woman said, glancing at Olivia.

"Yeah, this is Olivia. Olivia, this is Maggie. She's the woman I've been telling you about. We've been eating lunch together in the cafeteria."

"Nice to meet you," Olivia said. "Whatever you dropped rolled under the bed."

"Thanks," she said, bending down and grabbing a round Tupperware lid. "My grandma keeps bringing me food, and I forgot her lid. She's really particular about her Tupperware, so I ran back to get it before someone tossed it."

"How's your brother?" Emily asked.

Maggie shrugged. "The same. I'm losing hope. They say the longer a person is in a coma, the less chance there is of waking up." She wiped a tear from her eye and smiled. "Sorry, I try not to get emotional."

Emily gave the woman a hug. "Don't give up hope. They said he's healing well, right?"

"Yes, but still no sign of consciousness. He was in a car crash four weeks ago," she told Olivia.

"I'm sorry," she said. It was no wonder the woman looked disheveled.

"Thanks. I keep thinking he'll pull through. Jerron has always been hard headed and stubborn. I hope he fights his way back."

Olivia sat up straight and swallowed hard. "Jerron?" She looked at Emily. Her sister shook her head in a silent warning. She was probably trying to tell her there was more than one person named Jerron and not to upset Maggie.

"What is it?" Maggie asked, noticing the exchange.

"I know someone named Jerron," Olivia said, feeling lame for mentioning it. Her heart was racing. She had to see if it was him.

"Olivia, don't," Emily said.

Maggie cocked her head and studied them.

Emily sighed. "Do you remember how I told you about the dream my sister had during her coma?"

"Yes. That was quite the dream. You should make sure you write it down so you don't forget it."

Olivia took a deep breath. Her heart was racing in her chest. "The man in my dream was named Jerron."

Maggie blinked a few times. "That's a strange coincidence."

"I don't think it was a dream. Can I see your brother?"

Maggie looked at Emily, and Emily frowned. "What was Jerron's last name?"

Olivia thought for a moment. "He never told me."

"Maybe when you were unconscious, you heard a doctor mention Jerron, and the name stuck with you," Emily said.

"I have to see him," Olivia said. "Please? I'll never rest, not knowing if it's him or not."

"Olivia," Emily pleaded, "It's not him. Your Jerron isn't real. I'm sorry, but you need to get over it."

"I will if you let me see him. What is it going to hurt?"

"Olivia—"

"No, it's okay," Maggie said. "If it helps her get some closure, she can come look at him."

"I don't think it's a good idea," Emily said, biting her lip. "You should be resting. This might set you back."

Olivia swung her legs over the bed and grabbed her crutches. "I'll be fine," she lied. If it wasn't Jerron, she feared her heart might stop. They followed Maggie down the hallway and into a room.

A man lay in the bed, connected to a bunch of machines. Dr. Peters was standing in front of him, blocking his face. He turned and nodded at them. "Making friends?" he asked Maggie. She nodded.

Olivia slowly maneuvered her crutches around until she could see the man's face. "Jerron," she whispered. A tear ran down her face as she walked closer.

"Okay, you've seen him. Let's go," Emily said.

"It's him."

Emily frowned. "No, Olivia. Don't do this, please."

Maggie and Dr. Peters watched her with confused expressions.

"But it's him." Olivia moved a step closer and clutched her crutches. She felt like she might collapse at any moment.

"What's in his hand?" Maggie asked the doctor.

Dr. Peters picked up Jerron's hand and pried out a wooden wolf. "That's odd. You didn't put it there?"

Maggie shook her head.

Olivia smiled through her tears. "It's Finn."

Emily had her hand on her chest and she was staring at the small, whittled wolf. "It's not possible," she whispered.

"Olivia needs to get back to her room," Dr. Peters said, handing the wolf to Maggie.

"Wait," she said, propping her crutches against the wall. She hobbled closer to the bed and grabbed on to the bed rail to steady herself.

Emily shook her head. "Olivia, come on. We need to go."

"I'm the only one who can help," Olivia said, scanning the faces in the room. They all looked concerned. "Don't worry. All the stories end the same." Olivia leaned forward and pressed her lips against Jerron's. She could hear all the protests from the others, but they barely registered with her.

She felt herself being torn away, and she stumbled as Dr. Peters pulled her upright. "You are confined to your room from now on," he growled.

"Olivia?" Jerron croaked. The room went silent as all eyes fell on him. He groaned as he tried to sit up.

Maggie sat down hard in a chair and covered her mouth with her hands, and Dr. Peters released Olivia in surprise.

"Where am I?"

"The hospital," Olivia told him.

He lifted his arm towards her, then dropped it. "I feel so weak."

"You were just in time," he said with a small smile. His voice was as raspy as the worst chain smoker. "I was about to get eaten by some sort of dragon pig."

"I'm glad you weren't," she said, taking his hand. He smiled and kissed hers. "So we're back? We're home?"

"Yes." Tears ran down her face, but she ignored them. "I'd almost convinced myself it was a dream."

"I'm glad it wasn't."

Maggie sobbed from behind Olivia, causing Jerron's eyes to scan the room. They stopped when he saw Maggie. "Mags, I've missed you." Maggie rose to her feet and grabbed Jerron's other hand. "You don't look any older."

Maggie laughed and wiped a tear from her face. "I hope not. It's only been four weeks." More tears cascaded down her cheeks.

"Four weeks?" Jerron asked. "It's been years."

"You might as well save your breath," Olivia warned him. "They don't believe anything I say."

"It's impossible," Emily said, rubbing her temples.

"Then how do you explain it?" Olivia asked.

Emily just shook her head and leaned against the wall.

"I don't care what happened, I'm just so happy you're awake!" Maggie said, squeezing his hand. "It's a miracle if I've ever seen one." She dropped Jerron's hand and grabbed a tissue from the nightstand and blew her nose.

"Your wrist is still broken?" Jerron asked Olivia.

"From falling out the window."

"Why am I here?"

"Car crash," Maggie said.

Dr. Peters had yet to talk. He scratched the stubble on his chin and remained an observer.

"Why didn't you come back with me?" Olivia asked, rubbing the top of his hand with her thumb.

"No clue. I ended up in some crazy red limbo. Nancy came and said a bunch of garbage like usual, and the rest of the time, I was alone. Until the pig dragon."

"Nancy?" Dr. Peters muttered. He shook his head as if coming out of a daze and pushed the nurse's call button.

"Yes?" a voice said from the speaker.

"Ice chips in room 201," he said. "This is incredible. I can't even comprehend what just happened."

"It's easier not to try," Olivia said. Her heart was so full, she worried it would burst. Only a few minutes earlier, she had been ready to give up hope.

"Ice chips," a cheery voice said, entering the room.

Jerron groaned. "Not you."

Nancy practically bounced over to Jerron and stuffed a piece of ice in his mouth. He sucked on it and glared at her.

"Thanks, Nancy," the doctor said.

"You know her?" Olivia asked.

"Of course. Nancy is one of our best volunteers."

"I'm sure she keeps the coma unit well stocked," Jerron said.

"Wait," Emily said. "Nancy, as in the fairy godmother?"

"Exactly," Olivia said.

"My, what imaginations we all have," Nancy said, putting the cup of ice on the table. "It looks like we have a happy ending."

"So, you go around checking on all your victims?" Olivia asked.

"I have many responsibilities."

"I need to check some things out with Jerron," Dr. Peters said, coming back to himself. "Can I get everyone to leave for a while?"

"If you need me, I'll be checking on Terry," Nancy told him.

He nodded. "Don't go too far, Nancy. We need to talk."

"Terry is here too?" Olivia exclaimed. Everyone looked at her. "Don't stare at me. I'm not kissing that creeper."

"You better not," Jerron said. "If you want to kiss anyone, I'm right here." Olivia smiled a smile she worried would break her face.

"Terry, the bad guy, is here in a coma?" Emily asked, putting a hand to her forehead. "This is so overwhelming."

"I feel like I'm in a weird dream," Maggie said.

"Just a warning," Olivia told the doctor. "If Terry wakes up, get away and call the cops."

"Don't be so dramatic," Nancy said, rolling her eyes.

"If Terry was here all along—why couldn't you stop him?" Olivia asked.

"Stop him from what, dear?"

"Everyone out," Dr. Peters commanded. His mouth was in a tight line and his brows were knit together. "This conversation can wait."

"Nancy, stop!" Olivia called as she made her way down the hospital hallway. She tried to hurry, but the crutches made her slow. Nancy turned and smiled at her. Olivia, Emily, and Maggie approached the smiling woman.

"What can I do for you?" she asked.

"You have to stop doing this to people. How many people are here in comas because of you?"

"Because of me?" Nancy asked innocently.

"Emily and Maggie? Will you excuse us for a moment?" Olivia could tell the woman wasn't going to talk while they were there.

Maggie nodded and Emily looked like she wanted to protest, but changed her mind. The two women walked off, talking quietly to one another.

"You need to be careful," Nancy warned. "You don't want people to think you are losing your mind."

"So, how many people?" Olivia asked, balancing on her crutches.

"You three are the only ones right now," Nancy said. "I don't put everyone in a coma. I have many ways of doing things. It is interesting that the three of you were all in the same hospital, and you all came together. It must have been fate."

"I think the doctor is suspicious," Olivia said.

"Oh, I'm sure he is. Dr. Peters is a smart man, and he is in control of his emotions. He's seen a lot of unbelievable things—and he never reacts until he is away from his patients. He suspects I'm involved in some way, but what is he going to do? Tell people I'm putting people in magical comas?"

Olivia glared. "That's what you are doing."

"Sometimes. It worked out, though. Didn't it?"

"But now we are all injured, with crazy stories no one in their right mind would believe."

"Yes, but you are going to be happy."

"Are all the people you did this to happy? You said you don't usually put two real people together. That means even if people do fall in love, you send them back here without the person they fell in love with. Do you ever go check and see if they are still happy?"

Nancy shook her head. "I'm sure they are happy. They might not be with the person they learned to love, but now they know it's obtainable."

"Go check on them," Olivia said, cocking her head. "If they are all happy, I won't say another word about it."

"I might just do that," Nancy said. "I should have a chat with all of them. It will lift my spirits when I see how happy they all are. It will have to wait awhile. I'm in the middle of so much."

"I hope you'll stop if they aren't happy."

"I'm sure they are."

It was the middle of the night, and Jerron was tired of the hospital. The bed was anything but comfortable. He didn't understand why Dr. Peters wouldn't let him go. The doctor said he needed to keep a close eye on him, since he'd been in a coma for so long. Olivia was going home tomorrow, and he thought he was doing better than she was. He didn't have any broken bones. He'd only been allowed to see Olivia twice since he woke up three days ago.

Pulling on his slippers, he carefully stood. His legs were still a bit wobbly when he started out. His entire body felt weak. He grabbed his robe and put it over his ridiculous hospital nightgown. Peeking into the hall, he looked both ways. The only sound was someone typing in the distance.

Feeling like a criminal, he creeped down the hallway to Olivia's room. The door was opened a crack, and he quietly slipped in and closed the door behind him. The memory of her punching him in the face when he snuck up on her caused him to change his plan.

"Olivia," he whispered.

"Jerron?" she asked, turning in her bed.

"Did I wake you?"

"No. I can't sleep." She switched on the light and raised her bed so she was sitting.

He sat next to her on the bed. "I wish they'd let me go home tomorrow."

"Me too," she said, resting her head on his shoulder. "You're getting around a lot better than I am."

"I wonder if I'm allowed to demand to leave. It's not like this is a prison."

She sighed. "It feels a little like it."

"Maybe I'm trying to take things too fast. Just walking here wore me out. I don't like knowing Terry is down the hall. I wonder how long he's been here."

"Who knows? And from what Nancy said, I don't think he'll be waking up anytime soon."

Jerron rubbed a hand through his hair. "I have such strange contradicting feelings about Nancy. I don't think she should mess with people's lives, but at the same time, I wouldn't have found you without her."

Olivia nodded. "I was thinking the same thing the other day."

"I'm giving up on trying to convince her to stop. She doesn't listen at all. I wonder how many people she's done this to."

She looked up at him. "None of them could have ended as well as we did."

"Why do you say that?"

"We were the only two that were put in the same stories. That means the others didn't fall in love. They might have learned to believe in it, but they didn't find it."

"That's true. I guess we're luckier than most."

Olivia snuggled into his side. "I told that to Nancy, but she doesn't believe me."

The door swung open, and a frantic nurse poked her head in. "What do you think you're doing?" she asked in a loud whisper. Jerron didn't know you could yell a whisper, but this woman managed.

"Socializing," Jerron said, grinning at her.

"At this hour? And without permission? Dr. Peters left a warning about you, and I should have listened. Get back to your room!"

"Fine," Jerron mumbled, getting slowly to his feet. "Tomorrow, I'm protesting, though."

***

Olivia pulled a sock over her foot and rotated her ankle in a circle. There wasn't any pain. The cast had come off yesterday, but she was still trying to be careful. A knock sounded on the front door, and she smiled.

"Come in!" she called. The door opened, and Jerron came in carrying a pizza box.

She smiled. "Pizza again?"

"I know," he said. "But I really missed it."

"What are we going to do today?" she asked, as he placed the pizza on the coffee table.

He sank down on the couch next to her. "I'm feeling lazy. How about a movie?"

"Sounds good," she said. "Which one?"

He put his arm around her shoulders. "*Snow White*?"

She grinned. "No way. I may have changed my mind about a few things, but that doesn't mean I'm ready to watch anything I've lived."

"We have to get all the fun in before we start college next month. Maybe we should do something more exciting."

"We've had a lot of excitement already this year. We can have a lazy day."

"I just don't want you to think I'm getting boring."

She smiled. "Never." He leaned down and kissed her. Happiness filled Olivia's entire heart as she wrapped her arms around his neck. Breaking away, she pressed her forehead against his. "And now we get to live happily ever after."

Jerron kissed her nose. "So, I shouldn't say 'the end'?"

Olivia smiled. "No. It's a crazy beginning."

Also By Kristy Dixon

<u>The Silver Eclipse Series</u>
Akkron
Boztoll
The Other Continent

<u>Coming Soon</u>
Trapped Upon a Time
The Amethyst Crown

About the Author

Kristy Dixon received a degree in English. She started writing stories when she was seven and never stopped. She enjoys writing fantasy books for middle grade and teens. At home, she spends her time playing board games with her husband and kids and writing. Occasionally she takes part in a Super Mario marathon. She has six chickens and a cat that help keep life amusing. If she isn't playing with her kids or writing, she is usually eating cookies, or wishing she was eating cookies.

Made in the USA
Las Vegas, NV
10 September 2024

95068857R00173